Grab Bag 5

by

habu

GRAB

BAG

5

BarbarianSpy

BarbarianSpy
FOR LITERARY HEAT

This book is copyright © habu 2014
habu asserts his right to be known as the author of this work.
Published by BarbarianSpy in 2014
Cover design © S Bush 2014
Cover image: Manipulated, Man with bags © Wrangel at Dreamstime.com
ISBN E-Book: 978-0-9876093-6-6
ISBN Paperback: 978-1-925190-03-8
All rights reserved

BarbarianSpy
Jindalee St
Toronto, NSW 2283
AUSTRALIA

Table of Contents

Introduction   7

Enticingly Unnaked   11

Used   29

Pianoman   49

Position Interview   65

White Stripes   73

Each Time a Little Less   87

Pearl Fisher Ecstasy   99

Dressage Training   105

Last Laugh   119

Fuck a Duck   131

Hijacked   143

Winter Trial   155

The German   173

Carnival at Viareggio   189

David Vance Poses   203

Atonement or Exorcism?   211

About the Author   223

Introduction

The fifth volume of habu's *Grab Bag* series is a collection of sixteen stories never before released to the market.

It is the latest in a series of standalone stories with eclectic gay male settings and plotlines presented in the order in which they were delivered to habu by his muse, within the period since the previous *Grab Bag* collection was assembled. In addition to stories streaming down from habu's muse, this collection includes stories written for themed contests and ones specifically requested to be written by habu's readers. Setting is always important in habu's stories, and, as usual, the settings of these stories span the globe, from the United States, with the South heavily represented, to Europe, the Mediterranean, and East Asia. And, as always, there are unusual stories that take fresh approaches to men taking their pleasure with other men.

Three of the stories were written for erotica short story competitions. "Enticingly Naked," written for a Nude Day story contest, turns the concept on its head, featuring how *not* being nude can be sexy and arousing. "Pianoman," the story of a Vegas hotel bar pianist meeting his dream man as he is trying to escape his "now" man, was written for a Valentine's Day contest. And "Hijacked," written for Earth Day, combines the greening of technology with sex in the cab of a truck at a highway rest stop.

The stories span the globe in setting. Several are set in the American South. These include "Enticingly Unnaked," set in Savannah, Georgia, and two set farther south, in Florida. "Fuck a Duck" is a little ditty of a black bull being just a bit too sure of himself. "Winter Trial" explores relationships in the death throes of a circus act. "Dressage Training," written by reader's request for a specific fetish, brings us north to Virginia. The story follows the sexual training of a young horse groom with the same methods the trainer uses to prepare his dressage mounts. Farther north, in Baltimore, Maryland, "Used" finds a young man seduced by another man only to be pimped out to others. A few of habu's stories are set in Indiana. Representing that state in this collection is "Last Laugh," providing a tables turn sort of nastiness of thugs getting taken as much as they are taking. And what collection would be complete without a Vegas story, represented here by the contest story, "Pianoman."

One hallmark of the world traveler habu's writings is that he frequently takes his settings outside of the states. Germany is represented in this anthology by "The German," a tale of an international GM hooker's intriguing adventure in Munich, and Italy is the setting for the historical "Carnival at Viareggio," which takes the reader to an Italian beach resort in the 1920s to observe the various men buzzing around a bit of tasty young man bait. Two stories are set in unidentified European locales. "Pearl Fishers Ecstasy" is a flight of fancy on a take on the Act I duet, "Au fond du temple saint," that immortalizes Georges Bizet's opera, *Pearl Fishers*, from the aspect of the *Pearl Fishers* being staged as a homoerotic production. (It is best read accompanied by listening to a recording of the duet.) In the concluding story of the collection, "Atonement or Exorcism?", a young man returns to the European city where he believes he has wronged a man and receives the punishing atonement he seeks, from another man.

As always, there are stories from habu's Asian stomping grounds. "Each Time a Little Less," takes the reader to Okinawa, where a young airman is being coaxed into male

8

prostitution at a bar. An Italian manufacturer buys a Bangkok garment factory business in "David Vance Poses" just to seduce a male fashion model whose erotic photographs he has collected.

Three stories could be set anywhere in the United States. These include the contest piece, "Hijacked," and "Position Interview," which, set up as a job interview appointment, rolls along begging the question, "Just what is this all about? Where is this leading?" "White Stripes" finds a young prisoner on a work project in a municipal parking garage showing too much interest in breaking into a car and not enough attention to being stalked.

As is always the case with habu's *Grab Bag* anthologies, any reader interested in reading a fresh and stimulating perspective of one man taking his enjoyment with another man will find much to be pleased with and satisfied by the stories in this collection.

Enticingly Unnaked

"How about I treat you to a drink? You must be thirsty from all that naked time on the platform."

I had just climbed down from the velvet-covered bench on the platform where I'd been posing, in the nude, for the past hour for Chad Simmons' Savannah College of Art and Design night school art class. I'd barely had time to shrug my white cotton dress shirt over my shoulders. That didn't stop the man from sidling up to me and taking liberties, though. He had a hand on my bare butt. I wasn't surprised; I'd been expecting him to leap up on the platform with me and try to cover me since half way through the art session.

Truth be told, I was kind of aroused that I'd have an effect like that on a good-looking guy.

I looked over at Chad Simmons. He was cleaning some brushes and talking to the last of the other art students who were already filing out of the room. I'd only taken this gig to be near Chad, wanting it to be him asking me the "How about a drink at my place?" question. But the art professor was being very polite and standoffish about it all. I'd hoped when he saw me naked it would turn him on—like seeing him in a Speedo out at his Tybee Island beach house a couple of weeks ago had turned me on. But he was showing less interest in me naked than when we passed in the hallways.

"Drinks?" I said, turning my face back to the fiftyish local businessman—a very successful Lexus dealer, as I recall being told—with a large townhouse just off Chatham Square, within walking distance of here, that he had all to himself. He was tall and distinguished looking, with wavy gray hair, a manicured look about him, and a perpetual deep tan. His body obviously gym cared for. Some sort of South American. Brazilian or Colombian, which probably answered for how deep the tan looked. Maybe into more than just automobiles. Really smooth. Not so great with the painting, though, I could tell, because we were standing next to his canvas. He'd made my butt too big, and he'd obviously stood at my butt end to do the painting. Everyone else did side views. I'd heard rumors about him taking willing male students from SCAD to his place and paying them top dollar for a fuck.

I couldn't deny that I was a willing student—for a price.

"Sure, at my place; it's just a short distance from here, closer than any of the bars," Rafael Perez said. He still had his palm on my butt, but he was moving it around and squeezing a bit. It was obvious he was a butt man. The fact that I was letting him hold it there no doubt told him that I was for sale—and maybe I was—but only for the right price if I didn't want the guy. I'd give it away for free to Chad Simmons, but for the right price, I could be had by the Rafael Perezes of the world. I had college expenses just like everyone else, and the sex act—once that barrier was crossed—was a renewable resource. And, being a student in the drama and film-making department, I had plenty of offers too.

Letting him palm and pet me there helped him be pretty bold.

"I'd just need a couple of hours of your time. And I'd pay you $100 an hour. For a high-quality hour, of course."

I looked over at Chad Simmons, who, seeing that I was still here, walked over to us. Perez took his hand off my butt, stepped back, and turned and looked at his canvas like he was trying to decide what else to do with it. I thought he probably could make the butt smaller and there'd be a 100 percent improvement.

"Before you go, Jason . . ."

12

"Yes, professor?" I said, stepping into my jeans and turning to Chad as he walked up to me, looking every inch the sultry dark and sexily hairy young hunk that he was. He could have been a movie star as easily as an art professor. And I knew he was gay, because everyone knew he'd had an older lover who had died and left him that mansion with the private beach on Tybee Island that the art students had been invited to recently.

I left my shirt open and hanging off my shoulders and also left the fly of my jeans open and my dong hanging out. I'd just exposed it all for an art class, so there shouldn't be anything too shocking about my attention being arrested before I got it tucked away again. In reality, I knew I looked like an Abercrombie and Fitch model poster that even A&F couldn't hang on their walls—it was why I was asked to model for the art classes—and I wanted those charms to work on Simmons. It was why I accepted the modeling jobs. I wanted him to see me as naked as possible as often as possible. And as he came up to me, I did see a spark from him, an even stronger vibe of interest than when I normally saw him in the halls of the school, where I first thought that there was a connection to be had between us. And much more than earlier tonight, when I was posed, reclining and stark naked, on the platform over there. It might have been because he was teaching a class, but he was a cold fish in the face of my nakedness. That just didn't vibe with him being gay. I look pretty damn sexy when I'm naked.

When he reached me, he touched me lightly on the arm, and I felt like a jolt of lightning was going through me. I'm sure he could feel it too, and he was looking at me with lust in his eyes, I know he was. "I've meant to ask you if you're free Wednesday evening for a private session. I need another male nude sketch for my portfolio for the New Orleans show and I'm running short of time."

Hallelujah is what I thought, but what I said was, "Sure thing, professor. Any time. Even now if you—"

"I can't tonight. There's an art opening I have to attend. So, Wednesday at 8:00 would be convenient for you?" I noted a tinge of genuine regret in his voice.

13

"Yes, of course." Any time for you, I thought. But what were these mixed signals all about? I got the distinct impression just now that he'd like me to stay so he could fuck me.

I watched him turn and slowly walk away.

"So, you are free now to be with me?" Perez asked. He was back beside me and had a hand on my butt again, even though it had to be over my jeans now.

"Sure, why not?" I answered, tucking my dick into my jeans and zipping them up.

He fucked me in what obviously was a painting studio on the top floor of his townhouse—so he was a serious painter at least, or maybe just a dabbler from the looks of the paintings on his walls in the studio. He had a one-track mind in his painting. All young men with big butts, painted from the rear, most of them showing gaping holes like they'd just been reamed big.

He spent a whole lot of time on my buttocks during foreplay, so I could tell it was a real obsession of his. I was bent over a studio bed in the center of the room on my belly, with my butt sticking out and up, while he virtually worshipped it with his lips and teeth and his squeezing and revolving hands. I was as worked up as he was when he turned me on my back, grabbed my ankles, spread-eagled my legs, and fucked me with a thick cock that would ream me as big as those guys in the paintings on the wall.

When we were both done, he turned me over on my belly again and told me to go up on my knees, my chest pressed to the bed, my legs spread wide. He then took out a camera and his easel, canvas, and paintbrushes, and it was evident that my backside and my gaping hole, thankfully my buttocks painted large enough so I wouldn't be recognized, was destined for his wall collection.

The signal for when he was finished with his painting came when he came over, slapped my buttocks, and rolled the cheeks with his hands until my skin was red and he was ready to fuck me again—which he then proceeded to do with gusto.

I earned $300 for the session, but never was offered that promised drink.

14

* * * *

I gave a little cry as he entered me and pulled nearly all the way out and then back in, deep this time, making me open to him, but not as comfortably as if he'd given me more time and attention. And then slamming it home, again and again. A louder groan and a cry out this time. "God, you're fuckin' killing me." He was big, and he was taking me swiftly, almost brutally.

"Shush," George Garnett hissed. "You'll bring on the dorm counselor." Then he laughed.

He'd entered my dorm room while I was dozing on the bed, tired from a late-night play rehearsal. I wasn't even fully awake when he teased me to raise my hips enough for him to pull my cock through my legs and include that in the cursory attention he was giving to my asshole. And then it was all arms and legs, covering me, turning me on my back, forcing my legs to spread wider, and trapping me until his hard cock was in position to penetrate me. He bit me on the neck as he thrust his cock home, which had caused me to cry out in shock and momentary pain.

"You *are* the dorm counselor," I growled. "You're supposed to be the one protecting me."

"Got ya covered," he muttered, with another laugh, as he thrust it deep again and again and again.

"Shit, what's the hurry?"

"Got no time. Got a class. Came in to tell you something, but you looked too sexy laying there. There should be a law against a guy looking that sexy."

I groaned as he turned me on my belly; coaxed me up on my knees; crouched close over me, his chest pressing mine into the mattress, my arms out wide, my fingers digging into the crumpled sheets; and pistoned my channel with his cock. He was an athlete and in superb condition. All I could do was groan and take it. It wasn't like he hadn't been there before.

When we were stretched on the bed, my body pulled into his stomach and his arms and legs entwining me again,

15

both cooling off from our separate ejaculations, him kissing my ear, I asked him why again he'd come into my room.

"Well, I was hoping for a quick fuck. Didn't want to go to class hard and I woke up with a raging hard—thinkin' about you, of course. But I also wanted to be sure you'd heard about the beach party out at Tybee Island this Sunday."

"No, I hadn't heard."

"Celebrating national Nude Day. All guys, wearing nothing. At Professor's Simmons' beach house. He agreed to let us use the place. Nifty idea, eh?"

I'm not sure what George said after that. I wasn't more than half aware that he then was standing hovered over me sitting on the side of the bed, me cleaning his cock with my mouth, him getting hard again, but pushing me off with a laugh, saying he was late to class. And then me alone.

All I could think of was that I'd be at Chad Simmons' house, nude, with another chance to have him doing to me what George had just done—but, in my imagination, slower, more sensually, making me come again and again for him.

I had snapped out of it enough when George reached the door to my room that I called out to him and he turned.

"You know you can't just barge in here and fuck me whenever you want," I said, jutting my chin out.

He laughed. "Yes I can, and you know I can. You may have the cutest tail on campus, but it's mine whenever I want it—and you are a whore for it."

I couldn't look him in the eyes. I knew he was right. If he'd come back for me then, I would have opened my legs for him. I was such a slut, I knew it. But I was aching to be Chad Simmons' slut. And I would be Wednesday night. We'd be alone. I knew he wanted me. He'd have me—and I him—on Wednesday night.

But when Wednesday night came, I found that wasn't to be.

I was naked even before he came into the studio, posing myself in a reclining position on the couch on the platform in the center of the room, my thighs open for him. It would be OK with me if this session would involve no art and just fucking.

16

But he was as cold and clinical as he'd always been in my nude sessions. He never came close enough to me to touch me, and he had me rise from the couch and pose in an open doorway, leaning into the frame with an arm raised over my head and my hip raised.

I gave him the most sultry look I could muster while he sketched me. But forty-five minutes later, he just thanked me and told me that he was pleased with the result. He then said he was late to an engagement and that I was free to go.

After he left, I went and stood in front of the easel to see what he'd done. It was a charcoal sketch done in bold strokes. He had caught perfectly the sexy, sultry, "take me" expression I'd gone for and the openness to exploration of my body. I couldn't, for the life of me, understand how he could have seen that in the art and not seen the real-life implications of it. I knew he wanted me. I just knew it.

Earlier, in a panic, I'd wondered if maybe he was only a bottom—that it had been the rich, dead lover who was the sole top in their relationship. But, in asking around, I found that wasn't true. I also found that he wasn't above nailing SCAD students, so I still didn't know what the problem was with me.

* * * *

I didn't pay too much attention to what I was putting on to go to the Nude Day beach party on Sunday and I'd just come out of the gym, so I hopped on my motorbike wearing sweat pants over a jock strap and a gray athletic shirt with a ripped flap in it that exposed one of my pecs, the one with the silver ring in the nipple. I did shower first, though. It wasn't that I was wearing what I had on in the gym. It also, though, wasn't like I had to dress formal for this; it was a nude party. I wasn't planning on wearing anything for very long. And I wanted Chad Simmons to see me in the nude outside of the context of art modeling; it was my best aspect. I was counting on him being there. The party was at his beach house.

When I arrived, I was ushered upstairs to a room that had a bed in it but was mostly a study, I thought. Lots of bookshelves and books. Guys were leaving their clothes in

17

there on a studio couch. I stripped and left my gym clothes there too. Open double doors led into a large bedroom on the back of the house. Beyond that was a balcony overlooking the beach, and the noise from there led me through the bedroom and out onto the balcony.

There were a couple of dozen guys down there, all naked, and most of them well muscled and cut. A few horses too, including a couple of black guys talking with George Garnett. They were real bodybuilders and both were covered in tattoos. I didn't recognize them as students and guessed that they were from the city. They certainly were hung, both of them. There were several down there, as a matter of fact, that I didn't recognize as students.

The beach was quite private, which I suppose was why we were permitted to do this here. Chad's lot jutted out into the water and had high fences down each side. The lots on either side were unimproved and I thought it likely that Chad owned them too—inheriting the lots and this house from the manufacturer who had been his lover. Rock outcroppings ran down either side of the lot inside the fences too, extending from the grassy area below the balcony into the sand. The rocks created little pockets of sandy areas that could only be seen from the water—and from up here on the balcony.

What I could see from the balcony was that, although there was a volleyball game going, some tanning on towels on the beach, and a few guys out in the water, the more private areas already were being put to use by couples copulating. It wasn't just going to be a Nude Day celebration, it was going to be an action party. That was just fine with me if Chad Simmons was here.

I looked carefully at those down there, but I didn't see him. I paused to contemplate what I did see—what the party was supposed to be about. Did I find it more arousing, more sexy, to see guys nude rather than clothed? It helped in the shopping, I guess. I could see what was hanging and how fluid they actually were in movement, how comfortable they were with their bodies. It certainly stirred me to see what those two black dudes were packing—and how their tattoos flowed across their bodies and undulated as they used their muscles. I

18

admit I wouldn't mind a private meeting with either one of them. But did I really see the nude guys down there as more sexy without Speedos? There was something to be said about the mystery of anticipation and hidden possibilities, I thought.

When I turned to walk back through the bedroom and down the stairs, I noticed the décor of the room for the first time. It was a man's room. The walls were a dark green in a suede texture and the other color accents were brown and gold. The walls were covered with prints, lit up by track lighting. They seemed to be Oriental studies of ornately clothed figures in ancient costumes. The Oriental motif was followed elsewhere in the room as well. I was surprised about the artwork. This seemed to be the master bedroom. I expected that Chad's bedroom would have nude male figures on the wall—most of them probably painted by him.

Maybe, though, this bedroom had been decorated by his lover and Chad had decided not to change anything.

I approached one of the walls closer and saw that they were all Japanese wood block prints. And further, that they were Shunga pillow book art from the eighteenth and nineteenth centuries. I had been exposed to these in a class at SCAD. Pillow books were essentially sex manuals. These were distinctive in that the figures in the wood block prints all appeared to be males—in couples. And they all were having sex of some sort. In keeping with the technique, the figures mostly were clothed, with just bits of flesh here and there exposed—rather more than less in some of the prints. But it was clear that they were all having sex and that, walking around the walls, I could get a clear picture of the various sexual positions for male-on-male sex that were practiced at that time. I also "got" that the arousal of sex could be conveyed with just the expressions on their faces and the entwining of their clothed bodies. I didn't have to see naked cock in hole to "get" it.

I walked all the way around the walls, and by the time I reached the doorway out into the upper hallway landing, I was hard. As I descended the stairs, I saw Chad at the front door. He was in a suit and apparently had just arrived home. He

19

seemed surprised to see me descending the stairs. I admit I was pleased that he saw me in erection.

I expected him to make a move then, but although I could see the hint of interest in his eyes, I couldn't see enough interest to have hope that he would lose control and ravish me on the spot.

"You are part of this Nude Day gathering thing, then, are you, Jason?" he said, his voice sounding a little surprised, like this was the first time he realized I was gay. He took his suit coat off while he said that, but he folded the coat over his arm. Hardly the stripping down I'd been hoping for. And a check of his basket didn't reveal any particular arousal.

"Yes, George Garnett invited me."

"Ah, George. Yes, well, the others are out at the beach, I think."

"Yes. I just arrived. We were told to strip upstairs in that study-like space." We both were being awkward. I was wanting him to cover me right there on the staircase and take me and he just seemed tired from wherever he'd been.

"Yes, well. I hope you enjoy the party."

"You aren't going to be coming out?"

"No. I don't think so. Nudity's not really my thing. I have some work to do upstairs. But enjoy yourself."

I'd reached the bottom of the stairs and he moved past me, careful not to touch me, and slowly ascended the stairs.

Not into nudity? I thought. He'd thrown me for a loop there. The man's specialty was painting the nude male figure. Shaking my head, I padded through a kitchen at the back of the foyer and out onto a covered porch underneath the second-floor balcony and then out onto the grassy area.

George Garnett, standing, alone on the verge between the grass and the sand, saw me and waved me over. Now it seemed a bit unfortunate that I was still half hard. When he saw me, he started going hard too. He obviously thought he was the one who had excited me. He had every reason to think that. He was a horse, and I'd made it abundantly clear that I liked them big.

"Happy to see me, I see," he said as I came up to his side. He put an arm around my shoulders, his hand draped over my shoulder and his fingers finding the nipple with the ring in it, and he fisted my cock with his other hand. "I thought you'd never come. I couldn't wait for us to come together. Get it? Come together."

"George," I said. "It's early in the party. Let's wait for—"

"Come into the water with me."

"George."

"Come into the water with me."

He turned me toward the ocean and held me close to him as we walked down the beach and into the water. We waded out to where the water was chest high and then we kissed and stroked each other's cocks until we were both erect. Then George moved me in front of him, both of us facing the house, crouched down, and pulled me onto his lap. His bulb was pushing into me. I hadn't really been prepared for it.

"Uh, George. Some time, please. Take it easy."

He was gripping my waist and pushing me down on the cock. He was in a good three inches and I was gasping and groaning, still trying to open to him.

"Easy there . . . Fuck! Oh, shit!"

He had thrust his hips up smartly, pushing a couple of more inches up into my channel.

"God! Oh, shit. Oh, FUCK!"

He was slamming me up and down on the cock with his grip on my waist and laughing. "Good to get right to it," he said. "You love it. This is the way you were meant to be fucked."

He was fully saddled now, and although I was whimpering and panting, I was taking him. I lifted my arms up and locked my fists behind his neck and he ran his hands down my legs, grabbed my calves, and lifted and spread the legs wide, bringing my toes out of the water. His cock sank in deeper by an inch or two and he stroked me deep.

I was going with him now. Yes, loving it now. I was happiest with a man's cock—a man's monster cock—deep inside me. George wasn't wrong there.

As he plowed me from below and behind, my gaze went up to the house. A figure was standing on the second-

21

floor balcony where I once had stood. He was dressed in shorts and a cut-off T-shirt, showing an expanse of flat belly, with a trail of dark hair descending to the low-rise waistband of the shorts. I could tell it was Chad Simmons. He was drinking a beer and looking down at the party. I didn't think he could see George and me out in the water, and even if he could, he probably couldn't tell either that it was us or what we were doing. Well, he probably could pretty easily guess what we were doing.

George kissed me on the ear and whispered. "It's good for you." he was continuing to slam his dick up instead me burying it as deep as he could with each thrust.

"Yes, it's good for me," I admitted. It wasn't Chad Simmons, but it was good for me.

"You gonna come for me soon?"

"Just about now," I answered in a jerky voice. And then I did. George laughed and kept fucking to his own ejaculation, the waves carrying the stringy cum of both of us away.

We waded back toward the beach, and, as we reached the beach, the two horse-hung black studs approached us. I looked up at the balcony, but Chad was gone.

"He's all yours," George said to the two guys. "He likes it rough."

"George!" I said, but the two were already leading me toward a pocket of hidden sand in the rock formations, where, after they did pushups in the sand over my prone body while face-fucking me, one after the other, they fucked me in the ass in succession—not together, thank god—the first standing behind me and me reaching for my ankles and the second doggy style, with me on all fours on the sand. They were both thicker and longer than George—and rougher—and I thoroughly enjoyed the fuck, although I didn't tell either one of them that.

For the next hour, exhausted, I found a towel and laid out on the sand—on my belly, to minimize the approaches. Still I couldn't go to sleep because the offers did come rather frequently, and I dared not go to sleep anyway because I was sure that being asleep wouldn't stop any of these guys from sticking a cock up my ass.

When I was afraid that I'd get burned if I stayed out any longer, I rose, brushed as much sand off me as I could—fending off a few offers to brush it off for me—showered under the outside showerhead at the door up to the back porch, and dried myself off. I went upstairs and into the study and retrieved my clothes.

I had pulled the jock strap on, the sweat pants up, and the torn athletic shirt down over my chest and was looking down at the flap in the athletic shirt and fingering my nipple, thinking that the nipple ring might have come out—which it hadn't—when I heard the deep-throated growl.

"God, Jason. Take your hand away. Let me see that." Chad walked over to me from the doorway into the bedroom and reached out and touched my nipple with a couple of fingers. I could feel him trembling. He took the nipple ring between his thumb and forefinger and tugged a bit. I couldn't hold back a low moan, and I heard him catch his breath. Our eyes met, our faces moved toward each other, and we were kissing. Deep kissing. He pulled my body into his and I felt him hard. I was hard too. I was sure he could feel it.

Coming out of the kiss, I whispered in a whimpering, pleading voice, "Fuck me, professor. Oh, god, I want you to fuck me."

He leaned down and took my exposed nipple in his mouth and sucked on it. I lifted a leg, hooking it on his hip, trying to rub our cocks together as closely as possible.

He lifted his lips off the nipple and growled, "You want it? You really want it?"

"Yes, fuck, yes. I've wanted it ever since I saw you."

He picked me up in his arms and carried me into the bedroom, slamming one side of the doors between the rooms shut with his feet. He laid me down on the foot of the bed and then went back and quickly closed and locked those doors and then the door to the hallway. He returned quickly to me and crouched over me and kissed me on the lips. His mouth went to my exposed nipple again and a hand pushed under my waistband and the mesh of my jock pouch and fisted my cock.

23

I moved my hands down to push my sweats off my hips, but he brushed my hands away. He did the same when I gathered up the hem of his cut-off T-shirt and went to pull it over his head.

For some reason he wanted us to remain clothed—at least until he did the undressing, I assumed.

I heard and felt the rip as he tore the flap of material across my chest enough to expose the other nipple and attacked it with his mouth and teeth. I arched my back and moaned. My hands slid below the waistband of his shorts, careful now not to try to push them down, and I grabbed his buttocks in my hand and kneaded them while he devoured my nipples and made little growling sounds deep in his throat.

After several minutes of this, he knelt down between my legs as he spread them and his mouth went down my body, over the material of the athletic shirt. There was a little cut in the material of my sweats below the waistband, and he took hold of that and ripped the material down—but only down midway on my thigh, creating a hole that exposed the mesh of the jock strap pouch. He sucked me off through the mesh of the pouch, relentlessly, not satisfied until I had come inside the pouch. While he sucked, his hands slid up my torso under the hem of the athletic shirt and he rubbed and squeezed my nipples. His hand took hold of the flap across my pecs and he ripped that down to expose my whole torso and belly.

His mouth was raised to my navel and he kissed and teethed lightly on the skin there before moving down to my cock again to suck in my cum through the mesh. I was groaning, lost to him, willing to let him do anything he wanted to me.

After I'd come, he turned me and told me, in a hoarse voice, to kneel on the foot of the bed, and, when I'd done so, my chest resting on the surface of the bed, I heard the tearing of material, where he split my sweats apart along my butt crack. His palms went into the slit, which he tore apart more, exposing my buttocks, and he pushed my butt cheeks apart. I felt his mouth and tongue go to my hole. He kneaded my buttocks with his hands, and his mouth briefly left my hole while he licked and kissed and gently bit my cheeks and I

24

writhed under his attention. Then his mouth went to eating my ass out in earnest.

"Fuck me, fuck me," I whimpered.

"Yes," he answered in a breathy voice, continuing to work my ass. I continued imploring him to fuck me.

At length he stood and picked me up, carrying me in front of him and turning me away from the bed and over to a small ottoman. I went down on my belly there, my torso spilling over the far edge, my cheek on the floor, my arms extending out on the floor, my hands gripping at the pile of the carpeting, while he held my legs out at the sides and slipped his cock—proving to be a very, very long cock—through the slit in the seat of the sweats and into my channel. He had worked me so open that he slid right in.

He fucked me hard, deep, and fast to his ejaculation, him fully clothed, just his cock extending through his unzipped fly, and my clothes hanging off me in tatters.

He swung into a second fucking almost directly from the first, with little pause. Certainly with no time out to undress. He took me on the bed the second time, me on my belly and him saddled on my hips and fucking me more languidly than the first time.

We heard the noise of the party breaking up, of guys going into the study on the other side of the locked doors to get their clothes. I was trying to be quiet, but he was fucking me so deep and well that I couldn't avoid moaning and groaning. Chad reached over and turned the music on on the clock radio on his nightstand—and fucked on.

The party was pretty much finished and twilight was approaching outside the French doors to the balcony before Chad was done—at least for a while. Both of us were exhausted, and he just lay, stretched out on top of me and kissing my neck and my ears. Sticking his tongue in my ear and whispering to me what a good fuck I was.

"Why, Chad?" I whispered. "I don't understand."

"You don't understand what?"

"Why now? You could have done this weeks ago. I wanted you to. You didn't know I was gay and that I wanted you?"

25

"I figured you were gay, yes, but I didn't know—"

"I flaunted myself to get your attention. I did everything I could to be naked in front of you and to take on poses that would make you want to fuck me."

I heard a low laugh.

"What? What's funny?"

"I wasn't looking at you in a sexual way when you were naked. Painting nudity is my art. It doesn't turn me on. If it did, I couldn't paint."

"But then—"

"Seeing you partially clothed—your nipple in that torn T-shirt. You fiddling with that nipple ring. That's what aroused me. I knew your body was beautiful before. But it's the mystery of the body—the glimpses of sexy parts of the body in the gaps of clothing—that arouses me. When I saw you touch your nipple through that slit in your shirt—I had to have you. And then didn't you sense the heat of my arousal at discovery as I torn your clothes off you? Didn't you get that part?"

"Ah," I murmured. And yes, ah, I thought. The Japanese wood block prints on the wall. The male Shunga studies. This was his décor after all. I should have figured it out when I saw them. The arousal of those is in the facile expressions and the bits seen and felt in the gaps of the clothing as the men fuck. In his arousal, he had created his own gaps.

He was rolling off me, turning me over on my back, crouching below me, spreading and raising my legs, entering me again through the slit in the sweats. I cried out at the penetration, sure now that we were alone in the house and not holding back in my responses to him. He dug deep with that long, long cock of his and then held there. He leaned down to me and took my exposed nipple in his mouth, rolling the silver nipple ring around with his teeth and tugging gently on it. Then he paid attention to the other nipple too. I couldn't wait for him to find out that I had a silver ring embedded under my balls, in my perineum, too. I had worn none of this body ware when I was modeling for his classes. I knew now this was part of the key to him. When he'd seen the nipple ring, framed by

26

the material of the T-shirt, it was an unexpected surprise to him and his libido instantly jumped into gear.

He set my feet on the surface of the bed, my knees bent, his pelvis still between my spread thighs, his cock throbbing deep inside me, and, grasping the flap of torn material at my crotch, ripped it down both legs to my ankles. Starting at my ankles, he ran his hand up my calves, past my shins, over my knees, pushing the ripped material aside and exposing the knees of both legs. Taking each leg in turn, he kissed and gently bit my toes, my feet, my calves, and my knees, while I lay there trembling and shuddering and begging him to renew stroking me with his cock. As if he only then had heard me, he grasped my now-bare knees with his hands and began to stroke inside me, moving my bent legs back and forth with the hands working my knees like he was rowing a boat— maintaining the quickening rhythm of the stroking of his cock inside me. The shreds of the sweats flapped against my legs and the surface of the bed. I came in a flood that added stickiness to the inside of my jock strap pouch.

Chad pulled out of me and went down on his knees, sucked the cum out of my pouch, and mouthed and teethed my cock through the mesh of the pouch. Then he was back up on top of me, sliding his shaft inside of me again and his mouth going to mine in a cum-sharing kiss.

I ran my hands up under the hem of his cut-off T, not trying to pull it off him now, but exploring his pecs and his nipples under the material, able to understand how sexy that was just to feel them without seeing them. One of my hands went down to the root of his cock, stroking the material of his parted fly while I fingered where the root of the shaft, most of it inside me, met silky, curly hair. I move my hand lower, cupped his balls, my hand buried inside his fly, and squeezed. He groaned and began stroking inside me again. I laced his balls tightly in my fingers and pulled the balls out of his fly, extending them, pulling them tight, and squeezing them. With a jerk and a groan he ejaculated inside me.

I reached for his hand and pushed it under the waistband of my jockstrap, moving it down below my balls, showing him, by the discovery of touch, the other ring down

27

there, in my perineum, below the balls. He shuddered and fingered the ring . . . and hardened again and resumed stroking inside me.

In the darkness, later, as we lay in an embrace, still clothed, although in dishabille and now with his cock no longer in me, exposed to the air, standing up straight from his body as I stroked and squeezed it, he murmured. "It's too late for you to go home. You'll have to spend the night."

"I have nothing to wear."

"I have a silk robe I'd love for you to wear while I fuck you."

"Well, OK. If . . ."

"If what?" he asked.

"If tomorrow we go shopping in second-hand clothing stores where we can get clothes for me that turn you on and that are disposable. I can't afford to have any more of my own clothes torn up."

He laughed and I rolled over on top of him, nuzzling my head under the hem of his cut-off T; reaching for one of his nipples, buried in a nest of curly black hair; and, finding it, suckling on it. He didn't seem to object to that much exposure of his flesh but just lay there, humming deep in his throat. My fingers went to the other nipple, not wanting it to feel left out. Then my mouth took possession of the nipples, one after another. I worked my tongue to the matting between his pecs and then tongued his silky, curly black hair down his sternum, over his belly, and into his pubes. Licking up one side of his once-again-erect cock and down the other, I moved down to lick the balls that protruded from his open fly, swallowed them, and sucked.

With a roar, Chad lifted me and set me on his hips for the long slide of my channel down his shaft. I rode him, there in the dark, my hands inside his T-shirt, palms on his pecs, to what was, finally, a gloriously shared ejaculation, both of us, at least to some extent, still clothed. My cock had never left the jock pouch, but still I felt fully satiated.

And so much for that, I thought—so much for any need I might have for Nude Day.

28

Used

Phil came into the sauna as I hoped he would. He came up to the top tier and sat below me where I was lying on my back, just a white towel around me, the leg toward the wall bent, foot flat on the wooden slats of the bench, with the other leg straight. He sat close enough to me that the roughness of his towel brushed the toes of my stretched foot. I had started hardening up just in anticipation that he'd come. It had been Phil who had said "See you in the sauna" and had given me "that" look. And I continued to engorge now that he was here.

It had been my first visit to the gym I'd signed up to use on Tuesday and Thursday evenings, and, saying that he was a physiotherapist at Baltimore's Mercy Medical Center, he volunteered to spot me. I said that was fine with me. I liked the look of him already, dark-haired, maybe ten years older than I am, sparely built, but with the musculature of someone who gymed a lot. What really got me was that he was colorfully tattooed all over his torso and arm on his right side. I couldn't see it all because he was wearing an athletic T over his shorts, but it appeared to be one, swirly Oriental pattern. Very intriguing.

He had a gentle, sensual touch with strong hands and long, thin fingers.

I wasn't the only one he was spotting. He spent time with a small Hispanic guy about my age too. I could tell that he aroused me not only because I was hardening up while he was spotting me but also because I felt the loss when he was working with the Hispanic guy.

I had taken his "See you in the sauna," along with the look he had given me, as indications that he'd known I had hardened and was interested. I wasn't easy or anything and didn't go with a guy often, but I wasn't any virgin either. When I went with a guy, I wanted it to be casual, like this was, and I wanted him to take the initiative and control. And I wanted him to have a good body, which Phil had—with the bonus of the intriguing tattooing. I'd had no intention of going in the sauna before he'd said he'd see me there.

I felt his hand on the calf of my stretched-out leg. He was lightly massaging the muscle of the calf. I neither drew away from him nor responded positively. Not drawing away from his touch was an affirmation, of course, but I wanted him to be the aggressor. I went harder. I felt his other hand wrapping around the ankle of my bent leg and the one on my calf raised my right leg to a bent position as well. He gently coaxed my bent legs into a wide stance, and there I was, the towel around my waist spread wide and him scooting in and sitting close below me. He could see all the way up my thighs. He could see what I was packing; he could see that I was hard. And he could hear my shallow pant.

I opened the stance even wider, welcoming him in. It's as far as I was going to go, though. I wanted him to make the committing moves.

Both of his hands glided in, along the inner surfaces of my calves and thighs on either side, slowly. He was giving me time to object. I could have swung away, off the bench, and just walked out of there. I didn't. I wasn't doing anything to help him, but I was giving all control over to him. When he got there, one hand encased my cock and the fingers of the other laced themselves through my balls and distended them. My cock was throbbing inside his loose grip and my moan surely was audible to him.

There's was no fooling anyone now what was happening, whether I was open to it.

Letting loose of his hold on the balls but not the cock, he changed position, moving down to the bench tier below me and sitting below my waist, and turned toward me. He leaned over and took my lips with his and, while we kissed, he began to stroke my cock. Sitting back up straighter, he captured my eyes with his. Neither of us said anything, but I was breathing heavily and giving little whimpering sounds. I was overwhelmed by arousal and it didn't take long before I jerked, gave a little exclamation, and came in his hand.

Still we were silent; still he was holding my eyes with his. His cum-slathered fingers moved down to my balls, lacing through them and distending them again. A slick thumb moved around the rim of my hole and then penetrated me. I gasped and raised my buttocks to give it a better angle, and the long thumb entered me to the knuckle joining the hand, and he began to slow stroke my ass. He stopped occasionally to press in hard with the thumb and jerk it back and forth, causing me to raise my pelvis up, my body to shimmer, and me to groan deeply. That arm had gone under my leg and I raised my right leg and rested it on his shoulder on the tattooed side.

He was murmuring, barely audible, but I heard. "Nice. I'm gonna fuck you; I'm gonna fuck you good."

I *wanted* him to fuck me. I didn't do this often. But when I did, it was casual like this. I wanted him to more than finger fuck me; I wanted whatever he had between his legs inside me.

We both heard the sound of the sauna door opening, and he pulled his hand away and turned to a seated position as I quickly lowered my leg. It was the Hispanic guy, small of stature, but a well-cut body and a cute face. He came in and sat below me, his back to my face and beside Phil. Phil's attention went to the other guy, and I felt the loss. He put his arm around the Hispanic guy, and it wasn't long before I could tell that Phil was giving the guy a hand job. I could tell it from the moaning the guy was doing and the movement of his back in front of my face.

My feeling of loss was accentuated when I heard Phil murmuring to the Hispanic too. "Nice. I'm gonna fuck you. I'm gonna fuck you good."

"Yes, fuck me, fuck me good," the Hispanic was answering.

31

I knew the moment the Hispanic came. And I knew when Phil lifted him and pulled him into his lap and lowered the Hispanic guy on his cock, the Hispanic whimpering, "Yes, yes. Fuck me, fuck me. God, you're so big." And then I knew the moment Phil stopped pulling the small guy up and down on his cock and ejaculated. When Phil was done, the Hispanic wrapped an arm around his neck, arching his torso, and turned his face to Phil's for a passionate kiss. I didn't need any more evidence than that that Phil had fucked him good. I ached for it as well.

Letting the Hispanic play through like that did embarrass me, but I was patiently, or impatiently, I guess, waiting for my turn—either right there or in the shower or anywhere Phil asked me to go with him. I told myself that Phil was saving me, that he wanted to taking longer doing me.

But when he was finished with the Hispanic guy and they both stood up from the sauna bench, Phil just turned, leaned down and kissed me on the lips, and muttered "Later. Let's meet again later." I tried not to show my disappointment and he hadn't broken the connection. He'd said "later."

* * * *

"Interested in going someplace and shooting pool tomorrow night?" Phil asked as he was spotting me on the bench press Thursday night.

"Sure, but why not tonight?" I asked, not being in a hurry to be with him or anything.

"Can't tonight. I'm working the night shift. In fact, gotta get going now."

"Where should we meet and when?" I asked, trying not to let the disappointment in my voice show. I had been looking forward to tonight for two days—since he'd finger fucked me on Tuesday.

"How about the President Street Starbucks at about 9:00 p.m.? There's a good place with pool tables not far from there."

Friday night and Phil was late getting to Starbucks, by about half an hour. But I waited for him. It occurred to me

32

that it was done on purpose as a show of control, but that suited me. I wanted him to know he could control me. When he arrived he was dressed in green hospital wear—cotton-like trousers and a tunic-like thing over them.

"Might have to go into the hospital later," he said. "One of my regular patients isn't doing so well. Vertigo."

"Maybe we should cut the pool and go straight—"

"Naw, I'm sure it will be OK, and I want to play pool."

The place was full of atmosphere and testosterone. Everyone in there was male, and several looked like they were cruising. I got a couple of whistles myself on the way through the bar area to the room in the back with three pool tables. The air of both rooms was filled with smoke; it was hard to find a place in Baltimore these days that permitted smoking like this. I didn't smoke myself, but I connected it with being macho, and macho turned me on. All of the tables were in use when we got there, but there was just one guy at one of them, a good-looking tall, trim professional-looking dark-reddish-haired guy in well-pressed jeans and a navy-blue mesh T-shirt that closely fit his well-muscled torso and showed his beefy pecs off real well.

"Hi, there," Phil said to him as we sidled up to his table. "Mind if we join? This here's Shawn."

The guy and I shook hands as he said he'd enjoy having us shoot pool with him. Phil had said his name, but I didn't retain it. I was busy looking him over and liking what I saw. I did remember where Phil said the guy worked. He was an accountant in one of the big-name insurance companies that had its own skyscraper down at the nearby Baltimore Inner Harbor.

I wasn't good at pool, and Phil didn't seem much better at it, but the accountant was really good and was good about standing behind me and helping me to line up my shots. He got friendlier as the game progressed, as in he pulled in a lot closer to me when helping me line up those shots.

It wasn't long before Phil came back from a visit to the head and was holding his cell phone in his hand.

"Sorry. Gotta split. The patient I was worried about fell and may have broken something. Later, OK?" he said to me.

33

It wasn't really OK with me, but it had to be. He left me in the middle of a game with the accountant.

"Want to go grab a bite to eat after we finish this one?" the accountant asked.

"Sure," I answered.

"A Five Guy's burger OK with you? It's nearby and right next to my apartment building."

The conversation over the burger was easy. He showed more interest in me studying to be a vet at the Community College of Baltimore County than I was able to muster in what an accountant did in an insurance company. I kept not being able to match up a guy with a great body like he had to sitting behind a desk half the day. But he was attentive and we found other things to talk about. The discussion got around to sports, as it usually does between two guys, and to professional basketball. I was purely hometown and followed the Baltimore Bullets. He went further afield, saying he followed some California teams but was partial to the Washington, D.C., Wizards.

"Hey the Bullets and Wizards are playing tonight," he said, like it had just occurred to him. "A late game. It may have already started, but we could catch most of it if you like. It's on TV and my apartment's right around the corner."

Naturally, having cleared my calendar for the departed Phil, I said, "OK, fine."

He lived in a pretty snazzy building, and although he only had a studio apartment, a living and dining area with a kitchen behind a bar counter and then a sleeping el off to the side with a big bed in it, it was kept neat and was expensively furnished. He had a gigantic wall TV on one wall with a sofa in front of it, and this was where we sat. I had to sprawl on the deep sofa and lift my chin to focus in on the TV screen.

The game was already half way through the first half. He got us beers after he'd gotten the TV on and set on the right channel—two beers for each of us. When he came back to the sofa with them, he'd taken the mesh T-shirt off. I surfaced the question again of how a desk jockey could have such a finely developed chest.

We sat there, side by side, watching the TV. The players looked nearly life-size on his TV and I found the game mesmerizing at this size. I don't know when he'd put an arm around me, but it was sometime into the second beer. I do remember when, during a commercial, he'd turned my face to him and we kissed. It was right after that that he pulled my T over my head and we kissed again while he ran a hand over my torso and rested it on my belly as the game came back on the air.

"Do you mind?" he murmured.

"No, not at all," I answered. I was quite mellow at this point. And, god, did he have a great body.

During half time he left to go to the bathroom, delivering me another beer before he left. I had half of it drunk before he came back. He was naked and was carrying a couple of packets of condoms and a tube of lube in his hand. Most of my attention, though, had gone to between his thighs. He was horse hung, both long and thick. And a good ways erect.

I, of course, knew what was going to happen then, but I was too mellowed out to care and the guy was Grade A for the occasional casual sex I liked to have.

He came in close to my on the sofa when he sat down. "Are you going to let me fuck you?" he asked in a low voice.

"Yeah, I guess so," I answered. Might as well. I was planning on doing it with Phil anyway.

Before the second half of the game started, I'd downed the third beer and he had my jeans off and me stretched out on the sofa, my chest on an arm of the sofa, my head flopped over the side and my arms extending toward the floor, my fists gripping the sofa legs, front and back. His face was buried in my crack and he'd pulled my cock through my legs and was stroking it with one of his hands.

We'd done no talking since he'd come back, naked, from the bathroom and had pinned down that I'd let him pin me down. Until then I had been so absorbed in the game that I thought we were just fooling around a bit.

He didn't ask me a second time if he could fuck me, although it was quite obvious now that was going to happen. And I hadn't to him at any time that he couldn't either. He'd

35

taken control, assuming assent, and that was OK with me. The other guy being aggressive and self-confident went a long way. That had been more than OK with me ever since I saw what he had hanging between his thighs. One of my fascinations was in accommodating a huge cock—knowing that I had all of that inside me and could manage it. Not that I'd had a lot of experience with this—but enough.

When he rose from in back of me and came around to the side of the sofa to present his cock for sucking, he brought the TV clicker with him. As I took the cock deep into my mouth, seeing how far back into the throat I could get it before the gag reflex won out, he changed the TV to a gay male fuck video. The basketball game wasn't over, I didn't think, but he must have thought that the game had served its usefulness now, and I was too far gone with him to be concerned about the score in a basketball game. It didn't hit me until now, that he hadn't really been that much into the game anyway. He'd spent more time looking at me than at the screen.

He fucked me there on the sofa, with me in the same position he'd put me in to begin with and him stretched over my back. I'd given him some "yes, fuck me. Oh, shit. Slower, please. You're killin' me. Oh god, oh, god, oh, god" lip while he was entering me, but once he was saddled and starting to pump, I just lay there, whimpering and groaning and gasping and breathing real heavy as he plowed me. He'd put a towel under my midsection, and I stroked that with the underside of my cock while he fucked me. When I came, it was on the towel, leaving his sofa all nice and neat and clean.

He had this down to a science. Probably fucked three guys a week on this sofa, I was thinking. I had the presence of mind to wonder how I compared with the others.

After we'd both come and laid there, cooling down, as I felt his cock shriveling up—never really shriveling, though, always thickly possessing—inside me, we whispered, him telling me how nice and sweet I was and me complimenting him on the size and strength of his cock. He told me he didn't do this very often, which I knew from how he had it all set up was a lie, but that I was too sexy to resist. I told him I almost never did it either and that he was like to split me with that

36

horse cock of his. That pleased him, I could tell—and as I knew it would.

Neither one of us apologized or said it shouldn't have happened. He didn't say anything about a repeat date, though. This was OK with me too. Just a casual fuck. No threat, no chains. He wasn't Phil in my mind or plans.

When he let me up off the sofa, the porn flick still going on the screen, I went into the bathroom, peed, and cleaned myself off with a washcloth. I looked into the mirror, examining my face for some sort of self-remorse for being such a pushover on a casual meeting. I didn't see any sign of guilt. What I saw was a little smile, remembering how big the guy's cock was and how I'd taken it all. I tried remembering his name or even a sense of where this apartment house was in Baltimore in relationship to places I knew of, like the inner harbor, but nothing came to me. That did make me slip on a little frown.

I stood back from the mirror, took a "pose," and dipped my head down a bit, letting a lock of hair fall down in my face, and gave what I thought of as a sexy James Dean expression. I looked good and highly fuckable, if I did say so myself. "Please, Mr. Accountant with the huge cock, can you stick it in me again, pretty please?" I murmured, gave a little laugh, and then turned back to the bathroom door.

When I came out of the bathroom, he was sitting on the foot of his bed, swigging another beer. He had another in his hand, which he gave to me, and I stood there in front of him, pulling on the beer, while he did the same with one hand and palmed my cock with the other and slow stroked it. The porn was still going on the TV. I thought then that he must have it in some sort of loop. The actors kept changing, even though the fucking didn't, so maybe it was something that just played constantly.

He had a fresh condom on his cock and was hard. When he'd finished his beer, he latched onto my waist, turned me, and pulled me down onto his lap. It took a long time for me to slide down his pole, but when I could feel his reddish short hairs tickling my buttocks, he held there, one of his hands roaming my chest and belly and thighs while the other

37

one slow stroked my cock. He was waiting for me to finish my beer.

When I did finish it, he took it out of my hand, tossed it onto the carpet beyond danger of involvement in our fucking, and, arms encircling my waist, reclined back on the bed, taking me with him. He brought his legs up on the bed between mine, bent his knees, placed his feet on the edge of the foot of the bed and spread them. This spread my legs out wide too, but I managed to dig my toes into the edge of the bed and raise my pelvis enough to give him space to pull nearly all of the way out of me before stroking deep inside again— and again and again.

He fucked me in long, strong, ever deepening and quickening strokes, while I babbled how fully and well he was taking me and the porn continued on the gigantic wall TV screen across the room.

After he was done, he pulled me up with him fully onto the bed, used a clicker of some sort from a nightstand to turn off all the lights in apartment—with the porn still going on the TV screen—wrapped his arms around me, and pulled me into his stomach.

I woke up only once in the night—near dawn, it seemed, from the dim light now showing in the room from around the corners of the curtains on the two windows. The TV screen was flickering its never-ending porn film. I was on my belly, with the accountant straddling my hips and slowly working his cock inside me. For some reason—possibly because we both were half asleep or because we were more reliant now, in the darkness, on the sense of touch rather than sight—this was the most sensual of the couplings.

He worked into me slowly, his bulb kissing my walls as he descended, giving them close attention as they opened to him. I raised up on my knees and spread my legs to give him deeper access, and his cock gained every nano inch it could inside me. I was dragging my cock on the sheets to provide friction, and he snaked a hand in, grasping the sides of the cock with his fingers and increasing the friction of the underside of the cock on the sheets. The other hand cupped my chin and turned my face to his for a kiss. I could feel him shudder, and

38

from there he took me quickly, vigorously. When I came in his sheets, I remember thinking nonsensically, "Oh, shit. Now I've left DNA." and worrying whether he'd be mad that I had soiled them.

When I next woke, still on my belly, one arm dangling toward the floor, it was light and he was coming out of the bathroom, obviously showered—I could tell because his hair was still wet—in a white shirt and dark suit trousers, and fixing a cufflink. He looked up and smiled.

"Good morning. I'm almost late for work. Coffee's made and feel free to scrounge anything else you can find for breakfast. Just be sure the door is locked when you leave."

I was thinking that it must be rough to have to work on Saturday and wondering if that was what all accountants had to do as he walked into the living area, picked up the TV clicker, and—at last—turned the porn off on the screen.

It was suddenly very quiet in there, as he knotted his tied and pushed his feet into a pair of loafers. I kept waiting for him to say more, but he didn't. This was the first time I'd ever spent the night with a guy. I assumed there was more that they said to each other the next morning. For the life of me, I couldn't think of anything to say. Ask him if he had flavored creamers for the coffee? Where the sugar was? Something, probably, but I didn't know what.

Ask him if this was it? Should I leave a telephone number or something? Surely this wasn't the end of it. At no time, though, did he suggest we'd be doing this again. I almost felt the notch being carved on his belt.

I heard the click of the apartment door and was all alone. I closed my eyes, needing more sleep, because, frankly, he had exhausted me.

I probably *should* have asked him "what now?" He had a cock to die for and he handled it real well. I had always skidded away from any possibility of entanglements, and he certainly had treated this as nothing more than a casual check on his list of conquests, but I could see the possibility of something more with him. But I didn't even remember his name. I was out of the apartment, the door locked behind me,

39

when I realized that a little snooping probably would have rewarded me with his name at least.

It was then, too, that I decided I wanted to leave my telephone number. But the door was locked and I had neither pen nor paper of any sort with me.

* * * *

"How about taking a walk down at the Inner Harbor after the gym tonight."

Phil had whispered this in my ear as he held me when I'd come down off the chin-up bar. Tuesday night. He'd left me with the accountant on Friday night when we'd had what I thought was a date, just the two of us, but he hadn't said a thing about that tonight. Of course he'd given me warning Friday night that he might have to go to the hospital.

That entering my mind, I answered him with a change of topic. "How's that patient? The one who fell Friday night that you left the pool hall for?"

Was that a hint of panic I sensed in his intake of breath—that I wasn't just saying yes to going with him tonight after having been stood up on Friday night?

"Turns out it wasn't really my patient. But since I was the one who was called in, I had to feel her legs for possible breaks and stay until her doctor came in. Nothing broken; just bruises."

You can feel my legs again anytime you want, I thought. And this being the case, I quickly said. "Glad to hear it wasn't anything serious. Yes, I'd love to walk down to the Inner Harbor with you after we finish here."

Phil had been spotting the small Hispanic guy too, whose name turned out to be the pedestrian Pedro. But I still was surprised—and more than a little teed off—that it was Phil and the Hispanic waiting from me to dress and that Pedro was obviously going to do the walking with us.

The Inner Harbor of Baltimore is all gussied up with outdoor cafés and promenades, a yacht basin, and a large, popular aquarium. Even at 9:00 p.m., there were noisy crowds and a lot of partying going on, with lots of colored lights and boats out in the water, shimmering from the dancing light of the moon and the lights on the promenade.

We walked around a bit, with me wondering when and if we'd drop Pedro, or if Phil was in to taking us both on at once—which I was willing to try. Phil stopped, though, beside a table in an open-air bar. Two beefy black guys were sitting at the table.

"Well, hello there, guys," Phil said. "Mind if we sit?"

"No. Glad to have you," one of the black guys answered in a deep voice. "We're about to shove off for Mickey's, though."

"That sounds good to me," Phil said. "Maybe we'll walk on over there with you. This is Shawn and that's Pedro. And these are friends of mine, orderlies in the hospital, Buck and C. J." We shook hands. The one called C. J., by far the better looking of the two, and built to beat the band, wasn't real quick to give me my hand back.

Mickey's proved to be a gay dance club on Lloyd Street, east of the Inner Harbor, that I'd never been in before. I didn't go into gay clubs, normally. I took my few encounters as they came in straight-life venues. I didn't advertise and didn't go into this life all that much. The night with the accountant was probably the wildest time I'd ever had with a man.

Lots of smoke again, this time caused by a smoke machine, I was sure, and strobing lights, in various colors. A not-so-great-but-who-cares? band was playing and the dance floor was chock-a-block with gyrating men. The tables and bar were crowded too, although every time we went to the bar from the dance floor, spaces cleared for us. Buck and C. J. were commanding figures. Some would even say threatening figures. They were in silky soccer shorts and muscle Ts, and I had to admit that when we were dancing with them, they were both sexy and sensual in their moves. And very macho. Every gyration and thrust was powerful, sexy. We were almost having sex right there on the dance floor. I would have gone hard out there even if they hadn't touched me, but they did touch me. Both of them.

I was facing C. J. when the band went into one of its rare slow dances, and C. J. just put his hands on my waist and

41

pulled me into his crotch. I could feel the heft of him against my groin, and I knew he could tell I was hard. His hands went to grip and squeeze and separate my butt cheeks, and he ground our pelvises together as we moved against each other in place. I put my hands on the back of his head and our foreheads were plastered against each other. Our eyes were locked. If we weren't both clothed, he would have been inside me now.

"I'm gonna fuck you tonight," he murmured. "You want my dick."

"Yes," I answered in a whisper, not knowing if he heard me, knowing that it didn't matter to him if I said yes or no. God, the stud was nearly fucking me now.

A fast dance started, and, with a laugh, C. J. pushed me away from him and spun off to dance with someone else.

Phil was still on the dance floor with a willowy, rather effeminate blond when C. J. said he wanted another beer and he pulled me, while Buck pulled Pedro, to the miraculously space-available bar. The two black studs ordered beers for the four of us, and Buck enfolded the small Pedro in his arms and dry humped his leg, while C. J. pulled a bottle of different-colored pills out of his pocket, opened the bottle, and poured a stream of the pills out on the bar top beside the beer glasses.

"Your choice," he said with his mouth close to my ear. After he said that, he stuck his tongue in my ear, and turned my face away.

"None, thanks," I answered. "I don't do drugs." I wondered how he could be doing this so openly.

He shrugged, while holding me close to him in an encircling arm, picked out a pill, popped it in his mouth, and took a swig of beer.

I relaxed a bit, figuring he wasn't going to press the point. He turned my face to his with a hand under my chin, and we went into a kiss.

He pushed the pill almost all the way down my throat with his tongue. It only took a moment to take effect.

It was just a swirl of memories from there until the morning when I woke up slouched behind a dumpster in an alley off the Inner Harbor. Snatches of visions of the evening

42

before rose to the surface. The four of us were in a back room, probably in the same club, because this band was as shitty as the one that had been playing when I passed out. I was kneeling on the floor, my back against the wall, C. J. standing over me, the heels of his hands pressed to the wall on either side above my head. Face fucking me with a big, black dick.

Buck was plowing Pedro on a cushioned platform in the center of the room.

C. J. plowing me against the wall, with my legs hooked on his hips and my arms around his neck.

Buck fucking me on the platform while C. J. took care of Pedro against the wall.

Then just three of us in a car, no Pedro. C. J. fucking me in the backseat while Buck drove, and then C. J. driving and Buck fucking me in the backseat. Both of them with big, black, hard, cocks.

I would have liked to have been fully awake for it. But if I had been, I don't know if it would happened at all. Maybe, maybe not. They were both real studs.

The last I'd seen of Phil was him dancing with the effeminate blond on the dance floor of Mickey's.

* * * *

"Where'd you go Tuesday night?" Phil asked when we first ran across each other in the gym Thursday evening. "I was dancing on the floor and then when I went to look for you, you all were gone. Went to another club, did you?"

He burst my bubble of anger by being the first to speak. It made sense. We'd left him; he hadn't left us.

"Yeah, we went someplace else," I muttered, looking down at my socked feet. It was too embarrassing to give him any details. They were his friends—coworkers—apparently. In a big hospital, though. He wasn't responsible for what they did. And I couldn't say I wouldn't have gone with them without the drugging. I'd told C. J. I would, before I was on any sort of manufactured high. I couldn't say I didn't enjoy getting fucked by two big, black dicks. It wasn't what I'd ever done before, and it helped me feel better about it that I didn't have much of

43

a say in it happening Tuesday night. But I also didn't want to make the decisions and I wanted to be controlled. Couldn't have been controlled any more than that.

"Well, how about tonight after gym," he said. "We really do need to get it on."

Yeah, we really did need to get it on. It seemed like something that just wasn't happening, but I couldn't see that that was anyone's fault.

"That would be great . . . I thought—"

"We could go clubbing. Maybe back to Mickey's."

"Not there, please," I answered. "But, yeah, to a club somewhere. And then—"

"Great. Great. Let me introduce you to a new guy here. Randy. Randy, come on over here and meet Shawn. Randy is willing to spot other guys, but he doesn't know what to do. Mind if he tags along tonight?"

It depended on how far he was going to tag along, I thought, but I said. "Yeah, sure."

Randy was a big guy, maybe of Scandinavian extraction. Blond and big boned. Pretty much in shape, though. Big hands and big feet. I wondered if the old story of that meaning he was big elsewhere panned out in his case. It had in C. J.'s case. I didn't remember the accountant's hands and feet, and he'd been bigger and thicker than C. J. was. Randy had a sloppy "golly gee" smile that I liked.

So, I had two spotters all to myself this evening. Pedro hadn't shown up. I wondered at one point why not and worried a bit about when and how he'd dropped out of the mix Tuesday night. But I didn't wonder long.

The Scandinavian had a sensual touch. Not like Phil, who obviously was professional at touching other people, but in a strong, steady way. He was good at spotting, because he exuded confidence. He was open and humorous and seemed clean cut as well as well cut. He was wearing a wrestler's athletic T that was too big for him, with the scoop of the neck hanging down to his navel, showing bulging pecs and plump nipples and aureoles the size of quarters. He had a ring in one of the nipples, which made me see him as gay. It seemed that most of the guys coming to this gym were gay.

44

I had a revelation and went instantly angry, though, when I was coming out of the changing room and into the front reception area to meet up with Phil. Phil wasn't alone. Randy was there with him, obviously ready to go "walking" with Phil and me just as Pedro had done two nights previously. And more than that, money was exchanging hands between Randy and Phil.

Instantly I understood all. I don't know if Phil ever intended to give me a proper fucking. But it looked like he'd rent me out for as long as he could get away with it—and without cutting me in for all that I was giving out.

I turned and went out the service exit in the back and down a fire escape and to the street. Then I came around to the front of the building and waited in the bushes. The Scandinavian came down to the steps in front the building and stood there for a few minutes. He was joined in a few minutes later by Phil, who obviously was apologizing for not being able to find me in a search of the gym. Somewhat reluctantly the cash went back from Phil to Randy, and Phil walked off.

I waited until Phil was pretty far down the street and so did Randy, apparently not being sure where he was going next as it wasn't where he thought he'd be going.

"Hi," I said, as I walked up to him.

"Hi," he said back. "You're here. We were looking for you and Phil couldn't find you."

"Crossed signals, I guess," I said. "He told you you could fuck me, didn't he?"

"Yes," the guy looked somewhat embarrassed at having it said so openly. "He said that he arranged your dates for you—and handled everything."

"And you gave him money for it?"

"Yes. But he couldn't find you, so he gave it back."

"Just crossed signals," I said. "You can give it to me. I've got a place we can go."

I'd kept my place tidy. It was a small room with a kitchenette and a bath in something nearby but not much more fancy than a tenement. Mostly student housing, which I covered by working part time for a vet while going to school. I'd kept it tidy since that first encounter with Phil in the sauna,

45

because I also thought there would be a good chance Phil and I would wind up there some night—some night before this, of course.

I rode Randy's cock with him on his back and holding my waist as I straddled his hips. I was delighted to note that the adage about big hands and feet, big cock held true with him. It took some time for me to take his whole shaft in. After the first coupling, he whispered how good it was for him and asked me if it did it for me too. I answered that it did, mostly, but that I liked it better when the other guy took complete control.

"How far does that fifty bucks stretch?" he murmured.

"As far as you want," I answered.

"Through the night?"

"Yeah, if you want. You're good."

"Even if the bed collapses?"

"We'll do it on the floor then." I was thinking of Phil, what I was—and would be—denying to Phil with this encounter.

I had a loose but, it turned out, a resilient bed. Randy admitted that he liked the way it squeaked and the headboard and footboard moved dangerously with the rhythm of the fuck. I thought then that Randy was trying to bust the bed as he missionary piston fucked me and the bed squeaked and moaned in harmony with my moans and the headboard and footboard shimmered back and forth. I met him thrust for thrust until he exhausted me. And then he fucked on alone until my tongue was lolling out of my mouth and I was lying there, appendages every which way, like a Raggedy Andy doll.

He banged me twice more the next morning, taking complete charge, once with him standing at the foot of the bed and me arched back to the bed on my shoulder blades and him grabbing my hips and pounding my ass and once, by complete surprise, on the kitchen counter as I was fixing us something to eat. That was my favorite one.

When he had showered and left the apartment, me still in the bed watching his every movement, he left me an extra $50 on the nightstand. I would have liked to see him again, but I knew that, just like with the accountant, that wasn't going to happen. To these guys, thanks to Phil, the pimp, I was a

46

prostitute one-night stand. While he was showering, I had looked in his wallet. His name wasn't Randy. I made no attempt to remember what his real name was, though. I didn't take anything out of the wallet. Phil may have made me a prostitute, but I wasn't going to be a thief too.

I didn't go back to the gym, deciding that losing the money on that contract was better than contending with Phil again. I felt like I'd dodged a bullet by not bringing him back to my place. He didn't know where I lived. I'd just given my school box number to the gym when I'd signed up. I liked the fucking, and I'd liked the men he'd hooked me up with a lot; I just wasn't that fond of being used.

Pianoman

"First the tide rushes in, plants a kiss on the shore . . ."

Matt often started a set with something quiet and slow, like "Ebb Tide," when there was a convention or two in the hotel, like there was today—electricians and bankers. What a combination. Something quiet tended to settle and quiet them down to the point that he could stand it.

It wasn't a question of being a prima donna and needing the people in the bar to hang onto his piano playing and singing no matter how many years he'd gone to a first-class music school to learn these skills. He knew he was only there for background. But raucous noise put him off his game. It reminded him too much of Peter—the man he returned to during the day, the man who wasn't taking his recent forced retirement by a hostile buyout of his company well and who was taking much of his ire out on Matt. And Matt had the bruises to prove it.

The smooth, low, slow strains of "Ebb Tide" were working to some extent. The conventioneers close to the piano were speaking in lower tones than those out on the fringes of the room: bankers closer in, electricians packed in beyond and raring to go. Beyond a certain point his music couldn't be heard, so there was no consideration being given to the thought that someone was performing. He didn't resent them. They'd been penned up all day in meetings and this was their first chance to unwind. And the first opportunity to become frisky, for those who took advantage of out-of-town conventions to let loose in ways they wouldn't do at home. And this, after all, was Las Vegas, where the ads told you to let it all hang out.

This was OK with Matt too. He had put this to his advantage—increasingly so in recent weeks, having made the decision that the answer for this whole thing with Peter was for the two of them to split. The only problem was that virtually everything the two had belonged to Peter. It was the way he wanted it. If Matt was going to break away, he needed the means to do it—and to leave any backlash from it here when you went home.

The drinkers at one table nearer the piano were speaking louder than the others in his vicinity and Matt couldn't help but turn his ear in their direction and pick out the discussion. There were two women and two men, and one of the men was doing everything he could to put the moves on a younger, strikingly good-looking woman. From the dress of the men, Matt assumed they were executive level and from the youth and looks of the women, they were probably secretaries—or, as they called them these days, personal assistants. The man was concentrating on his moves on the young redhead so intensely that he probably didn't even know that Matt was playing the piano nearby and crooning softly into a microphone. The young woman, though, was listening to Matt—or at least pretending to, perhaps to try to tamp down the man's advances.

The man addressed the young woman as Laura, his voicing cutting right through the background murmuring. Almost unconsciously, Matt segued from "Ebb Tide," into "Laura."

"Laura is the face in the misty light . . . footsteps . . . that you hear down the hall . . ."

Matt had the young woman's complete attention. She obviously knew the song as about her. The man didn't notice, of course. He was on a mission and had his landing approach all mapped out and in gear. But the redhead—Laura—certainly paid attention. The dreamy-looking man with the curly blond hair and the smooth-as-silk voice at the piano was playing for

50

her—directly for her. And he was looking at her and smiling at her, for her.

"Excuse me," Laura said, after having jotted something on a cocktail napkin and standing up from the table. "I need to powder my nose. Coming with me, Tiffany?" She was speaking to the other three at the bar table, but she had eyes only for Matt, who smiled back at her—as he smiled for anyone in the audience giving him their full attention.

It probably hadn't even occurred to him that he had transitioned into "Laura." So well trained were his fingers that they could manage a complete set on their own, keying on something going on in the room, snatching it and matching it to a song tune, while Matt's thoughts were elsewhere all together.

The two young women walked away from the bar table with the campaigning executive looking slightly surprised and trying to keep track of where he had left off in his pitch so that he could pick it up again when Laura returned.

Laura and Tiffany brushed past the piano on the way out of the bar, and Laura dropped her cocktail napkin in his tip hat. This Matt noticed. He kept close tabs on that tip hat of his. That was undeclared income. Undeclared to Peter. It was for the stash Matt was trying to build to get out from underneath Peter.

After Laura and Tiffany had safely passed and were exiting the bar, Matt checked the hat. No added money. Just a napkin with a room number written on it. Room 717.

Matt sighed. He got room number notes like this three or four times a night. And sometimes he welcomed them when they led to added income. But not when they came from a woman, even one as gorgeous as Laura was.

Thus interrupted in his playing, Matt's fingers picked up a new tune, one reflecting his mood. The check of the hat showed that he was behind the curve on tonight's take. This put him into a "Deep Purple" mood.

"When the deep purple falls over sleepy garden walls . . ."

He sensed someone at the side of the piano. It wasn't unusual for a bar patron to come to the piano and lean over it,

51

savoring his playing, wanting to hear better amid the background noise of the drinkers, or waiting patiently to request a song. Matt welcomed such a presence. The patron usually dropped a few bills in the hat before drifting away. He turned his face up, bringing the brilliant smile to his face that always disarmed whatever patron it was bestowed on—male or female.

But it was only one of the bar hostesses.

"Hi," he said to Emily, keeping the smile, as it always was good to keep the other bar employees on your side. Emily had somewhat of a crush on him, so he was careful in traveling down the middle of that road with her—a tease of suggestive teasing and nothing more. She probably knew he didn't lean that way, but there was no reason to press that point. She looked good—dressed like the queen of tarts to celebrate Valentine's Day the next day, no doubt. She didn't look as good as the Laura who had slipped him her room number, though. So, he would be looking elsewhere if he was going to be tempted . . . which he wasn't. Not in that direction.

"Hi yourself, handsome," Emily said, giving him a sultry smile. "I come bearing a couple of fives and a twenty, the latter with a request for a song."

"Twenties are nice; fifties are finer," Matt said, as she dropped the bills in his hat. "Hope it's a song I know."

"You know all the songs. It's a good one."

"What's the song and who's the requestor?"

"He wants to hear 'Strangers in the Night.' That beautiful South American man over there."

Matt turned his face toward the crowd, directed by Emily's turned chin, and then he froze. The man by the elevator on the ninth floor.

Obediently, of their own, his fingers moved on the keys.

* * * *

It had been after his first set of the evening, another napkin dropped in his hat, with a fifty and a room number—932. A male this time. One of the conventioneers. Middle-aged,

52

maybe a bit of a paunch, but otherwise well-muscled. Ugly as sin in the face, but, in the dark, who cares? All he'd wanted to do—at least then—was to suck Matt off and stroke himself as Matt gave him sounds that made him feel Matt was having a really good time. He said he'd like more later but couldn't wait for at least this.

He'd wanted a kiss at the door as Matt left, too, though, while murmuring that they could do more later that night, after the businessman had attended his last session at the convention. Matt was noncommittal. After his last set, he'd do whatever was the most advantageous at that time.

Farther down the hall, the elevator door opened, and there he was. The hunk. A well-dressed, extremely well-put-together South American. Walking out of the elevator, his progress arrested as he saw the other man and Matt, close together, kissing, at the door of a room down the hall.

It was only a brief moment, but it had embarrassed Matt. The man at the elevator was so much more than the man who had pulled him close and surprised him with a kiss at the door to his room. Matt was still in the process of tucking his tux shirt into his trousers, so there wasn't much for the man at the elevator to misconstrue.

Maybe if the man hadn't smiled before he turned and walked the other way down the hall. Maybe then his image wouldn't have emblazoned itself in Matt's mind. Maybe also if the man hadn't been such a hunk—so much more so than the guy who paid fifty dollars to blow Matt and was angling for more later—at his convenience. Not bothering to ask Matt what would be convenient for him.

* * * *

The Hispanic hunk across the bar, maybe pushing forty-five, but not pushing it hard, and a beautiful man, with sensuous lips, was smiling the same smile. He inclined his head slightly to establish a connection with Matt from the smoky distance. Matt automatically acknowledged the salute and, with trembling fingers, began the refrain of "Strangers in the Night."

"Strangers in the night . . . exchanging glances, wondering in the night . . . what were the chances we'd be sharing love . . . before the night was through."

Matt sensed a presence at the side of the piano. He raised his eyes a bit, permitting his fingers, their strength increasing, to do what they did on the piano by habit. The gold cufflinks with the diamond insets were the first things that caught his attention. Then the manicured hands, meaty and strong, but very well taken care of, came into view.

The man was leaning his elbows on the top of the piano, comfortably, like he belonged there, in full command.

"Strangers in the night . . . two lonely people we were. Strangers in the night . . . up to the moment when we said our first hello . . . little did we know . . ."

"My name is Enrique," he murmured, as their eyes met. "After your last set tonight, if you are interested. The tip for playing the song, whether or not."

Matt watched as a business card, with a hundred-dollar bill wrapped around it materialized in one of the hands and was deposited in the hat. Then the man—Enrique—was gone.

Matt, shuddering slightly, his fingers, on their own, shifting into "The Shadow of Your Smile."

"The shadow of your smile when you are gone . . . will color all my dreams . . ."

He didn't bother to check the hat. He knew that the business card would have a room number on it. It did. Room 1425. One of the hotel's junior suites. He didn't give a second thought to what he'd be doing after his last set was finished for the night.

* * * *

He was all Matt ever wanted—or could want. More than Peter was; more than Peter ever could be. Expert, forceful, controlling, yet solicitous. And long and hard and thick. Virile. Fast to recover; unrelenting. The young, blond musician had no idea how Enrique sensed that he melted to slight bondage, something Peter never wanted. Matt's wrists were tied behind his back with the Brazilian's—Enrique having

54

told Matt that was his nationality—silk necktie. Not enough to actually incapacitate Matt if he wanted to break away, but enough to give the illusion of control having been relinquished.

Matt didn't mind the act with a stranger as long as there was the illusion that he wasn't complicit.

Enrique, solid and strong, heavily muscled, dusky-skinned, slightly hirsute with black, curly hair, sat on the side the bed, an arm encircling the slighter, nearly alabaster-white blond's waist, as Matt sat in his lap, facing him, knees bent and calves flat on the bed, encasing Enrique's meaty thighs, and arched back over the bedroom carpet, bound arms dangling toward the floor. Enrique's other arm moved from a hand cupping the back of Matt's neck to fisting and pumping the young musician's respectable—but put to shame by Enrique's—cock, while Matt raised and lowered his hips, with the strength of his knees, ever more rapidly on the cock buried in his channel.

Starting with Matt fucking himself on the cock, at the Brazilian's command, both of the men wanting to establish that Matt wanted it but that Enrique, his cock moving inside Matt's channel, caressing every undulating wall, controlled it. Then the finish of Enrique turning Matt, shoulder blades on the surface of the bed and bound arms over Matt's head, while the muscular Brazilian crouched between the young musician's thighs, spread wide and raised with Enrique's hands fisting Matt's slim ankles, and, pulling the young blond's pelvis off the bed to meet his, the forceful, experienced older man pounded, pounded, pounded Matt's slowly opening channel. First Matt, and then Enrique, ejaculated in noisy, animated explosion, punctuated with Matt's tenor-baritone and Enrique's bass flood of dirty fuck words off the street—some of Enrique's in Portuguese—that would seem out of character for each man in more controlled circumstances.

Enrique's laughed, "That was good. That was very good."

His shaft still buried deep inside Matt's channel, Enrique stood at the foot of the bed, bringing the younger man up with him into his arms. Matt hooked his knees on the muscular Brazilian's hips and, initially, nuzzled his face into the

55

hollow of the Brazilian's dusky and slightly hair-matted chest as Enrique held the younger man close and rocked back and forth, the lubricated slipperiness of the sheathed cock giving off a sucking, slap-slap sound as, healthy, needy, and virile, his cock regained girth and length. He pushed Matt's shoulder blades back onto the surface of the bed with his head, his lips finding the young blond's nipples, as Matt threw his bound arms over his head again and moaned to the sound of the forceful Brazilian's suckling at the younger man's nipples and the moist slap-slap of his cock inside Matt's channel, pulling Matt's hips toward him with each deep—deeper, thicker than the previous time—thrust, thrust, thrust of the insistent, digging cock.

Matt arched his back and emitted a little cry of passion as the two came simultaneously. Too exhausted now to say anything dirty, knowing now that the Brazilian needed no egging on.

Afterward they sat at the table by the window of Enrique's junior suite, he in a hotel robe, Matt naked, as they feasted on what was either a very late supper or a very early breakfast the Brazilian had ordered from room service.

The two explored each other in discussion in a way Matt had never done with any other man who had brought him to a hotel room from the bar for a far tamer tryst than the two had just enjoyed—in fact in deeper and more intimate detail than Matt had ever conversed with Peter.

In what was refreshing to Matt in these encounters, Enrique showed no reticence in talking about himself, and, seeming to understand that Matt was a bit skittish about it, he talked first.

"No, I'm not married. I've never made it secret that I'm a man's man. And, yes, my heritage is Brazilian, but I'm an American citizen. Ties back to Brazil, of course—mostly financial ties; I'm in international banking. But I've lived and worked in New York for over twenty years."

None of this seemed to be put on. Enrique had given him a business card with his room number on it. It identified him as a New York banker, manager of a branch of a Brazilian bank, and it gave a full name and contact numbers. Unless he'd stolen the card from someone and was playing with a false identity, he was being open with Matt. He certainly seemed to be Brazilian. Matt even got him to speak a bit of Portuguese— the words Enrique had spoken in Portuguese during sex, words that made Matt blush upon hearing the translation—which were offered without hesitation or embarrassment and were quite fluent—certainly graphic—as far as Matt was concerned. And there *was* a banking conference going on at the hotel.

"I don't usually do this when I'm on the road. But, you know, it's Vegas, and you are such a delicious treat. Achingly luscious. Compliant and resilient at the same time—and what you can do with your channel muscles. I don't often find a young man like you. And I have a weakness for young blonds."

His brilliant smile and openness disarmed Matt completely. In truth, he'd already laid Matt completely open with his lovemaking. Matt had thought of it as that— lovemaking. Not just fucking. It was something that Peter and he had, briefly, attained at the beginning of their relationship. Now, though, they just fucked. And argued.

"Me?" Matt, in turn, asked. "Why am I in Las Vegas? To play the piano and sing. Not much money in it in Tennessee, where I came from. Do you know where Tennessee is?" And then, at Enrique's nod, "Then you know why I had to leave. Certainly couldn't make the money that can be made here."

Then, in embarrassment, Matt went silent, his mind on that hundred-dollar bill that Enrique had dropped in his hat, confident that it would buy him what it had, indeed, bought him. Matt's thoughts went to what he had been denying to himself. He was just a whore. And Enrique had paid him generously for the lay. By talking about money just now, he'd sounded so mercenary.

"I'm not really money hungry," he blurted out, wanting to move to higher ground. "I'm making a change and need more than the piano playing pays to move on. It's just temporary . . . what I'm doing here."

"I know you're not a whore—or, at least, not mine. The hundred dollars was yours whether or not you came to my room. I wanted it to be something you wanted. But temporary? I got the impression you enjoyed me fucking you."

"Yes, of course. That's not what I mean. I mean . . . that . . ."

"I understand. You aren't really a prostitute, not really. That's fine. You are an outstanding musician, and drop-dead gorgeous. That should be—"

"Now you're mocking me," Matt said, a bit distressed.

"And you're an outstanding lay," Enrique said, with a laugh. "And men who enjoying it shouldn't deny any opportunity they have to do it. I know I don't."

Matt, completely disarmed by Enrique's openness—and compliment—laughed as well. He felt the tension draining from his body.

"A bad relationship? Is that why you need to move on?"

Matt felt completely naked before the Brazilian. He was physically naked, yes, but Enrique was completely stripping away all of his reservations, everything he'd been keeping to himself—and he found himself relieved and exhilarated by it.

And he opened the floodgates of his reserve and told Enrique of it all. Of Peter, who had swept him off his feet soon after he'd arrived, straight from Julliard, in Las Vegas and had begun working on the Strip. Of how forceful Peter had been, taking full control and taking care of Matt's every need. Just as Matt liked it.

So open was Matt that he told Enrique exactly what he wanted from a man, and Enrique murmured an "I've gathered as much."

Matt told Enrique of how Peter had founded a company that rented out party and restaurant supplies and that had done well in Vegas, even with Peter micromanaging everything—and despite his volatile temper. It had done so well, in fact, that it had attracted the attention of a larger company, which had worked to put Peter's company in a financial corner, had acquired the company in a hostile takeover, and had booted Peter out to an early retirement while he was still in his mid-fifties.

Although the takeover had made him comfortably rich, Peter was too young to retire and too old to start over again and was railing at everyone and everything, including Matt. His violent temper extended to the physical. He hadn't put Matt in the hospital—yet. But it wasn't out of the realm of possibilities. And it was always over something trivial, something Matt couldn't see coming. It kept him off balance, on edge, so that he only felt comfortable now here at the hotel, while he was playing the piano.

It was only a matter of time before he threw Matt out—his eyes were already roaming elsewhere—and Matt needed to find other arrangements before he was out on the street with no idea where to go. He'd always been taken care of. He wasn't a virgin when he'd come to Las Vegas. He'd had a forceful man to take care of him ever since he'd entered college. He'd still be back at Julliard if his mentor hadn't died. Matt had a "thing" for older, controlling men.

"So, you need an older, stronger man to take care of you," Enrique summarized. "And you enjoy the fuck—being fucked."

Matt wanted to object to the bald statement of it, but he couldn't say Enrique hadn't summed it up correctly. And Enrique already had another hundred-dollar bill out and was looking at him meaningfully.

"That's not necessary," Matt said. "I want it again as much as you could. I couldn't . . . now . . ."

"It will be here if you change your mind," Enrique said.

"Say those words again," Matt said. "Speak dirty to me in Portuguese again."

Enrique rose, smiling and letting his robe part, and moved around the table to pull Matt up close to him and whisper in his ear in a throaty voice. "*Trepar, fodor, funicar, sexo, porra,*" he whispered. "*Fazer sexo com alguém. Gostava de fazer sexo com Mateus.*"

"That last. What . . . ?"

"I said I enjoyed fucking Matthew."

Matt shuddered and grabbed Enrique's buttocks under the robe, holding the Brazilian close to him and feeling

59

Enrique's cock rise under his balls, penetrating between his thighs.

This time Enrique made slow, deep, quiet, total love to Matt, both of them stretched out on the bed, but changing positions so that Matt was on his belly with Enrique on his back. Then Enrique side-splitting Matt, and, finally, Enrique on his back, with Matt, facing the ceiling, stretched over him, feet and elbows digging into the surface of the bed and his buttocks rising and falling on the ever-hard, thick, and long cock. Throughout the early-morning hours, they were plastered to each other with Enrique's cock deep inside Matt's channel.

They slept through what was left of the early morning. Embracing. Matt cuddled into Enrique's chest, Enrique's cock still possessing Matt's channel. When Matt awoke, Enrique was gone, a note had been left saying he had sessions to attend for his conference. The hundred-dollar bill was still on the table by the window. Matt was tempted, but he left it there.

Matt went back to Peter's apartment, just down the street from the hotel and two blocks off the Strip, wary that there would be a scene with Peter for staying out all night. No matter what tricks Matt took at the hotel—which Peter didn't know about anyway—Matt had always been back home by 3:00 a.m. Always before. Not this morning.

But when Matt got home, there was no evidence that Peter had been there in the night either. Matt quickly mussed up his side of their bed, finishing just as he heard the front door to the apartment close. He came out of the bedroom drinking coffee, as if he'd just gotten out of bed himself. Peter didn't bother to tell him where he'd been—and, more important, didn't ask where Matt had been. He just grumbled and jabbed at Matt about this and that not having gotten done around the apartment, went straight to the bathroom, and turned on the water in the shower.

It was the first time that Matt was happy that Peter wasn't showing any interest in what Matt was doing.

* * * *

60

"Winds may blow over the icy sea . . . I'll take with me the warmth of thee, a taste of honey . . . a taste much sweeter than wine."

He had been there, at a table with four other three-piece suited men, in a back corner, when Matt had arrived in the bar for his first set. Matt hadn't intended to open with "A Taste of Honey," but his fingers, as they often did, just did their own thing—matching his mood, again, as they often did. He wondered if Enrique would be listening to the song and connect it with how happy he made Matt feel.

Enrique was deep in conversation, and if he turned his face toward Matt in acknowledgment, Matt didn't catch it for a while. But then he was looking over toward Matt and speaking to the man sitting to his right, another nearing middle-age, well-heeled-looking business executive, who also was giving Matt the eye while the two businessmen conversed.

The man Enrique had been talking to rose and moved toward the entrance to the bar, brushing past the piano in passing, and, Matt noticed, while he was playing "What I Did for Love," dropped a napkin wrapped in a bill into the hat on the piano. The man returned in a few minutes—probably from the men's room—and gave Matt a smile as he passed the piano. Matt automatically flashed back his "keep the patrons happy" smile. It was only as he was getting to the end of his set that Matt looked into the hat.

Another hundred-dollar-bill wrapped around a cocktail napkin. As, usual, the napkin had a room number written on it. But, to Matt's surprise, it wasn't room 1425, Enrique's room, but 1240. Matt's eyes went immediately to Enrique's table. Enrique was looking away from him, but the man who had dropped the note in the hat was looking at Matt, smiling at him.

Matt felt his stomach lurch and an immediate depression set in. His fingers went to the keys.

"When Sunny gets blue, her eyes get gray and cloudy. Then the rain begins to fall."

It had hit him like a sledge hammer—both that he cared and that Enrique obviously didn't—not only didn't care but was just passing Matt on to the next man willing to pay a

61

hundred dollars for his ass. There was no reason—no right—for him to have thought otherwise, of course. But it came as such a surprise—both that he cared and that Enrique obviously didn't. He was just another whore, good for a throw down and then a toss away.

Somehow Matt made it through the rest of the evening, the next three sets, punctuated with rest breaks standing in front of a sink in the men's room, soaking his face in cold water. Pretending that some of the moisture wasn't tears.

During the first two sets, he let his fingers play whatever they wanted. It would be a morose evening for the patrons of the bar. He knew that, but he didn't care. He wouldn't go. The man would have to tell Enrique the next day that his helpful bit of information on getting a good lay hadn't panned out. During the last set, though, he knew he'd go to room 1240. More than ever before, he needed a change. He needed to be done with Peter—to be done with all men who used him and threw him away. And for that he needed money. A hundred dollars was a couple of hundred more miles away from Vegas.

Matt went out on the Strip and walked up and down for an hour after his last set. It only made him feel more isolated—everyone swirling around him was exuding happiness. Many of them probably weren't happy inside, but this was Vegas. Having gotten here, they were going to have fun if it killed them. Suddenly everything in life was such a fake; nothing mattered much at all anymore. Having any scruples or principles—or hopes or dreams—didn't matter either. He laughed a dry laugh. He certainly was in the right city for that.

He returned to the hotel, threaded his way through the casino, where people were throwing their money at the machines with grins on their faces and gin and tonics fisted in their hands. Determined to have a good time being fleeced by impersonal machines. He hesitated before knocking on the door to room 1420, still struggling with himself on whether he was enough of a whore just to carry on with this. But then he knocked . . .

. . . And his eyes went big when Enrique, only wearing a hotel robe, opened the door.

"You're . . . this is 1240 . . . this isn't . . ." Matt stammered.

"Plumbing problems in my other room. They switched me. It's late. I thought you might not come. I saw my world collapsing."

"The other man—"

"Was going to the men's room and dropped off my note for me. What? What did you think?"

Matt tried not to tear up as Enrique pulled him into the room.

Hours later, after they had fucked in more positions than Matt had ever known existed, and lay, exhausted, watching the dawn creep in through the gauzy curtains on the window, Enrique whispered something in such a low voice that Matt had to ask him to repeat it.

"They have hotel piano bars in New York, you know."

"So I've heard."

"I'll take good care of you."

"So I hoped."

63

Position Interview

I tugged on the lapel of the suit and looked around the deserted reception room, admittedly a bit nervously. I felt quite alone here. The receptionist had checked me in, made a call, told me to take a seat, picked up her purse, and was gone. An end-of the day job interview appointment. I adjusted the knot on my tie and smoothed down my hair. I moved the heel of my right shoe back, feeling it encounter the end of the small duffle bag I'd placed under the chair. Didn't want to lose that.

It was all nerves. I knew I looked good. Eddie told me he liked sending me out on temp assignments like this because I looked so good in either a suit or a tux. Of course Eddie would probably tell me anything he had to to get me to do this.

Eddie had said, "Your name is Jeffery Walker. Remember that. And give him this résumé as soon as you enter."

"Résumé?" I'd asked. I scanned it. "This isn't anything I'd know about doing. I can't even pronounce half of these words."

"Don't worry, he won't look at it. Just make sure you establish that Eddie Jones sent you. He won't be concerned about anything else."

"Eddie Jones?" I'd asked, giving Eddie MacMillan a confused look.

He returned a pointed "don't ask, stupid," glare at me. He was right to. I'd done this before. It's just that Eddie had sprung this on me on short notice.

"We've got you backstopped," Eddie had said. "That's all that matters."

The room was starting to go to shadows. The receptionist had been gone for a good fifteen minutes now. It was well beyond the appointed time. I took several breaths. I didn't want to start sweating. Not in this special suit Eddie had given me to wear.

"Mr. Walker?"

I hesitated and then looked up at the door that had opened to an inner office. The voice was assertive and had cut through the silence like a knife. There was an accent in it. Spanish?

"Yes, sir, that's me."

"Step in here, please."

He was maybe in his forties. Good looking and built like a tank. Looked really good in his suit. Graying at the temples, but on him it looked good. Dark and sultry. Steel gray eyes. The Spanish accent. Yeah, maybe Spanish. He looked Mediterranean. He looked luscious. I was surprised. I had expected another sort of interviewer.

He stepped aside and grasped my hand as I entered the room. A warm smile and a strong grip in the handshake. "I'm Carlos Vendoza," he said. "Take a seat over there." He pointed to a chair on the other side of a big, wide, but not deep mahogany desk, swept clean. I sat, as I heard the door to the reception area close—and a lock clicked—behind me.

Vendoza came around and sat in the executive chair on the other side of the desk, facing me. We were really sitting pretty close together across the narrow desk. And when he leaned forward on his elbows, it almost was like he was invading my space—not that anything in this room was my space. It was all his, and he gave off the vibes of everything in the room being his too.

"You were sent by . . . ?"

"Eddie Walker," I said as I laid the résumé Eddie had given me that had too many unfamiliar technical words in it for

66

me to have had any hope of memorizing it, in front of him on the desk, the print turned toward him. It would be more accurate to say that I placed it under his nose and between his elbows. He fingered the edges of the document with strong-looking hands—long, sensuous fingers—but he didn't look at it. His eyes were boring into me, testing me without even starting into the questions.

"You understand what this position is, Mr. Walker? That it would be under me?"

"Yes, sir. I understand that. Mr. . . . Jones . . . hadn't specified what the business was, though." Eddie had told me to talk like this really was a job interview, to ask questions about the job.

"You could say that we work with imports and also . . . deposits, you might say. The company is based in Bogotá, Colombia. I'm the Miami connection, umm manager. I guess you could say I'm the inside man in Miami. Does that bother you, Mr. Walker? Me being an inside man?"

"No, sir. That suits me fine." Ah, that explains the Spanish accent then.

I had been looking above the man's head. I lowered my gaze and noticed that he had taken off his suit coat and tossed it aside on a side chair. His blue dress shirt looked expensive. Probably silk. And it was tailored close to his body, tapering down from bulging pecs to a smaller, but still solid waistline. The material was thin. I could see the shadow of the dark, curly chest hair swirling around on his pecs and descending in a trail toward his waist. And the material puckered at his nipples.

Although all of that was included in what I observed, that wasn't what caught my attention and made me take my breath in in a gulp. He was wearing a gun holster in his left arm pit with a godawful big and long handgun sheathed in it.

And then there was his foot. As I'd already observed, the desk wasn't too deep and the knee hole was open on both sides. His socked foot was resting on its heel on the edge of my seat between my thighs. Mostly on reflex, I widened my stance, and he pushed the foot farther into the chair, pressed his toes to my crotch, and began to rub. Any illusions that someone in my position could have had about this interview to this

67

point—although most anyone would have caught on with the empty reception room and the click of the lock of the door—what he was doing with his foot would dispel that. My reaction was to go hard. There was no doubt that he could feel that with his toes.

"You haven't asked what it is that we import, Mr. Walker."

"I was interested in that, but would it really matter?" I asked, as I watched him unbutton the top buttons of his shirt.

"No, not in serving under me—me being an inside man—no, that shouldn't matter to you. But I'll tell you that we work with pharmaceuticals and in moving money."

"Ah. Good to know." No saying later that I didn't know, that was for sure.

"You are interested in the gun, I see, Mr. Walker."

Well, I was initially, but now I was more interested in watching him unbutton his shirt and pull it off his back. The hint of a magnificent, hirsute chest and taut nipples that had been given through the filmy blue material was borne out. The man was a bodybuilder and was doing all the right things in sculpting his body.

"It's big and long, isn't it?" he said. "The gun. That's me. A big and long gun. I'm also what you could call an enforcer. You wouldn't be expected to do that as well—working under me—I would cover you as needed. Do you understand?"

"Yes," I said in a voice that was somewhat weaker than I intended.

He had his tie off and was winding each end through his fists. He moved much quicker than I was prepared for. He was behind me, looping the tie over my head and around my neck before I had time to react. He pulled me up from my chair and kicked it aside. I was gagging as he pulled my head back into the hollow of his neck while bending me over the desk, my chest landing on top of the résumé he hadn't bothered to read.

He fucked me from behind, bent over the desk, with that big, long gun of his. He took his time, both in the fuck and in the preparation. He'd choked me with the tie enough to

68

have me gasping for every breath of air I could get and not worrying about anything else he wanted to do to me. When he released me, I just lay on top of the desk, looking at the floor on the other side of the desk and moaning and gulping in air, as he ripped my shirt off my back, leaving the tie in place.

I felt the bulk of him come off my back and his hands go to my butt cheeks as he knelt behind me. I heard and felt the rip at the seam of my breakaway suit trousers and then my briefs as he opened up access to my now-bare ass. And I felt the colder air on the cheeks and then his warm hands, spreading them. And his hot breath on my asshole.

"Don't even think of moving," he growled. And with a thought to that gun in his holster and to his size compared with mine, I didn't. I lay there, chest on desk top and fists grasping the far rim of the desk, groaning and grunting, as he pulled my cock and balls through my spread thighs and worked them over with his hands and his mouth.

By the time his mouth had moved back to my asshole, with his hands spreading my butt cheeks apart, I was his for anything that he wanted to do.

And what he wanted to do was rise up behind me, grab and reverse my tie to my back, and arch my torso back toward him with brutal tugs on the tie that left me gasping for air again. Stuffing himself inside me, me grateful that he had opened me up well with his mouth and tongue, he took me in long, deep, ever-quicker strokes that had me forgetting the choking of the tie around my neck. I gave him an A in stamina and vigor. Just in case I thought of objecting to any of this, I could feel the leather of his holstered handgun banging against my shoulder blades each time he jerked my torso up to his chest with a tug on my tie. He rode my ass hard, without letup, for twenty minutes to, first, my ejaculation on my nice new, polished shoes, and then his. He'd worn a condom, although I had no idea when he'd sheathed himself.

He exhausted me with the first fuck, but if I thought he was finished, I was very much mistaken. After he'd ejaculated, he stayed inside me, embracing me from above while he let his hands roam and told me I was "a good one."

69

He was really good at fucking himself—and I told him so.

After he'd calmed down, he began heating himself up again, ultimately with me on my back on the desk top and him crouched over my face and feeding his cock into my mouth for me to get hard again.

He climbed down off the desk, pulled my pants and briefs—what was left of them—off my legs, and made love with his hands and mouth up and down the black silk calf-high socks with suspenders that Eddie had insisted that I wear. He enjoyed doing that enough—and it looked from where I was laying that it made him even harder—that I had to wonder if Eddie knew something about the demand I wear those socks that I didn't.

After I watched him roll another condom on and spritz his cock and my hole with lube, he grabbed my legs at the ankles, spread them wide, giving me a wide stance that I appreciated immediately after, and thrust back inside me. I think he fucked me even longer this time than the first. And he was just as vigorous as before. I had reason again to think that he had to be spending a lot of time in the gym.

I would have let a guy this good looking and built and endowed do this to me for free—at least that's what I thought until the point of his last ejaculation. As he was building up to one, signaled by his ragged breathing and the jerkiness and intensity of his stroking, he let loose of one of my ankles and pulled his handgun out of his holster. Scaring the bejezuss out of me, he rammed the barrel up into my mouth. Frightened out of my wits and too surprised to react—and well, about to hit my own shoot off—I lay there, paralyzed.

I heard the click as he ejaculated. And then the deep laugh. A click, not an explosion and then nothing. But who knows it if was just a misfire. We struggled for the gun. He was still laughing, maniacally, I thought.

I'll always remember the rush of adrenaline from having the gun barrel pushed in my mouth and the struggle with the guy for that gun.

* * * *

70

I heard the click of the office door behind me and went over to the chair I'd been sitting in in the reception room and dug the small duffle bag out from underneath it. I'd scouted out the men's room outside of the elevators on the floor when I'd first arrived, and I went there, stripped, and cleaned myself off with paper towels and water from the bank of sinks. I worked as quickly as I could. Eddie had said for me to get out of there as quickly as possible, and I certainly wanted to do that. I was exhausted. All I wanted was a beer and eight hours of sleep—in a very isolated place.

Shredded breakaway suit and shirt in hand, I looked around for the trash bin. Then I remembered that Eddie had told me not to leave anything like that behind either. Of course he was right. I stuffed them in the small duffel after taking out my jeans, T-shirt, and bikini briefs. An entirely different, completely casual look. I checked my face in the mirror to make sure nothing needed to be cleaned off and saw that my hands were trembling. I felt so numb that I hadn't known they were.

Out on the sidewalk, I looked up the side of the high rise, trying to pick out the window of the office where I'd been. I couldn't. I don't remember having looked out of the window of the office to get my bearings.

I laughed then, relieved by "mission accomplished."

Eddie had told me that these were good jobs and that they paid more because of the kinkiness of them. Other than the gun being pulled on me and stuck in my mouth, I had found it all very interesting and arousing.

His story had been a good one—if you take away Eddie having explained it all from the beginning. Not the gun, though. Certainly not the gun. And if you didn't know that this was the headquarters of a major insurance company and that the title "Insurance Agent" hadn't been stenciled on the man's door over his real name—Kenneth, not Carlos, Vendoza.

He'd almost had me fooled about being South American—not the drug cartel business, of course. That was over the top but really pretty hot, in its own way when matched with his Latin good looks and great body. And that dick,

71

oolala, that magnificent dick. He'd only dropped the fake accent when we were heavy in the clutches and he'd lost control of what he was saying.

All in all a good fantasy category assignment. And a great fuck. If the guy contracted for another fantasy fuck, I'd be happy if Eddie signed me up—the guy had said he wanted to see me again. But no guns next time. That was almost too real. I would have shit my pants on that if I hadn't cleaned out real good before going there. And if I'd been wearing pants. And if he hadn't had my ass channel stuffed with his big, long cock.

White Stripes

Chad saw the big, fancy sedan, a BMW 700 series, sitting all by itself back in a darkened corner of the parking garage as the bus drove around and around, spiraling up to the top, open deck, where it came to a stop. That had been the only car he'd seen in the garage. It was a Sunday, and this was a city workers' garage.

"Strange. No one in the ticket booth," the driver said to the man standing in the well by the door of the bus, a shotgun in his hands, pointed to the ceiling of the bus.

"Maybe the garage is unattended on a Sunday," the shotgun man answered, not showing much interest.

"That would be unusual," the driver muttered under his breath, thinking this guy was less vigilant and more just along for the ride.

"OK, everyone out." The bus had come to a stop on the top deck. The supervisor turned, facing the young men sprawled out across the seats of the bus, and added. "Grab a brush and a bucket of paint on your way out."

"We gonna be told what we're here for at some point?" Jareed, the black guy who usually asked the questions for them, asked.

"This is your lucky day," the supervisor answered. "You get to work indoors—sort of. Did you ever wonder who repainted the white stripes on those parking space dividers in parking garages?"

"Not really," Jareed said. A couple of the other guys snickered, but the supervisor just smiled.

"Loser jackasses like you guys, that's who. That's what you get to do today, men and girls. You get to slap new paint on the parking place dividers . . . all of them. And you'll get demerits for painting outside the lines or wasting any of the white."

"But there must be—" a thin voice piped up.

"Five stories. Yep, it's a five-story parking garage," the supervisor said to Larry, who was the runt of the group and never said anything that didn't come out as a whine. "And so, ladies, you need to get to it."

"Starting where?" Jareed asked.

"Way down on level one, from the ticket booth," the supervisor answered.

"Then why's the bus parked up here?" Another whine, so it was Larry who asked.

"Because you'll be working through your mandatory exercise period, so you're exercise will be in trotting down to the first level."

"And I suppose when we've worked our way up here, the bus will be down on level one," Jareed said.

"Do you have a problem with that, Jackson?" the supervisor asked. "Can your little girlie legs walk that far?"

"No, boss, no problem." Jareed could tell from the supervisor's voice that he'd had enough backtalk.

"Then it's time for you to stop lollygagging around here and get your asses down to the street level."

That was OK with Chad. He wanted to get another look at that sleek sedan on the third level and maybe someplace where stuff could be stashed between there and the street level that no one would see.

The sedan was still there when he reached the third level and there, on level two, was the type of city trash can he loved. He knew that the bottom of the can had space under it—that the side skirts lifted the bottom of the can a good six inches off the ground. He also could see that the can was just about empty. It wasn't likely anyone would be back to empty it for a month or more, and they wouldn't lift the whole unit

74

anyway. The actual trash receptacle was a separate can inside the outer shell. Underneath the whole thing, as he well knew, was the perfect place to stash something for days on end.

He'd be able to come back in two weeks—if he didn't get into any trouble in the meantime.

When they were down on the first level and divvying up who would work on what, Chad volunteered to work at the top of the first-level ramp and paint his way down toward those starting at the bottom. There were enough of them there that day that the supervisor and the bus driver wouldn't be able to watch and account for them all continuously. Like most of the other guys, Chad stripped off his T-shirt and hooked it in the backside of the shorts he was wearing. He didn't want to get paint on the shirt. He'd get shit for doing that. It was a jail-issued black shirt with white stripes. It didn't need any extra white stripes.

He knew he could slip away for the time it would take to check out the sedan and be back without them noticing there was one guy fewer painting for a while.

He told the two guys he was painting with that he had to take a leak and would be gone for a couple of minutes. He knew they wouldn't report him as missing for any time he took and that it was plausible that he'd go on up the ramps to an out-of-the way dark corner to take his whizz. There was no bathroom around. They all had to piss where they could from time to time. Homeless guys no doubt did that in here all the time. It was a city building, not a fancy shopping mall.

As Chad walked up the ramp, he rummaged around in the pocket of his shorts. He always kept some of what he called his "aides" with him, entangled with other metal rings and such that the powers that be thought it was just some sort of puzzle he liked to work during the times when the guys were just sitting around waiting for something to happen—which was most of the time.

One of the pieces he took out of the tangle as he moved up the ramps to the third level was something that enabled him to pop car doors and trunks quickly and silently.

The BMW was a real honey. It would have a nifty tape deck, but he decided to check out the trunk first.

He popped it quickly, raised the trunk, and reared back, with a loud "Yo!"

There was a body of a young man in the trunk. Not a dead body, Chad could see. The guy was trussed up and had thick tape over his mouth, but he was moving. And he was looking at Chad with his eyes wide open. But only at first. His eyes sifted to beyond Chad and got even bigger.

"You lost, buddy?"

Chad whipped around. The guy looked like he'd come right out of a casting call for Mafia types for a movie. Italian dark and swarthy. Muscular build. Bigger than Chad certainly. But looking mean as all hell. That gun he had pointed at Chad looked mean too.

"The trunk was already open, honest," Chad said, raising his arms away from his body in case the thug was trigger happy. "I didn't see nothin'. Just saw the trunk was open and came over. Didn't look in."

"I saw you pop the trunk, and I saw you look in and step back. Who are you trying to shit?" the man said. "So, now, what am I going to do with you? Looks like there's room for you in there too. A double-down day for me."

"Hey, man, you don't need to go—"

"But you were too handy by half with whatever you used to pop the trunk. Over by the side of the car and assume the position. You look like a guy who knows how to assume the position. I don't want you in that trunk with something you can use to open it from the inside."

"Look, man. I've gotta be back down on the street, or there will be—"

"What part of assume the position don't you understand, blondie?"

The "blondie" got to Chad. He looked at the guy for the first time. Really looked at him. He had the same expression on his face that any john did down on the street when Chad was hustling. The thug was interested. The last thing Chad wanted was to be put in that trunk with the other guy. He brought his hands down and slowly moved around to the side of the sedan. While he did so, he pushed the waist of

76

his shorts down low on his hips, low enough to show some butt cleavage.

He assumed the position against the car, but he jutted his buttocks out a good bit. This wasn't just a good position for a body search. This was a good position for one guy to cover another one for a little hanky-panky. As he assumed the position, he saw that there were DVD cases in the backseat. Gay male porn. So he was right about this guy. He had a chance here.

The man started to run his hands over Chad's bare torso—where he couldn't have possibly been hiding anything. And he was taking his time doing it. Chad could hear him breathing heavy.

The one thing Chad didn't want him to do was to feel all the way down to the hem on his shorts. There was some items Chad didn't want to be found sewn in the material there. One of them had always been a nuisance before, but it could be a lifesaver now.

"Here. This is what you'd be looking for. Here in my pocket. That's all I've got."

He started to reach in his right pocket, but the man pushed his hand away with the barrel of his gun and put his own hand in the pocket, bringing out Chad's metal puzzle, with the "aides" entwined. While he had his hand down there, though, he pushed it around to the front and got a feel of Chad's cock.

"Yeah, that's what I used to pop the trunk," Chad said. "It's all I'm carrying. I'm clean otherwise. But you don't have to stop feelin' me up if you want to. I liked that."

He really hated giving up the aides, but it was better than the guy finding out what else he had. He couldn't let the guy do that.

But the thug had his hands on Chad's hips now, over the material of his shorts.

"You're getting me all hot and bothered," Chad whispered.

"Am I now?" The man leaned into Chad's back real close and moved both hands around to his front and palmed his basket. "Got anything in here?"

77

"For you? Maybe, yes. Maybe something you'd like," Chad whispered. "Or maybe you'd like me to handle yours. Maybe give you a good blow job? If you promise to let me go, I could give you a great blow job, right here in your car."

If Chad could keep him right here for a while, the guards down below would surely be coming looking for him pretty soon. Both the supervisor and the bus driver were armed. It could be messy, but at least he'd have a chance. He was beginning to figure out what the young guy was doing in the trunk. He was young and good looking. A blond. Just like Chad. Just like those guys on the covers of the DVDs in the backseat of the BMW. The guys shown on the DVD covers were bound too.

The man was pulling Chad's wrists behind his back, and he felt the plastic restraints being snapped shut, binding his wrists together.

"Down on your knees by the open passenger door," the man growled.

"I could give you great head," Chad repeated.

"I said down on your knees, sweet cheeks," the man countered. He was palming Chad's butt cheeks underneath the material of the shorts, so Chad knew what cheeks he was talking about.

When Chad went down on his knees there, the man bound his ankles together. Then he sat down in the passenger seat, legs outside the car, unzipped himself and pulled his cock out, grabbed Chad's head between his hands, and lowered Chad's face to the cock. Chad opened his mouth over the cock and started to give the man slow, deep-throated head.

This wasn't a strain for Chad. This—hustling johns on the street—along with petty theft were the vices that had gotten him on a white-stripe-painting chain gang in the first place. Giving head came naturally to him. Being bound while he gave it was something new, though.

"That's nice, very nice," the man murmured. "A nice soft mouth. You do this a lot, I can tell. When you get me hard enough, we change places, but you'll be on your belly on the seat. We'll find out how nice another hole is."

78

"Chad! Chad Barnes. Where the hell you got to, boy? How long does it take to take a piss? There ain't no place to go here but up, buddy, so let's you not try anything."

The voice was wafting up the ramps from the next level down.

"Shit," the man exclaimed. He pushed Chad off him and rose out of the car. Showing that he was a strong man who Chad didn't want to mess too much with whether or not he was holding a gun, the man picked Chad up in his arms, walked around to the back of the car, and dumped him into the trunk beside the young man already in there.

"You make noise on the way out of this garage and you're a dead man—along with whoever is making that racket down there, you hear?" He gave Chad a mean look and then he slammed the trunk shut.

Chad had banged his head on the lip of the trunk when he'd been stuffed in there and was pretty dazed all the time it took for the car to clear the garage. He was too scared and intimidated to try to yell anyway when the car stopped briefly before exiting the garage. Chad knew that the supervisor had held the BMW up long enough to look inside the passenger compartment, but, not seeing anything, had let it pass.

The car bounced along for a good half hour, with both young men in the trunk gathering bruises and moaning in unison in the tight space.

But eventually the car slowed down, Chad heard a garage door open and the car roll inside and then the garage door roll down again with a hollow-sounding bang.

The trunk opened, with a blinding light invading the interior and a cheery voice said, "Wakey, wakey. We're home. Eeny, meeny, miny, mo. The choices. Maybe last one in, first one fucked."

Hands grabbed Chad and pulled him out of the trunk, not caring much that he banged Chad's head again, which sent his head reeling a second time with a blast of pain and colored lights. The man tossed Chad over his shoulder like he was a sack of mulch and entered a kitchen, leaving the trunk open and the other, trussed young man still in it.

79

The man carried Chad through a kitchen and a dining room and down a hallway. He kicked a door open and they were in a bedroom. The man dumped Chad on the bed on his belly. He was muttering to himself.

"Now, where were we? Hard all the way home, thinkin' about it. Got me all hot and bothered. Went for one, came home with two. God, I'm horny. Gotta get it off."

"Listen, I didn't see nothin'," Chad said. "I'll give you a good time. Just let me go afterward."

"Shut the fuck up, blondie."

The man jerked a nightstand drawer open. He rummaged around in it, pulling out various sex toys: handcuffs, dildos, bead strings, tit clamps. He came up with a ball gag. Leaning over Chad's body, belly at the foot of the bed, knees almost touching the floor, the man flipped the ball gag over Chad's head, forced the ball into Chad's mouth, and tightened the strap behind his head.

"Scream all you want now, blondie. There aren't any neighbors anywhere close anyway."

He reached around and unbuttoned and unzipped Chad's shorts and jerked them down to his knees. He went down on his own knees behind Chad, grabbed Chad's buttocks and pushed them apart, and pushed his face into Chad's crack. A hand snaked between Chad's thighs and grabbed his cock and he was being stroked and his ass was being eaten out. Chad squirmed. The sounds he was making were as much pleasure as anything, although he was scared as hell.

Then, after Chad watched the man pull packets of condoms and a tube of lube out of the nightstand drawer, Chad's channel was being lathered up. The man crouched over him, penetrated Chad's hole with his cock, and pumped him fast and hard to a long-coming ejaculation.

This part was business as usual for Chad, and he took it like a champ. The man wasn't particularly thick or long, but he was all about what he wanted and he could piston hard and had stamina. He just grunted and prodded and pinched at Chad with his hands, and thrust, thrust, thrust, as Chad moved his pelvis in rhythm with the fuck under him, making moaning sounds and moving with the thrusts, trying to convince the

80

man that he liked the cocking—which he sort of did. He certainly didn't mind having the cock inside him, not that he didn't get enough of it inside the prison. The fucking went on longer than Chad was used to, and various parts of him were cramping up before the man finished.

Chad lay there, where he was left, belly on bed and knees almost touching the floor, as the man pulled out of him and walked out of the room. Chad concentrated on the shorts still down around his knees—wondering if he could get to the wire strung in the hem there, or if what else was there was working. And wondering what he could do with the wire if he could reach it. If he could just convince the man to free his hands while they were fucking. The man hadn't said anything about being finished with Chad. He just said that Chad was a good lay and that he was thirsty and maybe ready for some variety.

"You think the guy in the trunk can take cock as good as you?" the man had whispered in Chad's ear. "Maybe not want it as much as you—put up a little fight? Be tighter than you? Cry for me? Make me mad enough to finish him?"

Chad took that to mean that the guy would be gone for a while—probably grabbing a beer or two and then sampling the other guy who'd been left in the trunk of the BMW. In any event, Chad going with the fuck maybe is what was saving him so far. Maybe the guy's blood-lust fetish was to be made mad—to have to take it hard, giving him an excuse in his own mind to snuff the guy.

How long, he wondered. How long would it be? He still had the shorts. The man hadn't had time to mess with them.

After Chad didn't know how long, the man came back into the room. He was naked—and in erection. And he was drinking a beer out of a bottle, but what Chad was eyeing was that the man had brought a straight razor in a sheath back with him and laid it down on the edge of the bed, well out of Chad's reach even if Chad hadn't been bound. The stood there and looked at Chad for several minutes while Chad tried his best to keep his eye off of the razor. Then, without warning, he was close to Chad again, pulling at him, raising him up to the bed, pulling Chad up to his knees, but pushing his chest down on the surface of the bed.

Chad's ankles were released, his shorts were stripped off him and thrown on a nearby chair, and his legs were being spread, with the man still insisting that he be raised on his knees. The man knelt behind Chad and Chad felt his butt cheeks being manipulated and spread. His cock was pulled through, held firmly at the root in the grip of one of the man's hands, and the man was alternating between sucking Chad's cock and eating his ass out.

So far, Chad could take this—even multiple times. It wasn't anything he didn't do for money. It was the fear of what came afterward that was worrying him. The longer he could keep the man interested in doing this, the better his chances were. Chad turned his head to the side where he could see his shorts. He took courage from them still being there.

The man stood, rolled a condom on his cock, and crouched over Chad's body, encircling the young blond's chest with his arms, entered him with a long slide, and began to pump. Leaving one hand on Chad's belly, he cupped Chad's throat with the other hand, and arched Chad's body back to him.

Chad moaned loudly, trying to convey that he was enjoying the fuck, wanting the man to want him again and again for as long as it was necessary. He moved his pelvis in the rhythm with the fuck and slowly took over the stroking to where the man just held his cock stationary and Chad moved his channel back and forth on it.

The man was moaning now too, enjoying Chad's response.

Chad was lying on his back along the foot of the bed, with one leg extending down to the floor and the other raised on the man's torso, Chad's ankle on the man's shoulder, and the man holding that leg with one hand and with one leg extending down to the floor and plowing Chad's channel when all hell broke loose.

The man had barely made it to the door of the bedroom when the room was swarming with cops. The cops pulled the man out of the doorway and down the hall. A

82

policeman in civilian clothes, apparently the man in charge of the raid, remained in the doorway long enough to admonish Chad to "Stay put until we sort this out."

Before leaving the room, he came over and pulled the ball gag out of Chad's mouth and released his wrists from the plastic cuffs.

"In the trunk. There's a guy in the trunk of the car," Chad said, his voice coming out in a squeak. He rubbed his wrists to get circulation back into them and exercised his jaw, working at getting it to stop aching and to start letting him speak in a normal voice.

"Yep. We found him right off. We think he's the ticket taker in that garage you're supposed to be in, son."

The cop looked down at the razor on the bed. "He put that razor there?" he asked.

"Yes," Chad answered.

"Lucky we can along when we did then, I reckon," the cop said. "You stay put right here, like I said, until we can figure out where you fit in all of this. Where is it? Did you even know you had it on you?"

"The iTrail GPS logger they sewed into our clothes to keep track of us? Yes, I knew I had it. That's what I was counting on you using to track me. It's there, in my shorts. Sewn in the hem. I knew it was there, honest. He took me just like he took the other guy."

"We'll see about that," the man said, sternly.

He was gone quite some time. Chad moved to his back on the bed, raised on his elbows, his feet flat on the floor at the foot of the bed, and facing the door to the bedroom, when the detective returned.

"It was quite a story that guy wove, Mr. Barnes. He says when he came back to his car in the garage, you had popped his trunk and were putting a body in it. He says you're here willingly."

"That's bullshit," Chad said. "He had the trunk open when I came up the ramp to find someplace to take a whizz, and he stuffed me in the trunk too. The guy in the trunk can tell you I didn't put him in there."

"The guy in the trunk's going to be OK, but not for a while. It could be a couple of days before he can tell us anything. I figure this razor on the bed and finding him fucking you bound tells me all I need to know. You were away from your work detail, though. If you were up there even to just rip off that guy's car, that would be a violation of your sentence. How much longer do you have to serve?"

"A week and a half."

"If you're written up for attempted theft, even if cleared of everything else here, you'll be in for your full sentence. How much longer on that?"

"Six months," Chad answered with a sad voice. As they were talking, though, Chad saw the detective looking him over real good. He, of course was still naked, and was lying there on his back, legs opened, and his torso propped up on his elbows. He was half hard too. He'd been enjoying the fuck and this detective looked pretty good to him too.

"I'm sure you'd hate to have to serve the full sentence," the detective said. He was talking to Chad, but his eyes were on Chad's half hard. His hand drifted down to his package too. Chad could see that his crotch was tented.

"What were you in for?"

"Petty theft . . . and male prostitution. I could be real good to a man who was good to me."

They both remained where they were for half a minute, neither saying anything. Chad was waiting for the man to do something—to tell him to dress and take him in or to suggest something else. The man just stood there, looking at Chad's package.

"Where are the others?" Chad finally asked. "The man who assaulted me and the other policemen?"

"The ambulance has been here to get the victim—the other victim . . . maybe it could be that way—and the other policemen have taken the man who was assaulting you into custody. It's just you and me here now. I'm supposed to bring you in myself."

"Isn't there something you could do? How you could report what happened? Something that wouldn't say I was

84

doing something wrong? Something I maybe could do to help you write up my side of this?"

"I could write it up so that the man came down to the second level and grabbed you while you were taking a piss."

"That would be great. Is there anything I could . . . ?"

"Did you see where the man kept his condoms?" He was already unzipping his trousers and pulling his cock out. He was hard.

"There, in the nightstand drawer." Chad wrapped his hands around his knees and lifted and spread his legs while the detective rolled on a condom.

"So, telling me that would constitute a yes, and your rap sheet is right—you're over eighteen?"

"Yes to both," Chad answered. "As long as we're being good to each other."

"Oh, I can be good to you if you make it worth my while."

The detective slapped Chad's hands away from his knees and took hold of his legs himself and wishboned them even further, as he thrust a cock inside Chad's channel that was appreciably thicker and longer than the one that had just previously been in there. Chad arched his back; grabbed at the detective's shirt, scrabbling at unbuttoning him and reaching in to grab his pecs; and cried out, "Yes, yes, fuck me hard!" as he settled in to what had been both the cause of and the solutions for his problems for some time.

When the detective tied his wrists together with plastic restraints and pushed the ball gag back into his mouth, Chad knew this wasn't going to be an easy ride.

Each Time a Little Less

I hunched down and looked away from the sentry as I walked through Kadena's Gate Two into Kozo City. It was a little silly, as the sentries knew that any airman walking into Kozo City in the early evening like this was looking for the bars—and for sex. And, if anything, they were wishing they were too. But the nature of the sex I was looking for had me slightly embarrassed, even though the sentries wouldn't have the foggiest notion what I sought. Well, one or two of them might. I was pretty free with my dick among the other airmen on the air force base in Okinawa—and I hadn't had any complaints.

But in the last couple of weeks, since I'd found Papasan's bar behind Mamasan's bar, I'd taken on a whole new interest—small, brown, boyish men. Really tight holes. Can't find many of them on an air base servicing jets. It takes a lot of muscle buildup and a pretty big man to service an air force jet.

Mamasan's wasn't too far into Kozo City, but it was far enough that I'd gotten plenty of offers of "a good time" before I got there. It was almost like the B-girls had a sense of the big wad of yen I had in my pocket. Of course, they might also have taken that bulge as evidence that I was hung—and excited to see them. Well, I *was* hung, if pretty much indifferent to what they considered their charms. It was a rough, jaded crowd out here on the red-light district strip. Given the choice, I'm sure they'd all want to go for the wad of Japanese money I was carrying.

I wondered how much this time. That's what I had been noticing the three times I'd done this. Each time it was a little less. If I reupped my tour on Kadena, I wondered if Takis eventually would be paying me for it.

Brushing two rouged figures off that I wasn't even sure were women, I dipped into Mamasan's bar. It was just like most every bar on the strip. Dim lighting, with colored lights in sconces around the walls; a long bar with a bamboo front and two overly painted, flat-faced and somewhat squat Okinawan women behind it—topless and jiggling big jugs as they shook the jiggers of whatever drink they were concocting. There was a smattering of men—all Americans from the air base; no Okinawan patrons allowed in this bar—slouched at small, round tables, with at least two B-girls in attendance at each, one in a Japanese kimono, because some men got off on that, and one in a barely painted on miniskirt and halter top. East or West, your choice—or both together, if you have the yen for it. A few humping couples on the small dance floor, swaying against each other, little attempt to disguise the in and out of that particular dance between the disheveled folds of clothing. A lighted stage beyond the dance floor, with panties-only girls making love to poles—at least until the panties came off. The music was piped in.

I gestured my noninterest in this section of the bar to whatever old, fat woman was parading as Mamasan this evening. She just stepped back and didn't hinder my progress to the doorway at the back of the bar covered in a beaded curtain. I'd been here three times before, brought the first time by a dishwasher at the NCO club I was fucking and, who, it turned out, was a patron recruiter for Papasan's. I didn't resent his bringing me there; I was grateful—and I still fucked him back on base when I felt like it and he was available. Small, brown body. A hole that opened right up for my big cock, but a talent for squirming and crying out like I was splitting him. He put me right in the mood.

Through the beaded curtain, past doors to rooms off either side of the corridor—private places to do your business for an extra fee, although from the looks of what was going on in Mamasan's, not many were too embarrassed to lap a "hostess" and do her right at a table or pull her close on the dance floor, readjust clothing, and enter her there, swaying against her and moving their cock inside her to the beat of the piped-in music.

Through another beaded curtain and into a smoke-filled, dimly lit bar room much like Mamasan's except that everyone was male—even those dressed as women were, or at some time had been, male. The two barmen were expatriate Westerners rather than Okinawans. They were stripped to the waist, one muscled, one lithe, appealing to whoever. The "hosts" here were a mixed bag. Some Japanese—or Okinawan, which was much the same thing. More Filipinos. A Thai or two. The latter more expensive than the others, as, I was told, they had "specialties." A few expatriate Westerners. Even an off-duty airmen or two. This had surprised me until the last time when I'd been hit with an offer to work part time there too. It was flattering, but I hadn't given it much thought.

"You huge; and balls like cannon balls," the papasan on duty had said, not talking about my physique, although I had enough pride and worked on my body enough to take the compliment in that area too. But as he had coaxed me, back to the wall of the corridor, and had me unzipped and was giving me a hand job as I was leaving the last time, I knew what part of me he was referring to.

"No, no," I'd said. "I no pay for this."

"No pay, no," he'd said. "My pleasure, you so big. You make a lot of money here," he had concluded. "And lots of jism," he'd added, with obvious approval, as I came for him. "You maybe fuck bareback if money good enough?"

That papasan hadn't been Japanese. He was Russian, I think. Bigger than me, and a handsome, well-muscled devil. Once he'd gotten me up against the wall and had fisted my cock, I was willing to let him finish me off. I'd thought he'd suck it, which would have been nice, but I found the hand job nice as well.

He had said he'd suck it but then backed off when I wasn't showing interest in working for him.

89

Tonight, it was the same Russian papasan as the last time—maybe the very papasan or record who actually owned the joint? I slipped him some money off the meaty roll of yen as I entered the barroom. He looked at the size of the roll and smiled. I gave him enough to cover a private room as well as his entrance fee, and he smiled for me again and said, "Room 3; go there with me first maybe? For you, free, if you let me hide it for you." As he was saying that, he stuffed what I'd given him back into the pocket of my shirt. He unbuttoned my shirt and ran a hand inside, onto my chest. The hand was surprisingly smooth for a bruiser that big. And arousing. He knew exactly what to fondle and to tweak to get the maximum response.

It was enough arousal for me to let him show me the room rather than just for me to take for granted it was back there and I could find it on my own. I'd been there before. I can't say I didn't know he'd want more once we got there or that I wasn't interested in what it might be.

Room 3 was much like the room had been the previous two times. It might even have been the same room. The same black-vinyl-covered, padded studio bed in the center. Two black, facing walls, mirrored ceiling; one wall, facing one side of the studio bed also fully mirrored, the mirror surface dull, though, with blemishes. Splashes of something, hardened. Probably semen, given the venue. The opposite wall some sort of movie screen across which danced the silhouettes of two, closely engaged hunky men. Two thick-metal hoops hanging from the ceiling, one over the bed and one off to the side. I hardened up, remembering how I'd helped use them before.

The Russian pushed me gently down on the bed and sat next to me. He was wearing a kimono-like robe, with a thick obi—sash—around his waist that, when he undid it and pushed it to the floor, caused the robe to open wide. He was naked under the robe, hard muscled, his cock in erection.

He moved an arm around me and dipped me to the side, searching for my mouth with his. But I turned my face away from him, and his mouth went down to my chest, my shirt having already been unbuttoned out in the bar room. He unzipped my trousers and fished my cock out. If he hadn't

90

been so fast doing that, and if my cock hadn't remembered the last time he did that, I might have gotten him out of the room and saved all my cum for later. I didn't come here to have sex with him.

"You can stroke me too," he murmured from inside the thatch of hair on my pecs, as he took possession of my cock and began stroking it.

I answered with what I hoped was a polite demur. It wasn't what I had come for. I had come for Takis. But the Russian was nice too. He'd given me a good hand job before. He was giving me a good hand job now.

When he told me what he had in mind and started to manhandle me, I let him know that I topped, exclusively. He laughed a low, guttural laugh and said that he supposed so, considering the size of my equipment and the cockiness of my walk. He didn't exhibit any resentment, content, at least outwardly, with sucking me off this time—which he showed was a real talent of his. He went down on his knees, pressing my legs open with his big, soft Russian hands gripping my knees, and his mouth went over the bulb of my cock.

My bulb is oversized, and for several moments before moving farther down the engorging shaft, he held the rim of the glans lightly in his teeth and sucked hard on the bulb, flicking the tip of his tongue into the pressed-open piss slit. Giving a guttural laugh at the long moan I responded to his attentions with, he let me lower my back on the narrow bed, with my head flopping over the other side. By looking at the ceiling, I could watch his head move up and down as he slid his mouth down the sides of the cock and then back up to suck hard on the bulb again before descending on the cock once more. I lost sight of that, though, when I grabbed his head between my hands to help control the movement of his mouth down and up my shaft. I didn't want him to leave now. It no longer was just about coming for Takis. I needed the Russian to finish me.

His hands glided up my torso, his fingers finding and rubbing and pinching my nipples until, with a jerk and an exclamation, I came down his throat.

91

He stood and offered his cock for suck, but I indicated I wasn't interested. I had come for Takis, not the Russian. I'd gotten off. The need for the Russian had then evaporated.

He took my refusal without rancor and asked me again if I wanted to work there—that I could only top, if I wanted to—that there were many who would want a cock like I had inside them. He commented again on the amount of ejaculate I produced, and mentioned the possibility of barebacking again. Once more I was flattered, and moaning low, because, while referring to my cock, he was holding it in his hand again and slowly stroking it. I recover quickly, which he seemed to appreciate.

I needed to get him to stop, though. I didn't want to give it all to the Russian.

I told him I hadn't made up my mind about working there occasionally. He repeated that he wanted to fuck me, noting that he had returned the entrance fee and the room fee to me—and that he'd given me a blow job that others would pay well for.

Not wanting to anger him, I complimented him on the blow job, but noted that I hadn't asked for it. Taking the hint, though, I pulled out my cash wad and gave him the entrance fee again—but not the cost of the room. He was satisfied with this, and I already was paying less than I had the last time I was here.

I didn't really have any intention of working here, but I wanted to spin out the offer as long as possible to see how much I could get for less cost each time I appeared. Under the right circumstances and money coming back to me, I could go farther the next time. I hadn't always been a top exclusively. But maybe, too, the Russian would be willing to bottom for me with the possibility that I'd say yes to working there. I had a feeling, though, that once I'd said yes, been identified to the local conveniently looking-the-other-way police force as an employee, and shown up for work, he'd take me into one of these rooms and work me over any way he wanted to. He was being much too polite and reasonable about it.

I went back to the beaded curtain of the doorway leading into Papasan's bar with him. Takis was on one of the poles on the stage. A small, berry-brown young man of perfect proportions. Not a full-blooded Okinawan, I was sure, as they ran to being squat and many had flat faces. His hair was an auburn red, and I'm not sure it was dyed. If it was, I had ascertained on the first visit that he'd dyed it all over. From the delicate beauty of his features, I'd say that he was mixed race—mixed with some Western background.

He was wearing only a gold lamé jock strap and was making languid love to the pole. Of the three dancers, he was the most artistic and the most flexible. He was everything arousing and desirable that I dreamed of since I found the charms of small Oriental men. That's why I was here for the third time. This was why I was playing the Russian papasan.

The papasan caught Takis' attention and gestured at me and then back toward the bank of rooms behind the beaded curtain, holding up three fingers to designate the room assignment. Takis smiled and worked his way off the pole just like the end of his set was preplanned for this withdrawal.

The Russian leaned over to me, putting a hand on one of my butt cheeks and squeezing as he named another price in my ear—unless, of course, I wanted to remain in Room 3 for him to fuck after I was finished with Takis. I smiled and whispered, "Not tonight." As a test, I only gave him half of what he requested. And he let that be enough. Once again a lesser amount than the time before. So far so good.

"You tease me," he murmured in my ear as he slid away toward the entrance to wave off one of the hosts and to take his position again. "It makes me want you more. I know you come back and let me fuck you. I give good fuck."

If his hand and blow job talents were any indication, I didn't doubt that he gave good fuck.

"You let me fuck you and then maybe," I answered back.

The expression he was wearing on his face as he moved away indicated that maybe he'd consider it. If he did, I was game. I liked them small and almost feminine like Takis. But I didn't mind them big and hard muscled either. A channel was a channel, and, with what I was packing, I could make the big ones squirm and scream too.

93

I was sitting on the bed in Room 3, facing the mirrored wall, while Takis was dancing for me, starting from the middle of the room and working his way over toward me. When he was almost touching my knees with his, he stood there gyrating slowly until I took the wad of yen out of my trousers pocket. I had zipped up, but my shirt was still open, my dog tags dangling on my chest.

I extracted a few bills and tucked them into the waistband of his jock strap. He ran his hand up my chest, closed his fist over the dog tags and gave them a tug or two, and then moved his hand down to touch the wad of bills again. All the time his face was smiling and he was licking his lips and puckering them up into air kisses. His hips were gyrating slowly—side to side and toward me and back. Two more bills in his waistband and I ran my hand over his basket—as he did mine, without any objection from him. He turned his bare butt to me and waved it over my lap until I inserted bills in the back of his waistband.

Full frontal again, with his hands gliding over my bare chest and mine over his, him giving me a lap dance over my lap, but off the surface of my thighs. More air kisses and a tongue in one of my ears. More bills in the waistband and he was unzipping me and pulling my engorged cock out. I leaned over, took the curve of his cock through the gold lamé pouch in my mouth, and slid my teeth down along the curve. His hand left my cock and moved to cover the hand holding the wad of yen.

I pulled off several more bills and moved to stuff those in his already-stuffed waistband, but he took them in his hand and let them float to the floor. Unsnapping his waistband at either side, he let the jock strap fall to the floor as well—accompanied by a downward flutter of all the bills I'd stuffed in there already.

I didn't stop him when his hand reached over and pulled four more bills off the wad of yen. After letting them float to the floor at his feet, he put his small, delicate hands on the back of my head and pulled my face toward his groin. I opened my mouth over his small, thin, but now-hard cock and slid all the way down. And then back up and down. He arched

94

away from me, letting his arms dangle at his side, in symbolic surrender, as I supported his small body with hands gripping his waist at the flare of his buttocks. He moaned, the first sound he'd made since we'd entered the room. He was moving in a languid dance, his thighs encasing mine, me scooted as far off the edge of the bed as I dared. I palmed his buttocks and spread the cheeks, the index finger of each hand searching for, finding, and entering his ass channel. He wriggled his buttocks for me, helping the fingers to sink deeper.

He murmured in Japanese and then whispered a few, accented English phrases—the usual, "Yes, do me like that, soldier," "fuck, yes," "Oh, shit that's good" phrases that seemed incongruent coming from such a small, boyish Oriental. I sensed movement and let my eyes lift as I continued to suck him off to find that I could see my cock-stuffed face in the mirror across the room. He had arched back and placed the palms of his hands on the floor behind him. The flexibility of him—imagining how that could be put into play—heightened my arousal.

I let my fingers sink deeper into his channel and started teasing it open. He moaned deeply and wriggled his butt.

I worked his little cock with my mouth for several minutes, but he didn't come for me. I ached to give attention to my own throbbing dick, but my hands were occupied with squeezing his butt cheeks and opening his channel.

He made the next move, bringing his body up and moving away from me. Just a few feet but just beyond my reach. He stood there, smiling, gyrating, and dancing in place, waiting. I knew what he was waiting for. I'd gotten clued into this move during the previous visits. More bills came off the wad and floated to the floor.

He moved back in, encasing my thighs in his, bending down and taking my mouth with his in a sweet-tasting kiss, while both of his hands went to encasing my cock, one hand over the other, not fully encasing what I was swinging, though. A thumb pressed on the piss slit and I shuddered. Now I was moaning, fully aroused by receiving the cock attention I'd been aching for.

95

He straddled my thighs coming down into my lap and encasing both of our cocks in his hand. Squeezing and stroking. We kissed again, and then he lowered his face to between my pecs and pressed me back with the pressure of his head. I still had my hands palming his butt cheeks, but now I had to move them to behind me to keep my torso inclined back, off the bed, straining to watch our coupling in the mirror across the room. His mouth went to my nipples and then to my dog tags, which he took in his mouth and sucked and tugged on with a slurping noise that made my cock bounce. If my cock could scream, "Me, me, suck me!" it would have done so.

Takis was in complete control. That was new to me in a fuck—except for when I had visited him before. Each time with him it was something new, something devised and controlled by him—and totally arousing. It probably was why I kept coming back to him.

We remained in that position, me moving toward an ejaculation, until I realized that this was going to be the end, a hand job ending in an ejaculation, unless and until more money floated to the floor.

When it did, he virtually jumped up off my lap and moved over to the metal hoop that was hanging from the ceiling across the room. He grabbed the ring on either side and pulled himself up, off the floor and into the ring, belly on the bottom of the ring, both his torso and legs hanging down. On my last visit, he'd sat in the ring, the small of his back on the ring and his buttocks pushed out to receive me, and draped his legs over my shoulders while I fucked him. His bending double over the ring on his belly was a use of the device I'd never imagined, although I'd tried to imagine a few uses of the ring myself. His hands went back to pull his own butt cheeks apart and give me a clear view of the puckering bud of his channel opening. The entrance was pulsating invitingly, and I figured out without any trouble that it was beckoning for my tongue.

He writhed and moaned and talked dirty to me in that funny little accent of his while I ate out his sweet hole.

When I couldn't take any more, I went back to the bed, slipped out of my trousers, and sat on the edge of the bed. I'd

96

taken the wad of yen, smaller than when I walked in, but still thick, out of my trousers, extracted a wad of bills larger than any I'd taken out before, and beckoned to him, with the hand holding the yen extended toward him. I could see him looking at me from between his perfectly formed little, spread legs as he was bent over the bottom of the ring.

He stared at me and smiled.

More bills came off the wad. Then he was off the ring and kneeling in front of me. I showered his head with the bills, which floated down all around him to the floor.

He placed his small hands on my knees, spread my thighs, and lowered his mouth on my throbbing cock. He couldn't seem to get the entire bulb in his mouth at first. And then he could. And then the struggle with the girth and length of the cock. And then he could, expertly deepthroating me. Showing that he'd been to the same cock-sucking school the Russian papasan had.

When I felt I was about to come—and he felt it too, he pulled off the cock and looked up at me expectantly. Obviously, this far only with what I'd spent. He was signaling that he would get me off—but with his mouth. No farther without more yen.

I showered him with more yen.

I have no idea where the condom came from, but it was in his mouth and he was expertly rolling it down my shaft with his lips and tongue. I almost came then. But, sensing that I was close, he stopped half way down and held until the urge had passed over me.

The ring hanging down from the ceiling over the studio bed was for him to grip with his hands while, facing me, he lifted and lowered his channel on my cock. Our lips had been locked until I decided to play with his nipples with my teeth. My hands, at least initially, were palming his butt cheeks again, spreading them, dealing with the difficulty of getting a cock of my size into a channel of his size.

Of course he eventually accommodated me all the way down. He did the work of raising and lowering himself on the cock. I let him. I'd paid for it—and he was wearing me out.

The little bugger had even more stamina than I did. I'd be embarrassed if it wasn't such a turn on.

When he reversed himself, facing away from me, with me watching him raise and lower himself on the cock in the mirror across the room, I fisted and stroked his cock hard, and, finally, he came for me. Then he went into overdrive in fucking himself on my cock, and, me obviously tired before he was, I laid back on the bed, my head flopped over the far side, watching him do his gymnastics in the mirror on the ceiling until I too, came and came and came, every dribble of cum pulled out of me by Takis' talents.

Afterward he told me I was the best. I told him I thought he was pretty damn good too.

I didn't count what was left in the wad of yen until I was back through the gates of Kadena and was safely in Little America again.

I grinned when I'd done the count. I'd spent less than the previous time. Each time a little less. Each time Takis required a little less to perform all the way for me.

I think Takis likes me.

Pearl Fisher Ecstasy

I am already panting shallowly in anticipation of the arrival on center stage of the fisher king, Zugar, and of the nightly effect he has on me—not Zugar himself, but the magnificent man who is playing him, the man who has been bought for me, the man I have sold myself to attain. With me singing the tenor role of the humble young fisherman, Nadir, we—Jorge Apoko, the black baritone, as Zugar, and I are about to enter into the Act I duet, "Au fond du temple saint," that immortalizes Georges Bizet's opera, *Pearl Fishers.*

The setting and costumes, both a gift to me, I know, enhance the homoerotic sensuality that rushes over me, through me, each night and that, in one duet, nearly wipes me out for the rest of the performance—but that holds me on the cloud of arousal for the fulfillment that comes after the performance. It is this duet that I look forward to every night—the fantasy of the performance version soaring above the reality of the after-performance "pay the piper" event. I lose myself to the experience of imagination in an ecstasy of the mind and emotion that is beyond all other roles I've taken in the theater. It is this role, this baritone, that Egor conjured just for me and with which he has bought me and for which I go home with him, to his bed, to his cock, every night.

The stage is bathed in aquamarine light to call forth the atmosphere of the men diving for pearls, in a grueling, but body-building and sculpting occupation, off the coast of ancient Ceylon. Egor has gone to great lengths to show that only the most beautiful, best-endowed young men are permitted to be pearl fishers in the fantasy world he has re-created and reimagined from Bizet's original vision. He has them relating to each other on stage, subtly but unmistakably, to foreshadow the homoerotic interpretation he's given the production—although anyone coming to performances by now would already have absorbed the media buzz Egor's vision has conjured. Behind us, behind the ruins of a Hindu temple, masses of beige sheeting, representing the shifting sand, bellow and swirl at the mercy of wind machines in the wings.

All on stage now are beautiful, muscular young men, bare chested and wearing only saffron-colored silk sarong skirts barely riding their hips, with the hems pulled up and tucked into the waist to create billowy short trousers and to show off their meaty and shapely thighs and calves, the hardness of their bellies, and a hint of what lies below. The costumes are known as the *kaavi mundu* form of a male sarong. I am attired just as the rest, blending in with the other beefy young men at the act's opening. The director, Egor Rustacovic, says he took this interpretation because he was impressed that his principle singers were as well built and endowed—and well he should know—as Jorge and I. But the mood of this production, of course, was no accident; it was one of the conditions I set for Egor to have his way with me each time he created for me the fantasy of the lusty duet with the imposing black baritone.

It is Jorge, a towering black Algerian with a powerful, deep chest, who has me unhinged and who Egor has bought to buy me with. He arrives on stage, as Zugar, declared to be the new fisher king and set apart from the rest of us by his overpowering, commanding figure. He overshadows all the rest, and only he wears anything in addition to a *kaavi mundu*. A bejeweled golden vest is on his chest, too small really for the bulk of him, covering little but serving to enunciate the massiveness of his muscular chest, the rouged erectness of his nipples that foreshadows his intent.

It is this, his chest, with nipples rouged and engorged in arousal, and his magnificent torso as it plunges down to a washboard belly and a dip in the front of the *kaavi mundu* that,

100

from my closeness to him, reveals the upper curling of his black pubic hair, that has me panting nightly. Although, that's not quite true; it's more what has not been revealed yet in tonight's staging of the opera, below that dip at the waist of his *kaavi mundu*. It is my fetish for huge, black cock—Jorge's cock. A fetish that has been satisfied with each staging of the opera.

I know the Egor has set the costumes as such to enhance the homoerotic sensuality of his production, to heighten my arousal—as well as his own. And I know he has chosen Jorge for me carefully—because Egor has known me and been known by Jorge. Egor knows that to have Jorge, to have Jorge inside me—again and again—both in fantasy and reality, I'll do anything for him. The duet is as much for Egor as it is for me, though. Each performance he is there, in the audience, to mount on his own arousal through his staging of the "Au fond du temple" duet, reveling in the sensual tableau he was created and joining and merging with me across the footlights. To pleasure himself as, for four fantasy minutes of ecstasy of mind and emotion, I let my imagination run wild— to satisfy my sensual needs and to prepare me for him, just as it prepares him for me.

Zugar has bounded in and taken center stage by right and by stage presence. His character focuses on mine, as I play a young pearl fisherman—just one of several on stage until Zugar singles me out. Our characters were once friends—close friends; very close friends, in the interpretation of the opera that Egor has given it and that has Milan all abuzz—before we both came under the spell of the Hindu high priestess, Leila. Zugar has won her from my character, Nadir, and Nadir has retreated to the edge of the sea, to dive for pearls and to forget not only the human pearl he has lost in Leila, but the man he has loved, who first coupled with him, but who stole the priestess from him after Nadir was brought under her spell and who, presumably, under Leila's spell, is coupling now only with her.

Zugar has been searching for Nadir, though, having broken the spell of the priestess on he himself and realized it is the love of Nadir that is paramount to him. The two men come together, explosively, at the center of the stage, and I, as Nadir,

101

quickly slipping into my imagination, start the duet, soaring up to an F, near the top of my range, but still a note I can deliver with power or sweetly, as I please.

Five measures in, Zugar mirrors my opening in a lower register but, after the initial three measures, releases me to soar again, alone. He doesn't leave me, though, as his voice pursues mine, slipping in underneath mine in punctuated tones, teasing and courting me. His voice weaves the taking of me in his arms in the fantasy I have completely slipped into. But then, playing the game of a pursuit with our voices, he lets me go to soar alone once more. Before I can break through the clouds with a high A, he captures me, pulling me into him where, giving foundation to my traveling on the clouds in my speaking of the delights of the Leila that I have lost, he reclaims me as his.

As his voice grows stronger, mastering mine, he reasons with me that there are far more delights in what he can offer me than Leila can. As I melt to Jorge's smooth but powerful baritone, undergirding my tenor aria, fantasy solidifies and reality totally evaporates for me. The stage and the other singers, the orchestra and the audience fade away. There are just Jorge and me. The huge black man, with the magnificent black cock that I know so well, want and need so much, have taken so often in my imagining, as we have sung this duet and disappeared into this fantasy world, nightly for weeks.

Once again, in my fantasy, he is going to possess me—fully—filling me to capacity and playing my body with the continuous experience of ever quickening withdrawal and possession, withdrawal and repossession, leading to glorious explosion. He is going to take me to heaven, riding on that huge black cock of his.

We no longer are singing side by side, arm in arm. In my imagination, he has pulled me to his chest. And in my initial solo singing, he has buried his lips in the hollow of my neck and reached down to unbind the *kaavi mundi* of both of us and let the saffron silk drift to the floor at our feet. The gasp from the audience floats out over my own. The hardness and strength of his magnificent black cock press to my belly, and I feel the edges of my voice take on the richness of melting chocolate—the chocolate of his body pressing into mine. I

102

want him inside me, filling me. I climb his thighs with mine, seeking the joining, the penetration, the complete merging.

Zugar takes over the solo voicing from me, my voice becoming quiet mewings of want in the background, under him, just as I ache to be under him. He sings of how the high priestess Leila had enticed and mesmerized him too until he realized that he and I have a bond that he could never have with Leila. Then, together, we sing of our burning affection for each other, a bond that becomes ever more sensual. Jorge—no longer Zugar, because the operatic production has melted fully away from my consciousness and only Jorge and I exist now in my fantasy—pulls me closer into him and lifts me up his body with his strong hands.

As our voices soar higher together, we become one, his voice becoming fortissimo, overpowering mine, mastering me, as I want him to, as he stands on strong legs in the center of the stage, me saddled on his hips, my ankles hooked at the small of his back. I reach between us with my hands, positioning the gigantic bulb of him at my entrance, rubbing it on my rim, opening to him. His baritone tones dip down into the bass range, gathering strength and power as, thrusting up with his black staff, he enters me, enters me, enters me.

My voice soars above his, reaching for the stars, as, with powerful hands he pulls me on and off the black cock—thrusting, thrusting, thrusting. Withdrawing and possessing, withdrawing and repossessing. My torso arches back, my fists clutch at the lapels of his vest, my mouth gapes open, singing to the heavens of the glorious taking. Feeling each deep thrust; warbling my want for the next one. Wanting the next one to go deeper, be thicker.

Our voices reach the clash of a crescendo, and, in my fantasy replay, night after night, of this glorious duet, Jorge releases his seed deep inside me, as I too issue my flow up his burnished belly. The chorus of fishermen behind us, heedless of the intimacy of our coupling sealing the strong bond between us that no woman can breach, rises in volume and pitch as reality begins to flow back into my consciousness and, closing my eyes to see and remember what I desired, I sink, in my fantasy, to the stage floor, my burning cheek pressed to the warm flesh of a calf, my arms and legs wrapped around the legs of my nightly master, standing there proudly and magnificent in his naked beauty, the king of the fisherman, head held high and beefy arms crossed over massive chest.

In reality, we are still standing, side by side and arm in arm, still wearing our *kaavi mundi*, still singing of our camaraderie, as the duet comes to a close and the voices of the men's chorus rise.

The opera goes on for two more acts, but the critics are right. They have always been right about Bizet's *Pearl Fisher*. The climax of the opera comes in Act I with the sealing of the bond between the fisher king, Zugar, and the humble fisherman, Nadir, in the "Au fond du temple" duet. Everything after this is anticlimax—even in interpretations that aren't as sensual and homoerotic as Egor's is.

Each night I barely manage to contain myself through the two concluding acts, my lust satisfied thus far only in fantasy, and I know, my eyes often drifting to Jorge's during the agony of our wait, that he feels the same way. I can only imagine how impatient the director, Egor Rustacovic, is in each performance, having given this sensual scene—and Jorge—to me solely to win from me what he wants—and, having created the interpretation of the opera and the arousal he himself desires, being forced to wait through two more acts to attain his own satiation.

But attain it he does, eventually, night after night after each performance, as, in Jorge's dressing room and before Egor takes me home to his bed, he lies on his back on a divan, with me riding his cock and Jorge, behind me, sharing me with Egor, as, for a second time that night, Jorge and I sing the *Pearl Fisher* duet while bringing the ultimate coupling to reality.

Egor has suggested that we perform an excerpt of the opera, just the keystone duet, "Au fond du temple saint," in selected clubs he frequents—that we perform the duet to my fantasy. I have already told him "yes, yes, yes." I await Jorge's decision.

Dressage Training

"The Hamiltons have asked whether you can go to Lexington with Mr. Hamilton for the Dressage at Lexington competitions in July, Santo. You'd be his groom for the three days there, and if you worked out well, you could stay on helping them here at Ash Creek Farms for the rest of the summer before you go back to school."

Santo flared up. "I'm not going back to Tech, Mother. I've told you that already. The first year didn't work out." But his irritation was immediately deflated by the trembling caused by what else she had said. "Mr. Hamilton has a groom," he said. "Pete Griswald."

"Apparently Peter no longer works there. And we'll talk about returning to Virginia Tech later. You were doing well there. You got a job grooming the horses right off for the equestrian club there. I thought that's what you were interested in—horse breeding. Winding up working at the Tech horse-breeding program over in Middleburg."

"It is," Santo answered. "But I can work over there anyway—and go to community college here in Northern Virginia."

"What should we say to the Hamiltons? They've been very good to us."

The Hamiltons had, indeed, been very good to Santo's family. His parents had a small farm outside of Middleburg, in the hunt country of Northern Virginia. And the Hamiltons owned a large spread—a horse-breeding farm—that enveloped three sides of the family farm. Winston Hamilton could have squeezed Santo's family out—easily—as this was an area for the ultrarich, and Santo's family was anything but rich. Instead, Hamilton had been friendly to Santo's family, and, knowing how difficult it was for them to make a living from their small farm, had provided seasonal employment for Santo and his father since Santo was a child. The father and son helped with the harvest of Hamilton's vineyard and Santo worked occasionally as a subgroom at the Hamilton stables during the fox hunt season. Santo's father, in turn, opened his land to the Middleburg hunt.

Santo's mother said he should be thrilled at the opportunity to work for Hamilton as a groom and to go with him to the Dressage trials in July down at the equestrian center in Lexington. And he *was* thrilled. But he was apprehensive too. It had been because of Mr. Hamilton that Santo had decided not to go back to Virginia Tech. Santo had made a fool of himself there and was too embarrassed to go back. And it was all because of Winston Hamilton.

Winston Hamilton brought out disturbing and arousing emotions in Santo. It had all begun for him back during the last harvest of the Hamilton vineyards, although that was just the first time Santo realized what disturbed him about Winston Hamilton. Thinking on it thereafter, Santo realized that he'd had an affinity for the man for years.

Santo and his father had been working hard in the vineyard—stripped to the waist. And Hamilton had ridden one of his dressage horses, the eleven-year-old chestnut Hanoverian, Hochkonig, over from the practice ring to check out how the harvest was progressing. Hamilton was decked out completely in his dressage outfit—a tight black jacket over a white shirt and tight white breeches, with shiny black boots up to this knees. A black top hat, white gloves, and a white cravat, as well. He sat there, astride his sleek dressage horse, smoking a cigar and watching the men work in the vineyard. Santo noticed Hamilton watching him, in particular, and he couldn't avoid stealing looks at Hamilton as well. The man—over forty, but in superb shape and handsome of face, with graying at his

106

temples—looked magnificent. Santo was shocked that he felt himself going hard. He had known that he had a preference for men, sexually, but he hadn't done anything about the urge with a man.

He had carried that image of Hamilton with him to his first year at Virginia Tech, and to get the older man—a family friend, so there would be nothing there for Santo—out of his mind, he nearly threw himself at a football player who he had misjudged on signals of interest. His faux pas, very publicly revealed and mocked by the other man, had made its way around the campus rumor mill, and now Santo couldn't go back there. He also couldn't tell his parents why he couldn't go back there in September for a second year. He had done well at the university stables, though. He knew he could get a job at the school's agricultural research station not far from his home, which had a horse-breeding program famous for developing champion racers and show horses.

"Santo, I asked you a question. We've always done what we can to keep the Hamiltons our friends. They've asked for your help."

"Yes, Mother, I'll go over there now to say that I would be happy to help."

Santo hadn't been to the Hamilton stables since that day, two weeks previously, in late May, that his interest in Winston Hamilton, despite all of his efforts, had spiked again. And Pete, the Hamilton's groom had been fully employed that day. And not just in grooming horses. Santo had come around the corner of the stable block only to stop in his tracks in shock and pull back around the corner. But he didn't leave. He took surreptitious glances around the corner.

Pete's cheek and chest were plastered to the wall between two stall openings. His feet were set more than two feet from the wall and were spread. His arms were raised against the wall on either side, with his palms flat against the wood of the wall. He had a pained look on his face and was moaning and groaning in a deep voice. Standing between Pete's legs in full dressage gear, one gloved hand on Pete's belly and other taking a cigar to and from his mouth, his groin nearly plastered to Pete's bared buttocks, Winston Hamilton was

107

slow-fucking the groom. Pete's jeans were draped around one of his ankles. Hamilton's privates, balls and all, were fully exposed outside the tight white riding breeches, and Santo could tell the man was horse hung because the balls hung low and he wasn't fucking Pete deep. He was pulling nearly all of the way out of Pete's ass, to the tune of the groom's gasps, and then sinking back in far, but not all the way, showing a good three inches of exposed cock root.

Santo pulled away as quickly as he could bring himself to do that and returned to his farm, determined not to come back to Ash Creek Farms—ever, if he could help it. It wasn't because what he had seen had disgusted him, but because this was what he had been trying to fight against his entire freshman year at Virginia Tech—the attraction to Winston Hamilton. The melting fetish of the older man in his dressage outfit, smoking a cigar, and, now, fucking another man.

Santo had never carried through with the urge, but he couldn't deny that he ached to be fucked by Winston Hamilton.

* * * *

"Do you like it? It's our hotel at the equestrian center in Lexington," Winston Hamilton said when Santo came over to Ash Creek Farms on the morning of July 10th for the drive down Interstate 81 to Lexington, near Roanoke. When Santo arrived, Hamilton was hooking up a truck-cab RV to a two-horse trailer. "Just bought it. It's a twenty-nine-foot Coachman Freelander model."

"Hotel room? But us? Both of us?" Santo could feel himself trembling. He couldn't reveal to Hamilton what he was dreaming of—the two of them sleeping in an RV. And not just sleeping. But Hamilton was an old family friend. This just couldn't enter into that dimension. Besides, Hamilton wouldn't want him. He was half Latino and his family could almost be called poor.

"It has a bedroom for me," Hamilton was saying. "And see the bump over the cab? That's a bunk for you. I want to stay as close to the horses as possible. The equestrian center has two campgrounds. It's time to bring out the horses now and for us to get on the road."

Santo went into the stables and took several deep breaths to bring his near hyperventilation into control. One after the other, he brought the two geldings out, the chestnut Hanoverian, Hochkonig, and the younger, seven-year-old, black Trakehner, Lowengren. Both horses were the best dressage horses that money could buy. It was the best of everything for Hamilton. Pete Griswald had been a real looker. He had been the best of the best for a man who wanted another man to fuck. Santo couldn't be anything that Winston Hamilton was interested in.

During the drive down the Shenandoah Valley, Hamilton talked easily of his love for horses and the hunt and, in particular, dressage. "Dressage is French for training, you know, Santo," he said. "Although military training and parading of horses goes back to the Greeks."

He talked in general terms about the sport and of his wish to enter the Grand Prix and Grand Prix Special versions of it in the summer Olympics. "There's no disadvantage of not being young to compete in this Olympic Sport. Older men can compete on equal footing. You don't think I'm too old, do you, Santo?"

"No, of course not," Santo answered almost breathlessly. He didn't think Hamilton was too old at all. He thought that Hamilton was in magnificent shape. His mind went back to what he'd seen of Hamilton languidly, but deeply, thickly, expertly fucking Pete, the groom. Yes, he thought Hamilton was in great shape. It was him being older that was a big part of Santo's attraction to him—that and how well he wore the dressage costume.

Hamilton spoke of the various gaits of the dressage— the Piaffe, the Passage, the Pirouette, the Trot, the Canter, the Flying Change—and of how precise they were. "The Trot and Canter you know. But the others are higher level—The Piaffe, prancing in place; the Passage, a rhythmic prance; the Pirouette, prancing side to side; and, most refined of all, the patterned changing of rhythm. I would like you to learn the gaits of the dressage, Santo."

109

"I'd like that, sir."

"Dressage is a sensual sport, Santo. It's all about building a balanced, harmonious team—a horse and rider communicating with each other and melding into each other, attaining a delicate balance of strength, flexibility, and accuracy. It's not just the rider lifting to the heights, but the horse as well, both becoming fully satisfied, both proud of what they attain together, as one. It's like making love."

He was quiet for a few moments, letting the almost worshipful way he'd expressed his thoughts hang in the air.

"Do you know that when I've reached that perfect balance with Hochkonig or Lowengren, I experience an erection and sometimes even ejaculate in the saddle?"

Embarrassed, Santo turned his face toward the passenger window of the cab—but not before having seen that Hamilton was watching him closely.

"Uhh, well . . ."

"Now I've embarrassed you, haven't I?" Hamilton said, keeping his tone light.

"No, sir, not at all," Santo answered with a weak smile that he showed to Hamilton only briefly before looking away again. He fought not to go hard himself, but he was losing that battle.

"I don't want to embarrass you. We're both adult men here. I've watched you grow up, but I've watched you grow into a man, and I think we can be straightforward with each other now. You don't want me to be false or distant from you now that you're a man, do you?"

"No, of course not," Santo responded in a quiet voice.

"I just want to get across the deep meaning that dressage has for me—that it has for most who engage in the sport. I want to indoctrinate you in dressage and help you see it, feel it, as deeply as I do. Isn't there anything in life that enthuses you so much—arouses you so much—that it makes you hard and gives you an ejaculation? I'm sure there is. You're a healthy young man, in fine shape."

"Yes, sir, thank you sir. I understand." Santo said this to the passenger window, picking a hazy answer to the questions, not wanting Hamilton to see the conflicted

110

expressions on his face—hoping that Hamilton couldn't see the tightening of his jeans at his crotch. It didn't help that Hamilton had reached one of his hands over and given Santo's thigh a squeeze.

Santo stole a glance over at Hamilton and saw that the man was ogling his crotch, which clearly showed that, indeed, there were things in life that gave the young man an erection to ponder.

They pulled into the equestrian center at Lexington and got the horses stalled in one of the eight stables at the center, dinner at a fast-food restaurant outside the gates of the center, and the RV berthed at the southwest campgrounds late enough that, exhausted, after showers, they both went to bed—Hamilton to his queen-sized bed in the bedroom and Santo to the bunk over the cab.

Santo couldn't help stroking himself in arousal, but he was weary enough that he went to sleep quickly before he could attain release. Hamilton seemed to be saying something to him directly as he dozed off, but what he had said was so direct and bald that Santo was afraid that he had misjudged it—just as he had misjudged that football player at Tech. But if he was saying something directly and with such confidence that he knew what Santo wanted, what Santo was willing to do, what Hamilton wanted him to do . . . unless in his own want, Santo had misjudged what Hamilton was saying . . .

* * * *

Winston Hamilton rode in six dressage classes the next day. Santo stood at the rails, his eyes glued to the magnificent figure of the man in his shiny black boots, tight white breeches, black jacket and white cravat, and black-satin top hat. Santo's eyes followed the white gloves, carefully watching every move the man made, every light flick of his riding whip that gave the horses their instructions, feeling the sensuality of the sport just as Hamilton had said existed—the sensuality that Hamilton had implanted in Santo's mind. By the end of the day, he could distinguish between the specialty gaits. Hamilton had been

111

right that he already knew the Trot and the Canter, but these specialty gaits were, indeed, sensual.

When the competition for the day was over, Hamilton had won the Reserve Champion honors, built from a red-ribbon second, two yellow-ribbon thirds, and a white-ribbon fourth. He was beaming when he turned the reins of Lowengren over to Santo and strode off to the campground. Before he strode off, though, Santo saw the wet spot on the front of Hamilton's white breeches. In fact, the breeches were so tight that Santo could follow the line of the man's half-hard cock, unusually thick, as Santo knew it to be from having seen Hamilton fucking Pete Griswald. It had been as the man had said in the RV en route to Lexington. Finding the balance with his horses as he had had made him come. He hadn't been exaggerating that.

Santo walked both of the dressage geldings back to the stables and prepared them for the night. All the time he was doing so, he was trembling, not being able to keep himself from wondering how many times Hamilton had come while in the saddle. He had entered six flights. He had finished high in all of them. The possibility that Hamilton was a virile man still didn't lessen Santo's own arousal for him. Thinking of Hamilton coming while he was in the saddle with Santo. Hadn't the man used the imagery when whispering to Santo last night as Santo drifted off to sleep in his buck over the truck cab—mounting him, riding him in the saddle?

When he entered the RV, he found Hamilton sitting on the sofa, still fully decked out in his dressage gear. He was drinking cognac from a snifter and smoking a cigar. His cock and balls were hanging out of his open fly. He was hard—and thick.

"It was a good day," he said, as Santo stood there, in front of him, mesmerized by the cock. "You have taken care of the horses. Now I want you to take care of me. Remember what I told you last night."

There was no hesitation, no hemming and hawing. It may have been arrogant for Hamilton to assume Santo would give into his wants and needs, but he hadn't been wrong. Santo sank between Hamilton's spread knees and sucked his cock to

112

another ejaculation, while Hamilton leaned back and languidly smoked his cigar and drank his cognac. Occasionally he lightly flicked Santo's cheek with his riding whip. When he did so the first time, he said, "The response to that is 'thank you, sir.'"

"Thank you, sir," whispered Santo as he lovingly ran the palm of his hand up the underside of the cock and opened his mouth over the mouth-challenging bulb.

Hamilton rewarded him with a flick of the whip on his cheek. Santo had never done this for a man before, but Hamilton moved the young groom's head with his gloved hands and gave him instruction in low guttural tones—and obviously enjoyed what Santo managed to do for his first time.

"Thank you, sir," Santo whispered again.

Santo wondered at what point Hamilton would make him stop sucking and would move them into the RV's tiny bedroom, the dominance of the bed there sensual in itself. After all the time of agonizing over his feelings for Hamilton— for men in general—and his fighting against the possibility of having sex with a man—and with Hamilton, in particular, Santo accepted without another thought that it would be Hamilton who took his male virginity. Hamilton didn't allow him to stop sucking, though, and ejaculated in Santo's mouth. Santo had gagged a bit but took the sucking and jacking off in his stride.

Afterward Santo stood and started to take off his shirt. "I guess you want to fuck me now."

"I want to fuck you, yes. I want to train you. I've known you wanted me for some time—back to last year in the vineyard during the harvest. And a couple of weeks ago when you watched me fucking Pete. Yes, I knew you were watching—and that you continued watching for a long time. And I've watched you since you were a boy. I knew I would take you some day. But I want it to be special. I want us to find that balance. I will fuck you tomorrow. Now I will take a shower while you broil up those steaks I brought."

This first servicing was all about conditioning. It was about Santo giving Hamilton whatever he wanted, whenever he wanted it. Nothing was given to Santo other than instruction— in much the same way that Hamilton trained his horses. The

113

smile on Hamilton's face as Santo padded off toward the RV's bathroom closet indicated that he was as pleased with Santo's unquestioned response to instruction that Hamilton received from his thoroughbred geldings. He had been cultivating Santo for this for years.

* * * *

"Push back on it. Slowly, slowly. Now a little faster. You do it all. I just provide the cock in this gait."

Santo was on all fours on the room-filling bed, naked. Hamilton was mounted on him, just as he would be on a horse. He was fully clothed in the dressage outfit he had come from the next day's competitions wearing. Only the fly of his white breeches was open, and his cock was buried in Santo's ass.

It was Santo's first fuck, so they had reached this position slowly and with much preparation and gasping and groaning. But reach this position they had. Santo had had to remain as steady as possible, gasping for breath and eyes watering, as his virginal hole slowly opened to the ultrathick cock. He had done so, following each of Hamilton's commands, though, in total subservience to his master, without question or objection.

When Santo had returned from stabling the geldings after Hamilton's triumphant day of taking two blue-ribbon firsts and thus easily winning the Champion ribbon for his class, he found Hamilton sitting on the sofa again, erect phallus rising from his open fly, smoking a cigar and sipping cognac. Santo moved to kneel and give Hamilton suck again, but Hamilton said, "No. Now we celebrate. Now you and I begin to train to meet the balance. Strip down for me please." He watched Santo strip. "Ah, very nice. Very nice indeed. To be young and ripped again. Now go to the middle of the bed and go on all fours, please. You are the next horse I ride."

Santo responded immediately and docilely. There was no question in his mind that he would give Hamilton whatever he wanted. As he went on all fours on the bed, he felt the white-gloved hands palming his hips and the moist tongue flick in between his butt cheeks, and shivered. His moaning started

114

and didn't stop for more than an hour. He only lurched and thought of complaining twice—first, when Hamilton twirled the damp end of his cigar into Santo's ass and used it like a dildo and then when he began to work his thick cock inside.

The young groom panted and groaned at the inching of the cock inside, filling and stretching him, Santo trying to divide his attention between the feeling of being fully stuffed and possessed and the velvety feeling of Hamilton's gloved hands—one palming his belly and the other cupping his chin, all three points of contact holding Santo steady, on all fours, under the mounted older man.

It didn't take Santo long after Hamilton was fully saddled to feel the two of them merging, a balance starting to form. Hamilton was crouched over his pelvis, fully dressed, the formal dressage attire adding to Santo's arousal. He didn't actively pump in the fuck of Santo in this first taking of the young man's anal virginity to other men, though, until near the end, so much as he instructed Santo on fucking himself on the hard cock.

"Push back on it. Slowly, slowly. Now a little faster. The Trot, as I taught you. Now the Canter. There good." Hamilton was breathing hard too and speaking in a low growl. It added to Santo's arousal that Hamilton obviously was enjoying the fuck.

Only for the last ten minutes or so did Hamilton pump Santo's channel—and then it was hard and fast, at a gallop. Before that he gently instructed Santo what to do to fuck himself on the cock. "Now revolve your hips," he said at one point, touching Santo with the gloved hands. "The Piaffe, the prancing in place." And Santo did, almost collapsing on wobbly legs as he felt the bulb of the cock caress him on every inner surface of his channel. He ejaculated then. He ejaculated again as Hamilton, groaning at the jerk Santo gave when he ejaculated, started to pump him hard and deep. Hamilton held out for several more minutes.

When Hamilton had ejaculated he let Santo collapse over on his side and lowered himself beside the young man, whose chest was heaving and thighs were trembling as loosely as rubber. Hamilton moved the gloved hands all over the

115

younger man's body, moving one eventually to encasing Santo's cock and stroking it gently.

It was only then that Hamilton leaned down and took Santo's mouth in his in a long, lingering kiss.

When they parted, Santo whispered, "Are you going to fuck me again?"

"Do you want me to?"

"Yes, oh yes."

"Not today. But we will sleep together tonight. Tomorrow I will teach you the Passage and the Flying Change."

"Excuse me?"

"You know the basic gaits we will use now, the Trot and the Canter at first. These were when I had you do the pushing by yourself on the cock, with the Canter being the more rapid of the two. When I fucked you it was a gallop—although that is beyond the world of dressage. And the revolving motion of your hips. That was the Piaffe. Tomorrow I will add the Passage and the Flying Change—and the signals with the flick of the riding whip on which you are to do when."

"The riding whip?" Santo asked weakly. He shuddered. "Are you going to whip me?"

"No more than I have. No more than I use the whip on Hochkonig and Lowengren. Just to signal a change of gait—as long as you follow my instructions. My geldings as thoroughbreds. You are a thoroughbred yourself of another kind." He then took up the riding whip, which had been laying on the bed beside where they fucked, and moved it around on Santo's cock, which began to engorge. Santo's was panting again. Hamilton gave the cock a flick of the whip. Santo's gasped and jerked. That was all, though.

Hamilton flicked the cock harder, and Santo gave a little cry. "What did I teach you to say to the touch of the whip?"

"Thank you, sir," Santo murmured.

Hamilton wrapped a gloved hand around Santo's ball sac and the root of his cock and applied pressure.

"Thank you, sir," Santo whispered through clinched teeth in a gaspy voice. Hamilton released the young man's balls

116

and moved the gloved hand up onto the cock and slowly stroked.

When he regained control, Santo spoke again. "You mentioned a bit and reins."

"Yes, a bit—not a horse bit; a bit men use in male-male sex, with a soft mouth piece—and reins."

"You will treat me like a horse?"

"Yes, I will mount you and ride you like a horse. We will have our own form of dressage. I will train you to be one with me, to merge with me, in a balance of strength, flexibility, and accuracy. This is not what you want from me?"

"Yes," Santo whispered, "that's what I want from you."

Hamilton stroked Santo to sleep with his white-gloved hands and then went and sat in the chair in the corner and smoked a cigar and drank cognac.

* * * *

Santo lifted his head at the slight pull on the reins attached to the bit in his mouth and waited for the flick of the whip. He had been instructed that the slight pull would warn that a change of gait signal was about to come. Hamilton and his other two horses had done very well on the last day of competition, winning him the class Champion ribbon again— and thus making him the Grand Champion of the competition. He was in a good mood. He also, fully clothed in his dressage outfit, was mounted on Santo's hips on the room-sized bed.

This was the second fuck. Today they would fuck into the night, Hamilton wanting Santo fully trained before they returned to Northern Virginia.

Santo was cooperating fully, taking whatever Hamilton wanted to give him. Santo was getting what he had been dreaming of for nearly a year—more than he had been dreaming of.

In the first fuck of the day, they had covered the Trot and the Canter and the Piaffe again, this time with the signals of the reins and whip that went with them—and once again Hamilton, overcome himself, had ended it all at the gallop.

117

Then they had rested. When he was ready again Hamilton put a docile Santo on all fours again and trained him to the Passage. In this Hamilton was no longer just a hard dick. Santo cried out as Hamilton suddenly thrust hard and deep. Then he held his breath as Hamilton paused there, deep inside him, leaning down and kissing him on the neck. Santo gasped at the long slide out, and then cried out again at the sudden, brutal, deep thrust—and the hold. "The Passage, a prance and then a hold of stance before resuming the prance" Hamilton whispered in Santo's ear. "Signaled by a tap of the whip on the right flank." Santo cried out again, as Hamilton repeated the pattern. Again and then again.

"The Flying Change," Hamilton declared. "I thrust twice, you push back once. Then repeat until I change the signal, which is a light flick of the whip on the left flank."

Hamilton didn't change the signal until they had both come for the third time.

As they lay on the bed, Hamilton moving his white-gloved hands over Santo's body, he said, "The job is yours. You train well. I feel the balance already. When we get back to Ash Creek Farms, I want you to move into the apartment over the stables. The groom job is yours—as long as you accept that this comes with it."

The arrangement was fine with Santo except for one catch. "Your wife and our families being so close. If either finds out . . . Pete got fired when you . . ."

"Pete was fired because I wanted you, because I was waiting for you to become a man," Hamilton answered. "And I wasn't the one who fired Pete. My wife did. She knew I wanted you. She is fine with this. She's the one who asked your mother to tell you I wanted you to go on this trip. And she's quite the filly when I mount and ride her too. She was quickly trained. Your family need never know about this."

"Then, yes," Santo answered with a sigh. He snuggled down, ready to drift off to sleep.

"Oh, no, young man. Dressage training is rigorous. Up on all fours. I feel like a gallop."

Last Laugh

Neal wasn't the sort of guy people noticed much. He could walk through a room of people talking—even a room full of people he knew—and get to the other side without being greeted or noticed. He could have conversations with strangers and then the stranger wouldn't recognize him if they met again. He was a guy of no standout talents, no distinctive looks other than being smaller of stature than his age. He wasn't ugly; he was just plain and forgettable—and a little scrawny.

He also didn't excel at anything. Well, there were a couple of things, but these weren't anything you'd brag about in public.

He hadn't done well in high school and thus was studying auto mechanics at a vocational school instead of going to college. This wasn't really something that interested him all that much, though, so he didn't excel at that either. And he didn't really have many friends in vocational school. He'd had a few undesirable friends in high school, but they hadn't really been friends and they had taken advantage of his weakness and lack of self-respect and had been what had made him the butt of jokes and derision—so much so that he'd embraced his "nonpersonhood."

Still, he did have interests and desires. And that's what brought him into the big box bookstore in Warsaw, Indiana, on a summer Saturday afternoon. He wasn't from Warsaw, and it was important to him that he wasn't. He didn't really want to be known around here, although there wasn't much danger of that.

What it looked like was that he had gone to sleep standing in front of a book shelf, holding a book in his hand, way in the back of the store, oblivious to the funny looks people gave him as they wandered down the aisle. He didn't care what most people thought, though. He was interested in one particular kind of person.

"That the only copy of the book on the shelf?"

Neal turned his face to see who had asked about the book, John Rechy's classic gay journey book, *City of the Night*. That was the book Neal had been standing and holding for all to see in front of the gay and lesbian book section—just half of one shelf really—for more than thirty minutes. He took a deep breath and gave the young man a wan smile. He was more than Neal had hoped for. He looked like a construction worker who had just come off the job. A muscular Scandinavian type, not much taller than Neal was but built like a fireplug. The "coming off a job" look came from the cut-off jeans, muscle T, and heavy construction boots he was wearing.

"You want this one?" Neal asked, broadening his smile a bit.

"I'd like something, but not that," the young man said. "Something with more feel and bite in it than you'd find between the covers of a book. What d'ya think of that?"

"I think you should have whatever you want," Neal answered.

"Interested in going for a drive in my new truck?"

"Sure, why not?" Neal answered. And why not indeed? This was exactly why Neal had come a third of a way across the state of Indiana to stand in front of the gay and lesbian shelf in a big box bookstore.

The truck was a black and shiny Dodge Ram 2500 double cab model, all polished up like it was the guy's pride and joy, which was probably right. On the way to the truck, with the guy palming Neal's butt to guide him in the parking lot, the guy said his name was Chaz. He also was pretty clear

120

about what he wanted and that he didn't want Neal to waste his time if that wasn't what he could have.

Neal introduced himself as an Indiana State University student named Jerry, home from Terre Haute on a short vacation—and said "no problem" to what Chaz said he wanted.

Neither of them believed the other as far as IDs.

Chaz drove the truck no more than four blocks before he nosed the Dodge Ram around to the back of a closed strip mall of five empty storefronts. He stopped the truck, reached over and palmed the back of Neal's head, and pulled him in for a short kiss. The kiss was short enough that it seemed like one fluid movement in which the palming hand moved Neal's head to Chaz' face and then down into Chaz' lap, where he had already unzipped himself.

As he fished his cock out of his shorts, he leaned back in the driver's seat and whispered a moaning, "Suck it, suck it, suck it, baby." With his head encased between Chaz' hands, Neal proceeded to do just that, having trouble opening wide enough for the dick. Chaz was built like a fireplug in equipment too—not long, but extra thick. Neal had some trouble covering the cock and gagged a bit as it pushed into his mouth cavity, but he kept at it. This is what he'd come to Warsaw for.

After a few minutes Chaz tightened his grip and pulled Neal's face out of his lap. "Geez, you've got a talented mouth," he gasped. "I want more, though, this time."

This time? Neal thought. I little chill of thrill went through his body. This wasn't just going to be a blow job and dumped out of the truck four blocks from his own car then, maybe.

Chaz opened the driver's door and rolled out of the vehicle. Turning, he grabbed Neal by the upper arm and pulled him out too.

Neal shuddered. He melted to rough.

Chaz slid Neal down the line of the shiny black Dodge to the tailgate, which he unlatched and let fall, with a bang. There was a pile of gunny sacks on the bed of the truck, which

121

Chaz quickly fanned out. With a jerk, he pulled Neal's T-shirt over his head and tossed it into the bed of the truck.

"What the fuck?" he exclaimed. He jerked Neal's shorts down off his legs. "What the fuck is this?" he exclaimed again.

"Try it, you'll like it."

"A slip? You're wearing a woman's slip."

And Neal was. It was a black silky number, with lace cut into the plunging neckline and spaghetti straps holding it on Neal's shoulders.

"Don't it make you feel horny? Feel how silky it is. You can have a lot of new fantasies with this," Neal said in a husky whisper. "You feel horny, don't 'cha?" He was cupping Chaz' balls. Chaz hadn't bothered to push his cock back into his shorts or zip back up while he was pulling Neal out of the front seat.

"God, you're right," Chaz growled. His cock was hard and throbbing. He placed his hands on Neal's waist and hoisted him up onto the tailgate of the truck. He stared into Neal's eyes as his hands ran over the silkiness of the black slip, gathering up material and bunching the slithery garment around Neal's waist.

"Shit. And black panties too." He started to pull these off Neal's hips, but Neal reached down and grasped his wrists.

"No need," he whispered coquettishly. "There's a slit."

And so there was. Chaz slipped a hand into the slit to find Neal naked underneath. The fingers of one hand went to rimming and then slowly invading Neal's hole. His other hand grasped Neal's throat, holding his head down on the surface of the truck bed.

Neal groaned and moved his hips, aiding in the finger fuck. He was whispering, "You're a real stud. Fuck me good. Make me feel it," in a small, breathless voice.

His hands went under the hem of Chaz' athletic T, rising to the young man's hard nipples. Chaz took time to move his hands to pull off the T and toss it aside in the bed of the truck, and then he moved back to holding Neal down with a one-handed choke hold and finger fucking him with the other. Neal lifted his ankles to Chaz' shoulders on either side and continued to run his hands over the man's muscular torso

122

and down to cup and squeeze his balls and shake and stroke his cock. Neal's own cock remained encased in the black panties.

"There. Rub me there again. Make me come for you."

Chaz was spending a lot a time in the finger-fucking phase, so Neal finally pointed over to his shorts and said, "Rubbers. In my shorts. Fuck me, stud. Give me your cock. Don't make me wait too long."

The young man snapped out of the rut he seemed to be in, let loose of Neal's neck, and reached over for his shorts, which had been tossed in the bed of the truck. He whistled and gave Neal a sharp look. There were a dozen packets of condoms, all connected in a long string. Chaz took time to count them out loud. A full dozen.

"You've come to party," he growled.

"Don't you know it? So party," Neal answered in a Betty Boop voice. He waited until he heard the snap of the condom being pulled up to Chaz' root, and then he reached down and guided the cock head to his hole. For the next twenty minutes all that could be heard were grunts, groans, gasps, and low moans, as Neal's channel slowly pulled the thick cock inside and the two set up a rhythm of the fuck.

Afterward, still inside Neal, Chaz leaned close down into him, their foreheads touching, and said, "You wanna be dropped back at the bookstore now, or do you wanna go for a beer? And maybe an afterward—or a bigger party."

"The beer sounds good."

While Neal readjusted his clothing, donning his camouflaging T-shirt and shorts again, Chaz went to the driver's side of the truck, pulled a cell phone from underneath the front seat, and made a few quick calls.

They drove to a seedy-looking roadhouse at the edge of Warsaw. The first thing Neal saw when they walked in were four beefy guys, looking as much like construction workers as Chaz did, sitting in a booth at the back corner of the place, the table top littered with full, but uncapped, beer bottles, and four sets of eyes glued to the entrance. The four faces, three white and one black, wore the identical grin.

"Bill, Alphonse, Mickey, and Jeb," Chaz said, in introduction, as they approached the booth. Instantly, all four

123

faces took on an expression of confusion, but they quickly were smart enough to catch that these were their names for the day. "This here's Jerry," Chaz told them. "All sweetness, he is. And *has* he got a surprise for anyone interested in checking him out."

With that, Chaz, slid in beside Bill and Alphonse on one side, and Mickey rolled out of the booth so that Neal could wedge between him and Jeb on the other side of the booth. Both Bill and Jeb tried to give Neal a bottle of beer at the same time, but Bill won the race. He took a moment longer than necessary to release Neal's hand and was giving him a warm smile. Both Jeb and Mickey put arms around Neal's shoulders on either side.

Truth be known, Neal wasn't worried or nervous at all. He hadn't been shown this much attention by a group of guys for some time. Entertaining groups of guys had once been a specialty of his, though. Even the slip and panties idea was nothing new for him.

The four new guys spent time trying to get Neal's attention and one-upping each other in their form of charm as they plied him with beer. As soon as Neal started to act woozy, though, they increasingly joked and engaged in sexual innuendo talk among themselves and acted like Neal wasn't even there— although he continued to be the center of attention.

"You'll be floored with this cutie's secret," Chaz said when he thought Neal's ears were buzzing too loudly to hear what they were saying.

"Give good head, does he?" That was Mickey.

"That and more," answered Chaz. "And a real surprise."

"I've put in for about all the beer I can afford," Bill said. "We gonna do this or not?"

"So, wanna take the chicken for a little ride?" Chaz asked.

"In your new Dodge Ram?" Mickey asked.

"Ram," Alphonse, the black dude said. Then he laughed. "The man said ram and my dick stood up and saluted. I feel like ramming something. Ram, ram, ram."

"Careful, big guy," Jeb said. "You could kill what you ram with what you got."

"So, again, wanna go for a ram . . . I mean a ride?" The offer was extended by Chaz again, who added his chuckle to the rest at his little joke.

"We could take him to my place," Mickey offered. "The old lady's at her mother's for the weekend. Neighbors not close enough to hear him."

"I say we make a picnic of him," Alphonse said. "Down by the river. On Zeke's—I mean Jeb's— river property. I've got firsties."

"The hell you do, Alphonse," Jeb chimed in. "You can use my place, but if you go first he won't feel any of the rest of us inside him."

"Let's stop for weed and beer to go on the way," Bill said.

Through all of this, Neal was moving his head back and forth, pointing it to whoever was talking the loudest at the moment, but giving a good indication from the sloppy grin on his face that he either didn't really hear any of it or was OK with it all. Just like he'd done in school for attention.

Five beefy studs and a scrawny Neal were loaded into the Dodge truck. Chaz and Alphonse were in front, the rest were in back, with Neal sitting on the lap of the middle guy, Bill.

"Jesuzz Chriist!" Bill yelled from the backseat while the truck was buzzing through the countryside.

"Found the secret, did ja?" Chaz called from the front seat.

"The guy's got on a black slip and panties," Jeb informed the front seat.

"So, enjoy," Chaz called back. "I found it a turn-on. There's a slit in the panties."

"Too late," Mickey said, with a laugh. "They're off. He's already on Bill's cock. Bill knows all about that slit."

All that could be heard inside the double cab for several miles were the sounds of sex from the backseat. Neal wasn't doing much more than groaning and moaning, but when he gave a sharp cry, Chaz exclaimed a "What the fuck?"

125

pulled over to the side of the road, and turned to look into the back. "Geez, guys, couldn't you wait for that. You'll finish him off before we even get there."

"Pull off more on the shoulder," Alphonse said. "We can all do him right here."

Bill was sitting in the center of the backseat. Neal was crouched in his lap, facing him, his legs bent on either side of Bill's hips and knees buried into the edge where the seat back met the cushion. He was still wearing the black slip, bunched up around his chest, but that was all. He was sitting on Bill's cock. Jeb had moved around to Neal's back, his own back pressed into the back of the front seat, and also had his cock inside Neal's ass, on top of Bill's. Mickey's hand was between Bill's and Neal's bellies, and he was stroking Neal's cock. Neal was flopping around between the two men double fucking him and moaning and groaning deeply. He had his eyes closed. His fists were grasping and digging into Bill's shoulders, the fingers opening and closing in the rhythm of whoever's cock was actively stroking inside him.

With a snort of disgust, Chaz put the truck back on the road. "Not here, Alphonse. The cops police this road."

Chaz parked the Dodge Ram at the end of a track a quarter of a mile off the main road into Jeb's heavily wooded river property. Jeb had cleared an area there, in a depression below the vehicle track and right next to a shallow river bed where water raced over exposed rocks. Jeb had put a picnic table down there, and whoever wasn't occupied with Neal up at the truck sat around the picnic table smoking pot, drinking beer, and joking about the gang bang they were sharing. They were all naked, for quicker transitions. They left their clothes in the bed of the truck.

Chaz had told them about the twelve condoms Neal had been carrying in his shorts—eleven when Chaz and Neal had gotten to the roadhouse, and nine when they had arrived at the picnic spot. They decided that they'd use them all—that would be their goal.

Chaz looked up the hill at the truck and laughed. He was high enough to be amused by the tableau of Alphonse, the big black stud, standing on a log behind the truck's tailgate,

126

between Neal's thin white legs, which were spread and raised and were quavering such that Chaz could discern every thrust of Alphones' dick. Glimpses of Neal's hands scrabbling around on Alphonse's torso and the rim of the truck bed as he screamed his taking of a cock thicker than Bill's and Jeb's together amused Chaz.

All the guys other than Chaz had already fucked Neal separately twice in the truck by the river—or en route to the river. Chaz had held Alphonse off. He knew that the big black would ream the scrawny little chicken a wide one. From Neal's cries, this seemed to be the case.

This was the eleventh fuck. Chaz was holding the twelfth condom packet. He was providing the chicken, so he would have the last helping.

When Alphonse was finished and had turned to climb down the hill to the picnic table, Chaz rose and made his way up the hill. He lifted Neal out of the bed of the truck and, making sympathetic clucking noises, helped Neal hobble around to the door to the backseat. He opened the rear door, and Neal made to sit on the seat gingerly. But with a laugh, Chaz pushed Neal onto his back on the seat, his legs still out of the truck. Neal moaned as Chaz rolled the last condom on his cock, and then, with a groan, Neal lifted his legs and spread them and planted his heels in the top frame of the doors on that side of the truck, arched his back, and gave a little cry as Chaz planted his feet on the running board, pushed his torso into the truck's backseat, suspended over Neal's, thrust inside Neal, and began to pump him hard and fast.

After putting their clothes back on, the beefy construction workers climbed back into the truck cab. They left Neal lying on his back on the gunny sacks in the bed of the truck, an arm flung over his face, and groaning.

Chaz let his four friends out at the roadhouse at the edge of Warsaw and then drove back to the shopping center where the big box bookstore was located. He pulled over to the far edge of the parking area, where there were no cars even remotely close, backed the truck to some trees, turned it off, and got out. He marched around to the tailgate, lowered it, grabbed Neal by one of his ankles and pulled him to the edge.

127

Then he lifted the moaning Neal out of the truck. Neal wasn't moving a muscle. He let Chaz manipulate him like a rag doll. Chaz laid him down on the mulch at the fringe of the parking lot. Neal had struggled back into his shorts and T-shirt during the ride back into town.

"Thanks for the party, bitch," Chaz growled. "The slip and panties were a fun surprise. Sorry, I don't know what happened to the panties. One of the guys took them as a souvenir probably. But that's what you get for taking chances like that. Bet you don't do that again anytime soon. No charge for the lesson."

Neal opened his eyes, peeking at Chaz' truck as it moved off, across the empty zone of the parking lot.

Bet I do it again next weekend, he thought. Although maybe not with as good results.

He scampered up, belying the weakness he had been displaying, and pulled back into the woods at the edge of the parking lot. He'd work his way around to his Camaro, parked at the other end of the shopping center from the big box bookstore. He suspected Chaz would be back—maybe sooner than later. Neal would watch for this as he went to his car.

He had just endured the riskiest part of all of this. It wasn't the pickup or the gang bang, or the double fuck, or Alphonse's monster cock, or being fucked twelve times. Neal had enjoyed all of that. That was one of the talents he couldn't brag about in public. He loved taking cock and could take it all day and in super sizes. Alphonse had been the best fuck of the lot—because Neal was an unabashed size queen.

It was because of his other talent. There had been a distinct danger that one of those dummies would notice that they'd all been stripped of their credit cards and folding money during the gang bang. While one was leaving him and the other arriving at the truck's tailgate, Neal had been rifling their wallets. The roadhouse gang would discover that as soon as they tried to pay for beer at the roadhouse. Chaz could realize it even sooner than that.

But Neal had disarmed them all with his act that he couldn't hold his beer and that he had become so incapacitated that he just let them gangbang him. The truth was that he'd

128

never lost control over himself and he loved being gangbanged. He loved being the center of attention for groups of beefy and hung men.

And Neal would be at it again next weekend—standing at the gay and lesbian shelf in some big box bookstore in some new town, waiting for some dummy to pick him up, give Neal the fuck he craved—today had been a bonanza—and then gift Neal with all his folding money and his credit cards, which Neal would fence for a tidy sum. Neal wasn't from Warsaw. He lived in Fort Worth. And he would never hit the bookstores there.

Next week Kokomo maybe. That was far enough away from Fort Worth—and from Warsaw. These guys had laughed at him while they banged him. Neal was used to that. But Neal always had the last laugh.

Fuck a Duck

I liked them small—short, but otherwise perfectly formed. And the stripper was all of that. I'd stopped in Orlando on my way down to Key West for my usual winter gay cruising fix, having been told that Orlando was a secret Key West. Parliament House at Orlando's Rock Lake, on North Orange Blossom Trail, had been recommended to me, and thus far it was panning out. Ten acres of musky male lust. I'd been hit on three times in just walking across the hotel lobby. Maybe it was something I wasn't wearing. I had wondered how I would go over down here in the south, but I'd never had a problem in Key West, and I wasn't to have any problem here either. If anything, I attracted more interest than most, thanks to the legends, which in my case rang true.

I could see through the lobby window that I'd barely walked away from my Chrysler Crossfire parked out there before two guys were having sex on the hood.

I went immediately hard as I was checking in and the hotel clerks and I checked each other out.

"Will there be anything else, sir," one was saying. "Anything at all?"

"Maybe later," I answered with a smile. About thirty minutes later if I couldn't set up a better hookup before then. I was horny as hell, and the desk clerk looked ready to go.

The hotel room was nice enough, and at $70 a night was a steal. It overlooked a pool of young, ripped men having a

131

ball and the queen-sized bed was firm, just the way I liked it. It later was amusing to think that less than an hour after check-in I'd find that the bedsprings had a little squeak to them as I lay on my back, and the small, perfectly cut body of a male stripper bounced up and down on my cock, whimpering "Black cock, black cock, big black cock."

That's me, a black bull.

I arrived thirsty, so I headed for one of the resort's several bars—just one of the resort's amenities in addition to all sorts of other ones, including a nightclub—as soon as I'd stowed my bag, taken a leak, draped myself on the balcony railing for a few minutes to pick out my favorites among the men at the pool, and bounced a bit on my butt on the bed—but not heavy enough by myself to have discovered the squeak.

I was feeling raunchy as well as thirsty, my mind dwelling on the two guys I saw fucking on the hood of my Crossfire, so I went into a bar that I could see had a stage with male dancers on it. I sidled up to the bar, ordered a scotch from a beefy tattooed bartender wearing just a Bike jockstrap and knee-high soccer socks and giving me the eye of interest, and turned to find that they weren't just dancers. They also were strippers. Having already gotten the measure of this place, my guess was that they were rent-boys as well.

They apparently had started off as firemen and policemen, and now were in various stages of being down to G strings. They came in all sizes and coloring, even another black guy, filling out his pouch better than any other stripper up there—but not, I'm proud to say, as well as I would. Something for every guy. And every guy in the audience seemed to be pleased—those who weren't intimately paired off and having eyes only for each other, that is.

My eyes went to a short Latino who was perfectly formed other than being maybe no more than five foot three. I was six five myself and built solid and muscular like a football halfback, but I very much appreciated little guys. I appreciate them so much that that my dick flips right up when I see one I like. I like to hear them squeal as I spike them with every possibility, given the relative sizes, that I'll see my cockhead waving at me from their tonsils as I fuck them.

132

I really liked this one, and I'd changed into a pair of loose shorts, a cut-off athletic T, and open-toed sandals when I'd come down both because I wanted to be more comfortable after a long day of driving south and because this attire showed me off to great advantage. I was stopping in Orlando for two days. I wanted to score well and often.

And I wanted to score first right now. I was so rock hard that my balls ached. It had been a long drive from Detroit.

I stared at the little Latino hard, taking in all of his moves and licking my lips. I was a specialty; not just every guy would go with me. And a few ran away screaming when they got a real good look at me.

He didn't seem to have that problem. He must have picked me out of the crowd as special and his king of special, because he began to dance just for me—or so I fancied. I'd seen movies where two people connect across a crowded room and the movie emphasized that by putting spotlights on just those two and having the rest of the crowd dimming into the background and otherwise absorbed in small conversation groups away from the center of the action. I had always thought that was fake, but that's what it seemed like this was now, and it didn't seem a bit fake.

In the movies too, they sometimes suppress all background sound at these moments to something in slow motion like sound heard under water, and that was happening here too. I could feel the beating of my heart—it was matching the rhythm of the throbbing of my cock. I wouldn't say I was in love like this often depicts in the movies, but I was in heat and lust, with a hard, throbbing cock that I was fisting through the silky material of my sports shorts.

I wanted to take the little stripper and fuck the stuffing out of him—see my cockhead waving at me from behind his tonsils—and I wanted to do it right now.

I knew the dancer had picked me out; his hand went to his crotch too, and he grabbed his nuts as he blew me a kiss with the other hand. You can't engrave an invitation any better than that.

133

I could see a couple of guys from the audience going up on stage, and it hit me that the underwater tones of an announcer floating over the music on the stage was an invitation for guys to come up and dance with the strippers.

I made a beeline for the little Latino, who was obviously waiting for me, because he brushed off a couple of guys before I could get to him. We danced close, his arms raised and draped around my neck, his face looking up at mine and mine down into his. My dick pressed into his torso somewhere between his navel and his pecs, and there was no hiding that I was in heat. He would have had to be a dummy not to know I was built big. They usually were trembling at this point, but he showed no fear.

So, I didn't waste time in preliminaries. I dug into my pocket and came up with a hundred-dollar bill. I'd put bills of various denominations in there and folded them differently so I'd know which was what. I didn't catch up with that many little guys and this one was a real honey and wasn't backing away from me, so I went for the gold. I waved the bill in front of his eyes so he could see Benjamin Franklin staring back at him. I always laughed at using Franklin this way, because I had the feeling that, of all the Founding Fathers, he was the one who would approve of being used in this way.

"Wonder what this can get for me around here?" I asked, as we swayed against each other, the feel of his hard chest rubbing against my covered cock to the swaying of our bodies driving me nearly to distraction.

"Just about anything you want, for just about as long as you want," he answered. His voice was a high tenor and it had sort of a funny, squeaky sound to it. "I have a break in about ten minutes," he added.

"I've had a long drive today and I'm horny as hell."

"So, I noticed," he murmured.

"You say you get off in ten minutes. I'm not in the mood for a tease. I want to get off in thirty. You can do that, or do I go looking?"

"Sure, for a Franklin I can do that."

As I stuffed the banknote down the front of his jockstrap, he both raised his lips to mine in a kiss and moved a hand down to creep up under the leg hole of my shorts and rise to grip my cock. I wasn't wearing briefs.

As he came out of the kiss, he murmured in a voice tinged with awe, "Shit you're big. Long and thick."

"I'll bet you say that to all of the johns."

"Not like I'm sayin' it to you. Is it as black as you?"

"Darker." He shivered, and I added, "Sure you can handle it? I don't want to waste any time here."

"Yes, I'm sure."

"Scared of it?"

"Shit yes," he said with a big smile.

And handle it he did, although at one point where he arched his back and his eyes were rolling up into his head and his mouth was open in a silent scream as I tested out how deep I could go, I thought maybe I'd lost him. I looked in his mouth and didn't see my piss head staring back at me, but I bet it was close.

Seven minutes after we'd left the bar I was on my back on the bed in my room—he had cut out for his break early— and he was astride my thighs, his knees pressing into the outside of my thighs, and he was rolling a condom on my cock. That done and lube applied on the condom and his hole and with a fist around the root of my cock to keep it erect, he saddled himself and lowered his channel on the cock.

He was whimpering, "Black cock, black bull, big black cock," over and over again and was doing some groaning and chuffing, but no more than I was. He had a loose hole you could drive a truck into, so, in time, he was able to slide nearly all the way down me. (Later, when I took control, is when I gave it all to him and he nearly passed out on me.) I made the customary, "You're so tight" comments, but we both knew that wasn't so. If it was so, he couldn't have taken me nearly all in. Still, as soon as my cock was sheathed, he managed to tighten the channel up on it. And he could use those channel muscles to undulate all over the cock. I moaned. He was perfect.

I just lay there as long as I could contain myself, with him doing most of the work, pumping his channel up and down on the cock, faster and faster. Breaking the pumping

135

occasionally to rotate his channel on the cock, making both of us groan with pleasure. Still murmuring "black cock, big black cock" like he meant it. Taking nearly all of the cock and then exposing nearly all of the cock with each pump, setting the bed springs chattering. I started off holding his waist and helping him with the rise and fall, but it was quite evident he was fully capable of doing this all by himself, so I used one hand to grip and stroke his cock that had been beating against my belly and the other one to worry his plump, brown nipples with.

Eight minutes into the fuck, he reversed himself on the cock, leaning toward the foot of the bed, grasping the ankles of my spread legs with his fists and pushing hard back into my groin with his butt cheeks. Taking me to the root. I was jerking and shuddering. Almost no one took me to the root. I had images of seeing the bulb of my cock coming out of his mouth. Where in the hell was he putting it all?

Seven minutes of this and I felt like I was going to explode—and that I needed to take control—and I raised my torso up, embraced his torso with my arms and laid back again, taking him with me. I used my thighs to spread his legs wider and roll his hips up, and I began the pumping action inside him myself. I fisted his cock with one hand and grabbed his balls with the other and began stroking and squeezing.

"Want you to come for me," I growled into his ear. And he did so, shooting a little arc of cum up into the air, which fell back on his belly. Within thirty seconds I had filled the bulb of my condom, and he was scrambling around, ripping the condom off, and sucking the last bit of cum out of my bulb, as I huffed, fisted the bedspread, and lifted my pelvis off the surface of the bed.

When I had lowered my hips with a sigh, and his mouth slid farther down on the cock, I turned my head and looked at the clock on the nightstand. I had shot off thirty-two minutes from the moment we'd left the bar. Not bad.

Having licked me clean, the stripper turned his body and reclined into my embrace. We lay there like that, both panting, for several minutes.

"That was good," I murmured. "You're very good. I was going to float, but I think I want to do you again."

136

"You're not just good; you're great. I love black cock," he answered in the funny little tenor voice of his. "Any time you want me I'm available. Cocks that big, thick, and black are hard to come by."

That's when I got him under me and gave it all to him—and when he nearly passed out. Fifty minutes from the bar and I almost had a dead stiff on my hands with a cockhead swabbing his tonsils from the inside and a smile on his lips. God, I loved the little guys.

I gave him a rest then and time to revive before setting up the next round. I thought he'd cut and run as soon as I heaved my body off him, but the tough little guy was hanging in there with me.

"You available after dinner?" I asked "I'm famished. I mean for food. But I came here to fuck too."

"No, not tonight. Sorry." The response sounded genuine—not just putting me off. "I work my other job tonight."

"Your other job."

"You don't really want to know."

"Sure, tell me. I've always wondered what other jobs male strippers have. Altar boy?"

"No, I'm a duck."

"A duck?" I couldn't help but laugh. And not just at what he said, but at the connection I immediately made with his strange voice. A little manipulation of that and he'd sound just like the cartoon character, Donald Duck.

"Yes. I work most evenings at Disney World in a Donald Duck costume. I'm small enough for that, you know."

"Yes, right," I said, trying to suppress the laugh. Not only short enough to wear a Donald Duck costume, I thought, but a voice that could be made to go with it as well. "Well, OK, guess I'll see you around."

"I do want you to fuck me again," he said. He already was lightly fingering my cock, like he wanted me to do him again already. My cock was engorging like it had the same idea. My mind was already considering whether he'd want another Ben Franklin to do it.

"It's OK. I know you have to say that to all . . ."

137

"I do want you to fuck me again," he repeated. "I don't say that to every guy who fucks me. But I have to be over to Disney shortly."

"OK. It's OK. I'm going to take a shower now. You can see you own way out."

I was in the shower when I heard the door open, and he was standing there. He hadn't dressed, and his body was absolutely gorgeous. My cock was interested again. I made no objection when he entered the shower stall.

"Back against the tiles," he said.

"You don't have to do this," I said, as I backed up to the tiles. "You'll be late for work."

"The brats can just wait," he said—and he said it in a Donald Duck voice that made me laugh.

"Well, then, how much more for . . . ?"

"No charge for this one. I told you you were big and thick enough for me to want your cock. And I melt to black cock. I want you to believe that—to know that I can't get enough from a black bull."

He put his hands under my thighs and coaxed me to move my feet away from the wall and crouch a bit, letting my back slide a little way down the slick tiles of the shower wall. Water was cascading over both of us from the showerhead. He climbed my thighs with his, and I encircled his back with my arms to give him support. I felt him rolling another condom on my cock before he positioned it at his hole and skewered himself. Then he did a crab thing, motioning for me to hold his waist in my hands and then palming the tiles on either side of my biceps and raising his feet to the tile walls beside my waist and spread, and then using them for leverage as he fucked himself on my cock until I couldn't take him having all the control anymore. Then I pulled him hard and fast on the cock, coarse black pubic hair jamming into silky black, curly pubic hair with each thrust. His cries of "black cock, black bull, big black cock" echoed around the tiled bathroom. I briefly worried that we were making too much noise, but this was a men's fuck hotel. There was probably fucking going on all up and down the hallway of rooms.

138

With heavy panting and moaning we came nearly simultaneously, and he sank to the tiles on his knees again, jerked off the condom, and cleaned my cock with his mouth. He didn't let me go, though. He kept sucking and sucking the cock until I gave him an after ejaculation and, knees weak, sank to the floor of the shower to join him in kisses while I moved my hand between us and brought him to another jack off.

"That was a nice surprise," I murmured afterward, still in position with the water raining down on us.

"I like surprises too. Surprise me sometime," he said. And then he was gone, leaving me to finish my shower. He wasn't in the room when I came out of the bathroom naked. I went out onto the balcony and looked down at the pool. I didn't realize at first that the wolf whistles were for me until the propositions started being called up to the balcony.

"Hey, up there. Black beauty. Hung just like I like 'em. Tell me your room number and I'll come up and show you a really good time. I can sheath all of that. You'll love it."

I smiled and waved. But I also shrugged and returned to the room. The fucks and a blow job after a long day on the road had been exhausting. Besides, I think the guy was being way too optimistic about what he could sheath of me. One of the reasons I liked doing the little guys is that I'd found that, interestingly enough, they often were able to handle the big dicks better than bigger guys could.

I laid down for a short nap before dinner. I dreamed of little guys in Donald Duck costumes and chasing them around an amusement park and fucking one in the bushes, his little white tail wagging and tickling my belly as I spiked him. I woke up with the thought of combining this dream with surprising Donald, as he had suggested I do.

That was his real name. He had told me his name really was Donald. And we both had laughed at the coincidence.

* * * *

I was in a bit of a daze when I turned from the ticket booth at Disney World. This was almost as much as I had paid to fuck Donald earlier. So, I was feeling a bit screwed. Already

139

I was thinking that this little surprise wasn't the best of ideas. And I hadn't been wholly sold on it from the beginning. After dinner I had roamed the pool area of the Parliament House resort, and although I'd gotten a lot of offers, several willing to do exactly what I was looking for, Donald's slight image kept springing to mind. I wanted to do it with—to him—because his body was exactly what set me off. I didn't find anyone else at Parliament House with his body and I was only here for two days. I wanted to do him as often as I could.

I didn't have that much trouble finding him. All of the cartoon characters were gravitating toward the central circle on the island at the end of the Main Street section. The park would be closing in another couple of hours and many of the people, especially the ones with children, were filtering out of the park. The cartoon characters were gathering for last-minute photo ops with the children.

I picked out Donald in his little white, feathery fat suit and large yellow bill, and positioned myself in front of him, but away from the kiddies. I called out "Donald" to him and waved. He waved back.

When there was a break in the children, he turned and entered the park area called Adventureland. I followed at a discreet distance. He waddled with his little white tail wagging back and forth—I can't describe it in any better way—through that park area to the last building on one side, with the sign "The Pirates League." At the edge of the trees beyond that, he went down a path at the side of the building. He obviously wanted me to follow him, which I did.

I walked faster, catching up with him at the doorway into another building in back of The Pirates League building.

He quacked—quite convincingly—as I wrapped my arms around him and forced him deeper into the wooded area. Finding a pile of logs, I bent him over the logs on his fat, white tummy, found what I wanted to find—a zipper underneath him that exposed his ass.

I almost laughed at how furiously his little white tail was wagging as I slowly pushed my cock inside him. His channel seemed tighter than it had been back in my bedroom, but I managed to mount him amidst quite a bit of quacking.

140

The quacking subsided fairly quickly into moaning though, and soon he was pushing back at my thrusts inside him and murmuring "Yes, fuck me, fuck me. You're so big," in a weak tenor voice.

When I had come, I stood up and away from him, tossed out a "Surprise, Donald! See you back at the resort," and left him there, panting and moaning.

I returned to Parliament House thirsty, but happy and decided to go to the resort's strip bar for another drink.

Entering the bar, I did a double take. Donald was dancing a pole in just a G-string.

He saw me, but it was several minutes before he was able to leave the stage. "Couldn't get enough of me?" he asked with a smile.

"Got that right. But how did you do it?"

"Do what?"

"How did you get back from the park before I did? There some quicker back route between Disney and here than Interstate 4?"

He gave me a quizzical look. "Don't understand what you mean. I was called off my evening shift at Disney tonight. So I took another shift on the pole here."

I said nothing, but I felt so traumatized by the mistake I had made that I had to take him back to my room and fuck the quack out of him all night long.

Hijacked

"What's good for the earth and all that."

"I often wondered how that worked," the young man behind the counter of the diner just south of Santa Fe said. He was leaning over the counter, having delivered Andy's breakfast, but not all that anxious to move on. Andy was a real looker. A regular Paul Newman, but with more muscle. And the young man behind the counter had his interests. Besides, the looks he was getting back indicated that the trucker, Andy, had similar interests—and they might include him if he played it right.

"Yeah, gotta do what we can to keep the environment clean," Andy said. He had been trained well to parrot his company's policies, but he did, in fact, support keeping the environment as clean as possible.

Sadie, the older woman behind the counter, snorted in passing, "Ya mean getting the environment *back* to clean don't ya, sweetie? Make up for decades of screwing it up." She nudged the man behind the counter, "There's an order needing taken at the end of the counter, Stan, if you can get your eyeballs back into your head." As Stan reddened and scurried off, she turned to Andy. "Top off that coffee, sweetie?" She didn't have any objection to hunks herself. And they were safer in the long run if they swung a different way. She'd wrangled with too many hunks already in her life. Andy sure was nice on the eyes, though.

143

"Yeah, thanks," Andy said, as the man behind the counter moved to the far end of the barstools. There was a young guy, some sort of mixed breed, perched on a stool down the counter. Some part white in him, Andy thought, but something else. Native American? Hispanic? Whatever it was, it was a good mix. He was kind of small, but well formed and with a real good face. Andy wouldn't mind getting his dick into that one. And the glance the young guy gave him after he'd given his order to the counter man indicated interest too.

Andy loved this diner. His kind gravitated here; made him feel real comfortable. He smiled a bland smile back at the mixed breed. He didn't have to be the one on the make. He had no trouble picking guys up on the road to fuck silly in the compartment behind his cab. He knew he looked like Paul Newman and was hung. There were guys who came to this diner from cross county just for the chance to hit on him.

While eyeballing the honey at the end of the counter— well both of them; the mixed breed perched on the stool and the guy behind the counter, although, of the two the mixed breed was the winner—and being eyeballed in return, it hit Andy that something seemed a bit strange. Then he figured out what it was. When he'd seen the mixed breed walking across the windows outside before entering the diner, he'd been chatting with three other guys. Where were they? Andy looked around the diner and saw that the three were over at a table. A surly lot, he thought. He must have been mistaken about the really sweet-looking mixed breed having been with them. They looked like ranch hands just off a dusty cattle drive, and looking for trouble.

Sadie had made a pass at serving them coffee but had backed out of their aura as fast as she could. She was at the end of the counter now, pouring for the small mixed breed. They exchanged a few words, and then she turned and called down the counter to Andy.

"You driving that fancy new rig out there now, Andy? Guy here asked about it, but I was curious too."

"Yeah, that's my new company ride," Andy said. His semitrailer was parked across the parking lot, all gleaming silver.

144

"Guy here says he ain't seen nothing that fancy around here before. Neither have I. He said that's got to have the biggest compartment behind the cab he's ever seen."

"Yep, it's a special model," Andy answered. "My home away from home." He'd jumped at the chance to switch to the new rig when it came onto the lot—and wholly because of that larger sleeping compartment behind the cab. But Andy thought of it more as a fucking compartment. He liked to pick guys needing a ride, in more ways than one, off the road, and a larger cabin supported more exotic fuck positions.

"And the truck's a new-fangled design," he continued. "Anderson's producing a few hybrid semi trucks now to see how they go. My company's motto is 'Anything for the Environment,' so I'm helping to test a hybrid model to see how it copes with hard hauls like the one from Santa Fe to Phoenix. So far so good. Good mileage for a semi, fewer emissions, and it's pullin' OK so far."

And there's that extra roomy sleeping compartment too, he thought.

"What'yer hauling this trip?" the counter man asked.

"Electronic gear. TVs and computer monitors mostly. Taking them from Santa Fe to Phoenix."

Sadie snorted, "So much for the environment. Fancy earth-friendly truck haulin' ozone killers."

Andy was about to respond to that, when there was a growl from across the room. The three dusty cowboys wanted to order. Sadie pulled a pencil out of her hair and a notebook out of her pocket and sauntered off across the room.

Andy finished his coffee, tossed his money down on the counter, and went to the head to take a piss before going back on the road. He was standing at the urinal, pissing a strong arc onto the porcelain wall when he heard the bathroom door open. He turned his head a bit as the good-looking mixed breed entered and sidled up to the urinal beside him. The young guy unzipped and turned and gave Andy a grin. He then lowered his eyes to Andy's urinal—well, more at what was pointed into the urinal. Andy turned a bit to give the dude a good look at his package. He was proud of it—and had every right to be proud of it.

The other guy gave a little gasp, and Andy had to move a bit to his right, afraid that the mixed breed would piss on his pant leg in his loss of control at seeing how Andy was hanging.

The truck driver might have said something, as the come on seemed pretty obvious and the little guy was a really nice piece—and was equipped pretty well too. He was half hard just from looking at what Andy was packing, and Andy was about to give him an even better look, when the bathroom door opened again and the man behind the counter entered.

The idea of a threesome—all the signals had been there—raced through Andy's mind. But he didn't really have time for that, and he was a bit worried what that Sadie would say when the three had been in the head for some time. She had a mouth on her and didn't seem to put much restraint on what she'd say at full volume—and to the diner at large. And she seemed smart enough to have caught the vibes going on between the men out at the counter. She certainly seemed to have had the number of the guy behind the counter. Andy just didn't want to endure the walk from the head to the diner door—and there was always something he could pick up on the road. He'd never had trouble that way.

So, he zipped himself up, having emptied his bladder essentially before the mixed breed had entered the room, winked at the mixed breed, and relinquished the urinal to the counter guy. There were only two urinals. If Andy didn't back out fast, there obviously was going to be some action or some embarrassment at misreading signals. The counter guy seemed much more interested in what Andy and the mixed breed were doing than in taking a leak.

Andy marched quickly through the diner and out to his fancy environmentally correct semitrailer. He had to walk around an old Mustang convertible with a faded red paint job and an even older beat-up truck that had once been a U-Haul van but had been indifferently painted over in white to get to his rig. He checked around the semi for anything that looked like it might be trouble. Finding nothing worrisome, he pulled himself up into the truck cab and drove out onto Interstate 25 for the short leg to Albuquerque through the Santo Domingo and San Felipe Indian reservations. He'd been a while checking

146

the truck and the Mustang and van were still parked by the diner when he drove out.

His mind went to the bathroom he had hastily left and to what maybe the counter man and the cute little mixed breed were still doing in there. He sighed with a bit of regret, almost sorry that he hadn't stayed for some action. It was true he could pick a guy up between here and Albuquerque, but chances were good he wouldn't be as nice a piece as that little mixed breed.

It wasn't long while he was driving through the desolate sage brush area and alongside a steep ridge before he noticed that a convertible was riding his tail. The tailgater looked like a faded-red Mustang. The little piece from the diner maybe? And sure enough, not long after he noticed it, the Mustang pulled out beside him, coughing smoke out of its ass that made Andy frown. He couldn't keep the frown on very long, though.

The cute mixed breed was driving and was alone in the car. Andy looked down into the open-topped convertible from his high perch in the cab and did a double take and a little swerve of the semi in his lane followed by a big grin. The little guy had his cock out of his shorts as he drove and was beating himself off. He grinned up at Andy and then let the semi surge ahead and pulled in behind it again.

Now, if that wasn't an invitation, Andy didn't know what was. He'd see how interested the little guy really was.

In Albuquerque, with the Mustang still hot on his tail, Andy turned west on Interstate 40, headed for his destination in Phoenix. He knew, though, that he was taking a break soon, because the Mustang turned onto 40 with him.

Hot on my tail; tail hot for me, Andy thought. And he laughed at his joke. He had to spread his legs a bit because he'd gone very hard and his basket needed added room. He put a hand on his basket and rubbed. He was more than ready for some tail. He'd get a taste of the mixed breed after all.

He turned into the first rest stop he came to and parked far back in the truck lot. The Mustang didn't follow him into the truck parking, but he knew the guy had parked in the car lot. Andy had done this a hundred times before—hook up

147

with a guy in a car on the road and both pull off in a rest area to rock around in the compartment behind Andy's cab. Not usually this blatantly. They usually established contact at one rest area, and the guy would follow Andy to the next rest area and park in the car park and walk over to Andy's rig. This way there was no misunderstanding what the guy wanted.

Andy was all the harder for it the straightforward way the cute little trick was playing it, though. He leaned on his wheel and looked out of the driver's window until he saw the mixed breed appear and start walking toward the truck across the expanse of asphalt. A real sexy walk. Oh, yes, he wanted it.

If he could go any harder, Andy would. What a sweet lookin' piece, he thought, as he climbed down from the driver's cab and opened the door to the spacious compartment behind the cab.

The young man, who sometime during the process identified himself as Hector, which Andy didn't believe as he identified himself as Sam, pulled himself up into the aft compartment as Andy held the door for him, followed him as far as climbing up on the running board, looked around the lot to see if anyone was looking, and then entered the compartment. Andy had no more time than to sit on the narrow bed in the rear of the compartment than Hector was kneeling between his knees, unzipping his pants, pulling out his hard cock, and starting to give him head. Andy leaned over and pulled the compartment door shut and then started searching around in a pouch on the side wall. Anticipating him, though, Hector pulled a condom packet out of his pocket and handed it up to Andy without losing a stroke of his mouth on Andy's cock.

After several minutes of what was a really excellent blow job, Andy tore open the packet. Hector reached up and clasped Andy's hand in his and came away with the disk. He lifted his head off the cock, popped the condom disk in his mouth, and then smiled up into Andy's face before lowering his mouth again and managing to roll the condom onto Andy's cock with his teeth and tongue and a couple of good examples of deep throating.

148

Andy shuddered and gave a growl from deep in his throat. This was going to be good. The little piece really knew what he was doing.

Andy rose up, grasping the small mixed breed by the waist, and turned him to where Hector's back was on the bed. Andy grabbed the hem of the young man's T-shirt on either side, Hector's torso briefly rose up off the bed as Andy pulled the shirt over his head. Then he stripped Hector's shorts off and unbuckled his own pants and let them and his briefs slip down to the floor of the compartment.

"You're huge, and gittin' bigger," Hector said. It came out in sort of a gaspy squeal though.

"You think you can take it all?" Andy growled.

"Or die trying," Hector responded. He laughed and spread and raised his legs, finding footholds on the walls of the compartment. He grabbed for the back of Andy's head with both hands, and guided Andy's face down to his. They hungrily went into a deep lingering kiss. Andy's hard cock was poking at Hector's flat belly, and the young man reached down with a hand and encased the dick and beat it against his belly as they kissed.

Breaking out of the kiss, Hector growled. "Don't make me wait, you rodeo stud. Fuck me, fuck me hard."

Andy wasn't ready yet, though, and he assumed Hector wasn't ready for the thickness of him either, so he slowly worked his mouth down the perfectly formed berry-brown torso, down to where he could swallow Hector's cock, while the young man arched his back and cupped the back of Andy's head. Andy already was working his fingers into Hector's hole, which was opening up to him nicely.

"Oh shit, oh fuck. fuck me, fuck me," Hector whined as he ran his fingers into Andy's hair, pulling his head as closely into his groin as he could. "Now, now. Shit! Do it now! You're a stud. Spike me!" he cried out.

With a laugh, Andy pulled his head out of Hector's lap, raised his body over the young mixed breed's, slowly forced his cock inside the channel as Hector writhed and moaned and ran his hands inside Andy's unbuttoned shirt and up his hard-muscled torso, to grasp the truck driver's bulging pecs and then to travel on to dig his fingernails in Andy's shoulders, as Andy did it "now" . . . did it hard . . . did it deep . . . did it with increasingly possessive vigor.

With a cry, Hector shot up Andy's belly. But before Andy could come, the young man was scrambling out from underneath the older man and was turning them both on the narrow bed so that Andy was on his back and Hector was crouched over him. Hector sank his mouth over the sheathed cock, scraped his teeth back up the sides, and repeated the action again and then again and again. Andy arched his back off the bed and growled, ready to come, but Hector didn't let him come. He held the older man immobile for nearly a moment, while Andy came off his high.

Then Hector began working his mouth up from the cock, nibbling and licking at Andy's beefy torso. The younger man grasped Andy's biceps and pushed his arms over his head. Hector held Andy's arms over his head while he worked on Andy's nipples and Andy groaned and grunted. Andy shuddered and jerked once as he felt Hector straddle him and begin a long descent of his channel on Andy's cock again. Down Hector's hips came, as Andy moaned at the warmth of the channel and the undulation of the sweet little piece's channel muscles on his cock. Up and down. Andy gasped. This was one talented, tight channel. Up and down, and Andy gasped again.

Hector rocked back and forth and sideways on the cock and Andy raised his torso in ecstasy and embraced the young man tightly with his arms. They rocked back and forth, moving Andy's cock inside the tightened channel, Andy's moans a bass, Hector's a baritone. Once more Andy's body went rigid, ready to blow, and Hector held him in suspense of movement until the urge had passed. Then Hector gently pushed Andy on his back again and restarted a slow ride of the cock.

Hector's hands were gliding up Andy's arms, pushing them above his head, as Hector's tongue slurped into one of Andy's pits. Andy could feel that there was something in one of Hector's hands, but he didn't know what it was until the handcuffs had been snapped on one wrist, pulled through a

150

metal handle bar in the side wall of the compartment, and then snapped on the other wrist.

"What the shit?" the trucker muttered.

"Go with it," Hector said with a low-throated laugh. "I'm going to give you the fuck of your life."

Andy shuddered. The little fucker already was giving him the fuck of his life.

The mixed breed swung around and pounded on the closed door and then he swung back toward Andy and began to fuck himself in earnest on Andy's cock. Andy groaned and grunted and arched his back in pleasure as the young man rose and fell on the cock and broke off from the rhythm to revolve his hips. His channel muscles were working the cock for all they were worth. Andy groaned each time Hector took it all and then held, squeezing his channel walls on the throbbing cock. Andy noisily took in his breath as Hector slowly pulled up the cock and then gasped and grunted and his pelvis jerked as Hector slammed himself all the way down again. Again and again and faster and faster.

Andy gasped and muttered his, "Yes, yes, like that, there," mile-high pleasure. The sweet little piece was good . . . really good . . . the best. Andy had never picked anything this good off the road before.

Andy heard the rasp of the hinges on the rear door of the semitrailer, and he turned his head in slight concern. But Hector lowered his lips onto Andy's and they went into another deep kiss. Andy didn't care under the circumstances what was happening at the back of the truck. Who the fuck cared about that junk? Sadie in the diner had been right—it was all just a scourge on the earth. All he cared about was that he was building to an explosion. And Hector had to let him have his ejaculation this time.

He heard the rummaging in the back of the truck. But he didn't care. He was in paradise and on his way to new levels of heaven.

The explosion of his ejaculation was matched with a pounding on the compartment door, which was jerked open. An angry raspy voice yelled, "It's a bust, Pete. We gotta beat it. Get out of there."

151

Hector was pulling himself off of Andy, while, still exhausted from the thunderous ejaculation the young man had given him, Andy wearily raised his head and managed only a, "What the fuck?"

"You were great. Wish we could do it again," Hector, perched at the opening to the compartment, said. He was grinning as he pulled his shorts and T-shirt back on.

"Wait. You can't leave me like—"

"Here's the key to the cuffs. You can keep them," Hector said, as he flipped the key onto the floor of the compartment, well out of Andy's reach, and, with a grin, was gone. As Pete, as Andy now knew the young mixed breed to be named, dropped out of sight, Andy got the blur of a van truck speed across the opening. It was an old U-Haul truck with an indifferent slapping of white paint over it.

Andy lay there for an eternity, his feelings mixed. He knew he'd been hijacked and that Hector's ardor had all been to serve that. But, god, what a beautiful brown body. And man could he fuck.

A shadow fell over the open door to the compartment, and the body of a beefy young man filled the space.

"Lookin' might fine like that, Andy," the young man said. He was wearing a big grin. "Always dreamed to find you this way. Would have preferred that it be after you'd fucked *me*, though."

"What the fuck are you doin' here, Kurt?"

"What a way to talk to your savior—especially seein' as how you are all trussed up like this—completely at my mercy."

"What the shit happened? What'yer doin' here?"

"I'm driving a load of junk to Phoenix for the company today too. Pulled into the rest stop and saw your semi with all that electronic crap out on the ground. Decided I'd check you out. Glad I did. You check out real nice."

"I was hijacked," Andy said.

"Yep, I can see that. Used a real nice diversion, I see. In fact, it reminds me of old times. While I'm ridin' that cock of yours, I'll be thinkin' that, if I'd used cuffs like that, I wouldn't have let you get away. I guess those hijackers were expectin' something else back there other than broken and

152

used TVs and monitors goin' to them special incinerators in Phoenix."

"They fingered me in a diner south of Santa Fe. If they'd come in a little sooner, they'd have heard me telling the waiter that this was an environmental waste trip, not a load of new electronics. Now pick up that key down there and undo me."

"Think I'll just do you first, seein' as how you can't just slip away from me this time," Kurt said. He pulled the door to the compartment closed, reached into his pocket and pulled out a condom packet, and rolled the spent one off Andy's cock. "Wooie, what a load of cum you gave him," he said as he dropped the used condom on the floor. "Hope you saved some for me."

Winter Trial

"Are you sure? The trial starts tomorrow. You'll need your strength." Jason hadn't entered this territory with Carl before, but he thought it had to be said, that it was time that they both faced it.

Carl didn't answer in spoken words; he showed what he was interested in by embracing Jason closer from behind and pressing the bulb of his cock at Jason's entrance. Jason could feel the bulb move past his hole and the underside of the throbbing cock rub up and down across his hole. Carl was hard.

"I know I haven't been giving you enough attention, baby," Carl answered in a low voice. Jason felt the fingers of one of Carl's hands enter and spread him. With a sigh he lifted his leg and moved it over Carl's and rolled his buttocks up to provide a more convenient angle. Carl buried his face in the back of Jason's neck, gently attaching his teeth to the scruff of Jason's neck as a dog would to subdue and hold a pup in place, and Jason gave a little groan as the cock entered him, obtained purchase, and began languidly to press in, withdraw, and then press in again. Jason turned his face to the bicep of the arm Carl was embracing him with and kissed and licked it. He was panting shallowly, willing Carl to dig deeper, to fuck more vigorously. He knew Carl could do it—or could have done it a few months earlier. Carl could dig deeper than this, fuck harder than this.

155

But that didn't happen. With a sigh, Carl came, in a weak flow. Jason felt the wetness at his entrance and Carl going flaccid almost immediately. Jason hadn't come. He hadn't come for months—in hand jobs, yes, but not from a proper fuck—and Carl seemed to increasingly be weaker and more despondent. He'd had such confidence before the Great American Circus had canceled his act at the end of the summer. Now it seemed that each day was a trial for him.

"Jason," Carl murmured. "If I should . . . if you should become completely free . . ."

"Shush, Carl. Nothing's going to happen to you—or to us. You're going to get this job and we're going to happily tour the South all season."

"Yes, I know. But if . . . if, you know . . . I want you to get right back out there. There will be money for you, but I don't want you to just sit back on it. I know I haven't . . . and that you need . . . and I want you to have it all, all that you want."

"Shh, now. There are years to think about that. Just sleep now and get your rest. Important day tomorrow."

"Yes, an important day tomorrow," Carl whispered in a half-awake voice.

Jason waited for Carl's breathing to become deep and regular, and then he slowly struggled out from underneath him and sat up on the side of the bed. He was hard but was losing it. He gave his cock a couple of strokes but then thought, why bother, and rose and walked over to the open-door closet in the dormitory room they were sleeping in. Half the clothes hanging in the closet were show clothes, all spangles and glitter. They were Carl's costumes, not Jason's. The costumes Jason wore in the magic act were also spangled and glittery, but they were skimpy enough to be folded and stored on the shelves across from the closet—form-fitting brief shorts and tight athletic T's mostly. Jason had learned the act routines well in the almost three years he'd been with Carl, but, as far as the magic went, he was there mostly for eye candy. He understood that.

But that's magic too, he thought, with a smile. The stuff that dreams were made of. And that was magic he'd

156

always been good with—and with serving the dreams of other men.

It had been revolutionary for Carl to go with a young blond man rather than a shapely female for an assistant in his magic act, but it had paid off in attendance at first—both women and a certainly kind of man flocked to see the act. But the powers that be in the Great American Circus were puritanical, and as soon as they understood the appeal of Carl's magic act, they had been thinking of excuses to sever their ties with him.

The final reason they had given had crushed Carl. It wasn't that the act was too sexy or homoerotic. It was because Carl was getting too old. Carl wasn't more than fifty and could fix himself to look like no more than thirty-five across the footlights and at a remove from an audience, but it was true that he was getting grayer and more prone to fatigue and wasn't moving as supplely as he had even when Jason had first met him.

He had been handsome, trim, and mysterious then. Not more than three years previously. The Great American Circus had camped at the edge of Peru, Indiana, at the well-established circus and fair grounds there, Peru and other towns in Indiana having been historically great money-making stops for circuses. Jason's life was just limping along at that point. He worked the counter of a fast-food restaurant by day in a job that he'd started in high school and had just continued with after graduation with no better prospects in mind. After graduation he had supplemented this with dancing a pole at an all-male strip club on a country road between Peru and Wabash.

Jason had been blessed with a small, but perfectly formed body, blond good looks, an innate sexiness, and a supple flexibility. It hadn't taken him long to realize that the better money wasn't in slinging burgers or even in dancing poles and stripping down to a sock jock but in servicing the older men who came into the club.

Carl had been one of those men. He had come into the club twice, in those spangled costumes of his, straight from night performances out at the Peru fairgrounds, although Jason

157

didn't know that until later, before he approached Jason, who danced the pole on a raised stage not more than four feet from the gawking and whistling clientele. Jason had picked Carl out of the crowd immediately. He was a handsome man who, though quiet in contrast to the raucous noise those around him were making, exuded confidence and mystery—not the least because of the flashy stage costumes he wore.

That second night, backstage at the club, Jason enjoyed the smooth, exotic feel of the satin of Carl's pants on the tips of his fingers as he unzipped them and gave Carl a slow blow job for $20 and a ticket to the circus. Having led a dull, insular life to that point with nothing really going for him but his looks; perfect, small body; the allure he evoked in men; and his willingness to give men sex, the circus was an explosive revelation for Jason. He loved everything about the gaudiness and overpowering invitation and celebration of it. He was equally impressed by Carl's magic act.

Jason had perfectly understood what the free ticket to everything the circus had to offer entailed for him, and he was more than willing to be lying on his back on a small couch in Carl's trailer with Carl's knees pushed under and raising his buttocks and Carl's hands gripping his waist and pulling his passageway on and off Carl's cock.

Carl was a good lover, unlike most men Jason went with. He started slow and methodically and worked Jason to the point of Jason pleading for it—and then finished quickly and expertly, having Jason writhing under him with pleasure and timing the ejaculations so that they were nearly simultaneous. He made Jason feel not so much that the other man was getting his rocks off as that he was making love to Jason, concerned that Jason be fully satisfied too, even though it was Carl who was paying for it. Ultimately, it hadn't been much of a decision for Jason to make to come live with Carl.

Afterward that first fucking Carl begged Jason to stay, and Jason never went back to his small room above the drugstore in Peru or the fast-food restaurant, or the men's club out of town. When the Great American Circus packed up to move to Fort Worth at the end of the week, Jason had signed on to be Carl's new assistant in the magic act.

To Jason's thinking, Carl had saved him from a dull life buried in Indiana. Without Carl he would have gone nowhere—not even here to a closed college campus in Ocala, Florida, where the Clyde Seeley Circus was having winter trials to put together the acts it would take on the road in the summer. It seemed that Florida was the winter center for all sorts of trials like this—The New York Yankees were down in Tampa for spring baseball training, and there was a multiteam football training camp going on over in Orlando. Carl's trial to compete with other magic acts would start tomorrow in the former college's auditorium. Carl had been despondent, never having to try out for a place in a circus before, but Jason was doing everything he could to keep Carl up to the challenge.

Jason didn't care all that much for the circus life—the glamour of that had worn off, though it was better than slinging burgers and dancing poles in the Indiana outback—but he did care for Carl. He'd grown to care for Carl very much. Carl had been true to him and had saved him from Peru, Indiana.

Running his fingers over the satin of Carl's costumes hanging in the closet, Jason gave a sigh. He could tell that Carl was slowing down, but he'd never tell Carl that, at least not directly. He wouldn't even admit that Carl wasn't satisfying him sexually anymore. But that was true.

Carl had taught Jason that there was more, much more, to a relationship than sex. Over the past several months, after the Great American Circus had let the act go, Jason had tried, in subtle ways, to turn Carl's interests elsewhere. The problem wasn't money. Carl had plenty of it. He had saved and even had inherited a nest egg. But the circus was Carl's life. "I'll die in the circus," Carl had said, and Jason could tell that Carl meant that.

Now, the possibility of doing that was on the line.

Jason would adjust. He had to. With another sigh, he grabbed up a towel and padded down the hall to the communal shower that was the only head facility the old college dormitory offered on this floor. It was midnight. He'd enjoy a shower by himself, he thought. It would be a relief from showering with other guys and having them ogle him, and him maybe be

159

interested in them—seeing what they were packing—but unable to do anything about it.

But it turned out that he wasn't going to enjoy a shower by himself. When he entered the communal bathroom, Jason could hear the water running in the shower room. Shrugging his shoulders, he dropped his towel on a bench between a bank of lockers and moved into the shower room.

He almost backed out when he got there. The big Turk, billed as Halem the Magnificent, was all soaped up and standing under a steady stream of water from an overhead showerhead. He turned when Jason entered the shower, and his eyes slitted and Jason could see an immediate response in the man's huge cock. The man didn't bill himself "The Magnificent" for no reason. Then a big grin blossomed on his face.

Halem's was one of the magic acts Carl was competing against, and his competition was the most stiff—as stiff as his cock was becoming.

"Well, look who's here. Come on over here; I've got something for you."

Jason shuddered, guilty at the aching want he felt, and slid up against the tiled wall beside the entrance to the shower, not knowing whether to just try to ignore the man or to turn and leave the shower. The big Turk's intent was clear.

How far back into the communal bathroom did Jason think he could make it? How far did he want to make it? He was aching for sex. Carl's feeble attempt earlier had only inflamed and frustrated him. Before Carl he'd had no trouble going with any man who had the price of the servicing, was half-way decent enough looking, and/or who had a nice cock. Jason liked being fucked.

The Turk indeed was magnificent. He was young, not much over thirty, and he was over six and a half feet tall and built like a brick house. Dark skinned, with a profusion of black curly hair covering his chest, his arms, his legs. His bush thick, untamed. There was a wild and nasty look about him. Jason hadn't been fucked rough since before Carl. He was overdue for it. The best times he'd had were with primitive brutes.

160

The hesitation was just long enough for the Turk to circle around to the entrance into the shower room and to extend his heavily muscled arms in both directions, closing off the entrance. Jason moved along the wall, around one side, toward the showerheads.

Halem leered at Jason. "I've had my eye on you," the Turk growled in a heavily accented voice. "I know you want it. I know you take it. I saw how you and the old man you assist act with each other. What you need is a real man, though. A big cock like mine."

Jason moaned, trying to press himself into the wall.

Halem laughed. "You're going hard. You're going hard for me. I know you want it."

Jason *was* going hard; there was no hiding that. After months of frustration getting it from Carl, there was no hiding he wanted it from the Turk.

He stood there, shuddering, but not moving, as the Turk bore down on him. He whimpered an ineffectual, "No, don't," as Halem grabbed his waist with strong hands and turned him to the wall. He continued whimpering in a small voice that neither of them could decipher or cared about as Halem sank to his knees behind Jason, spread the smaller man's butt cheeks with the palm of his hands, and stuck his tongue between the cheeks. Jason squirmed and moaned deeply as the Turk opened and prepared his opening with his tongue, only once breaking away to laugh and mutter, "I was right. Someone's been here tonight already. But what a weak glob. I'll have your eyeballs swimming in cum."

Jason's only answer was a low moan and a shudder. Halem had a hand running between Jason's spread thighs and was milking his cock. There was no hiding that Jason was hot for what was happening. The Turk stood, grabbed Jason's hips, and pulled the small blond's pelvis away from the wall. Jason pressed his cheek to the tiles and raised his arms up the cool wall. He gave a jerk and a little cry and expended a long breath of air as the Turk worked the long, thick cock inside him. Then both just grunted and groaned as Halem pumped the channel, slowly at first, but building to a pistoning action.

161

Tears of frustration and mixed feelings rolled down Jason's cheeks as he thought of the betrayal of what he was letting Halem do to him. But he wanted it so badly and Carl wasn't providing it. It didn't change his loyalty to Carl, Jason kept running over and over in his mind as he found himself moving his hips back at the Turk to meet the thrusts, reveling in the size of the cock he was accommodating. There had been one stud this thick and long back at the club . . . but Jason couldn't think of that now. That was before Carl. Carl had given him so much, meant so much to him.

But, god, this Turk could cock. And it had been so long. Halem snaked a hand around Jason's slim hips, stroked his cock three times, and then grabbed and squeezed Jason's balls. The young blond shot off against the wall and started to collapse inside himself. Halem encircled his waist with a meaty, hairy arm, and lifted him off the floor. He pulled away from the wall, and, exhausted, Jason flopped over, bent at the waist, still attached to the Turk by a cock deep inside his ass. Jason's head, arms, and legs dangled toward, but off the slick, wet floor of the shower room, as Halem, knees bent, crouched a bit and continued to pull Jason's passage on and off his cock until, with a shout of triumph, he exploded, once, twice, three times in strong spurts deep up into Jason's passageway. He was still hard, though, and fucked furiously, the slide helped by the cum slathering Jason's passage and Halem's cock and balls, as the cum oozed out of the ass opening and dribbled down Jason's thighs.

Jason dangled there, sighing and moaning. He hadn't been fucked like that for three years. He hadn't ever been fucked like that.

But Halem wasn't finished. He slung Jason over his shoulder and padded back to his own dormitory room, where he fucked Jason twice more in the night before finally letting the young man go.

"It's what you wanted," he whispered in Jason's ear the last time as he was crouched over Jason, on all fours on the narrow dormitory bed, after fucking him doggy style.

"Yes," Jason answered in a voice laced with guilt but also with satisfaction.

162

"It's what you needed."

"Yes," Jason answered. That too, oh, yes, that too, Jason thought.

"You will lay down for me anytime I want you."

"Yes."

"You will come work for me now, be my assistant now."

Jason didn't answer that. His needs, weighed against his loyal to Carl went only so far. Halem was Carl's primary competition for the magic act slot in the Clyde Steeley Circus.

Halem laughed, pulled his cock out of Jason's ass, stood up, and slapped Jason on the butt cheek. "You'll come to me. You don't have to say it now, but you'll come to me. The old man you're with is finished in this business. I'm going to get this job."

Jason crept back into the room he shared with Carl and climbed into Carl's bed, stretching himself along the back of the lightly snoring man rather than going to his own bed. He was racked with guilt, and Halem's words that Carl was washed up kept ringing in his ears. But there was more to a relationship than melting, rough sex—which the Turk certainly could provide. Jason and Carl had more working for them than sex—or even the circus. Jason had given in on the sex outside the relationship—now at last. And he was a realist; he knew he couldn't pretend it hadn't happened. He knew that it would be easier to give in the next time—and then even easier the time after that. Maybe not to the Turk, but there were a lot more sexy men around these circus trials. The sex with Halem had been something he did need. It would be easier to do the next time. But as long as he stuck with Carl, no matter what, he wouldn't let it destroy their relationship.

* * * *

The first round of the magic act trials were conducted on the stage of the former college's auditorium the next day. Carl arrived rested and optimistic, which gave Jason an excuse to feel justified that they hadn't worn each other out with sex the previous night—not that Jason didn't feel worn out by sex with the Turk, Halem the Magnificent, who was energetic and sassy this morning as well.

For his part, Jason was keyed up. Having had good sex for the first time in months, the floodgates on his desires had opened. The sex had satisfied him greatly, but it hadn't satiated him. He wanted more. Now that he'd had a taste of it after so long, he wanted to feast on it. It didn't help that Halem was slitting his eyes and giving him meaningful looks every time their eyes met. Jason was walking around with a perpetual hard on in his skimpy gold lamé briefs and half T-shirt that left his flat belly bare. He was eyeing every built, good-looking man in sight, and more than a few of them were eyeing him back with interest. The Clyde Seeley Circus was known to be gay friendly—Clyde Seeley was gay himself, people said. This was why Carl had even been able to land an audition with the circus for an act that accentuated sexy maleness. It stood to reason that some of the men working to support the acts were gay as well.

There was a lighting technician, dark haired and Mediterranean complexioned, tall and lanky, but well muscled across the chest and biceps, who Jason's eyes kept going to. There was Clyde Seeley himself, sitting in the middle of one of the rows closest to the stage, who was giving Jason the eye and smiles. But he was older—almost as old as Carl. And he was meatier, well built at one time but a bit of extra padding now. But Jason's eyes kept going to the lighting technician, who was proficiently going about his job as lighting needs changed between and during the acts on trial.

Five acts were there in the morning. In the afternoon it was down to two—Carl's act and that of Halem the Magnificent. Jason didn't know why there still were two acts. Carl started off strong, but as they rolled into the afternoon, he began to flag. Halem never wavered. He was magnificent and mesmerizing each and every time he went on stage to exhibit a new trick. And he knew it and reveled in it.

They were taking a break before a final round of sets between just Carl and Jason, on the one hand, and Halem and his willowy assistant, Selena, on the other. Clyde Seeley was huddled with Carl and Halem down in front of the stage and was asking them both more detailed questions about what they expected and could give in a deal if they were hired.

Jason was standing beside one of the flying curtains at the edge of the stage when he felt his waist being encircled by a strong arm and he was pulled back into the dim light of the backstage and pushed up against a cinderblock wall. A man was standing behind him, pressed into his body, covering him close, with one hand holding Jason's wrists together and over his head. Jason could feel the hard need of the man at the small of his back. He turned his head to see that it was the lighting technician, who had been called Bud and who Jason had been not too subtly flirting with across the footlights.

"You've been teasing enough," the technician, who didn't seem much older than Jason was, growled in his ear. "You just a tease, or you wantin' it?"

Jason was breathing hard, but he didn't answer. A hand snaked around his belly and sank under the waistband of his shorts.

"Yes you want it," the man growled, his hand cupping Jason's balls and the root of his cock. And, indeed, Jason was hard. He'd been hard most of the day. The inside of his pouch was slick with precum. A finger was pressing into his cock head, working on worrying his piss slit open, and Jason shuddered and moaned.

"The question is whether you want it from me."

Jason didn't hesitate. He'd been in heat all day. Halem had taken him beyond the barrier of noble denial the previous night. Carl need never know. He'll actually be relieved that, unable to stop himself, Jason wasn't after him for sex that went beyond a hand job.

"Yes, but when?"

"Now," the man growled as he hauled Jason away from the wall and shepherded him out the stage door, down a dark hall, and into an unused classroom. Bud perched on the edge of a desk, trousers, socks and shoes off, legs spread and the soles of his feet leveraging off the linoleum floor while Jason, naked, his nipples covered by the palms of Bud's hands, sat in the young technician's lap, facing away from him, legs bent, calves on either side of Bud's hips, leveraging his knees off the

165

surface of the desk, as he bounced up and down on Bud's buried cock.

Before they had finished, Jason had swiveled around to where he was facing Bud, still lapped. His shoulder blades were resting on Bud's thighs, and Bud was pulling him on and off the cock. When they had both come, Bud pulled Jason's chest up to his, embraced him with his arms, and the two kissed and whispered to each other as Bud's cock went flaccid inside Jason. He'd worn a condom and Jason somewhat regretted not being able to feel him skin on skin and the flow of the semen inside him. But he appreciated the technician's thoughtfulness. Neither Carl nor the Turk had had such a concern for the future.

"That was good. No, it was great. You're a great lay," Bud whispered.

"Thanks. You are great too," Jason answered.

"You wanted it bad, didn't you?"

"Yes, I want it bad," Jason admitted.

"Give me a couple of minutes and I'll do you again."

"We should be getting back. The conference will be over. Carl will be looking for me."

"I want to do you again."

"Later maybe . . . don't take that wrong. I want you do fuck me again."

"I'm afraid there may not be a later," Bud murmured. "Your act is going to lose. Surely you know that."

"Yes," Jason asked, his voice full of regret. "I can see that."

"He's not well. Your old man isn't well. You can see that."

"Yes, I can see that. More the reason for me to stick with him, though."

"He doesn't satisfy you anymore, does he? I can tell. You responded to me with hunger for the fuck."

"There's more to a relationship than sex."

"But I can tell that you need the sex. I can make you happy. I'm young; he's old. I can fuck you again and again."

So could Halem, Jason thought. And he wasn't old either. But, yes, the technician was rising inside him again

166

already. And he had a very nice cock. Not as thick as Halem's, but thicker than most. Nice enough that Jason was panting and squirming on the reengorging cock.

Bud was rising off the desk and turning Jason without losing the purchase of his cock inside the small blond to where Jason was bent over the desk with his belly against the surface. He raised his arms over his head and gripped the opposite edge of the desk with his fists to hold himself steady as Bud began pumping him hard and deep and rapidly.

"Yes, yes, yes," Jason cried out in a gaspy voice. "Fuck me, fuck me hard. Just like that."

"You want it. You want me. Just like this," Bud growled, as he reared his hips back and then thrust. And then again and then again.

"Yes, yes, yes," Jason whimpered.

"I could take you home with me. You could stay with the circus."

"He needs me," Jason moaned.

* * * *

"If you come back to my trailer and . . . talk with me, I think I could help your cause."

Clyde Seeley had pulled Jason aside and whispered this in the young blond's ear after the last set of magic acts had been performed and Seeley had declared that he'd give his answer the next day on who got the slot in the circus's summer run.

It wasn't going to be much of a surprise unless there was a dramatic change in circumstances in some way. Even Carl seemed to be resigned to the inevitable—or at least cognizant of what it likely would be. The day had taken a big toll on him. He had stumbled through his last set, with Jason having to whisper to him what he should do or say next at several points. In contrast, Halem the Magnificent was sparkling and magnificent to the end.

The Turk had moved toward Jason after the last discussions with Seeley and was giving Jason triumphant and knowing looks. Jason knew he'd go with Halem again if the

167

opportunity arose—if he could do it without Carl knowing—something that he earlier would have thought he'd never do again even though he'd told Halem he would. But the night with the Turk and what Bud had just done with him in the classroom made Jason admit that he couldn't do without sex like that. It didn't mean that he wouldn't stick with Carl, though. There was much more to their relationship than sex. But Jason knew now he'd have the sex whenever he thought he could get away with it.

Hadn't Carl told him he needed to get what he needed? But not necessarily when Carl was still around.

Before Halem could reach him Clyde Seeley was bearing down on them, and Halem veered off. Carl already was limping out of the auditorium. He'd said they'd meet in the dormitory room next—that he needed to rest.

Jason knew there was time for him, for an hour or so now. He'd had sex just two hours ago, but he was aching for it again. If Halem had told him to follow him to somewhere private, Jason would have gone with him.

When Seeley invited him to his trailer to talk then, Jason knew it was for more than talk. The man wasn't ugly and he wasn't even as old as Carl was. He was a bit heavy, but he also was muscular, and Jason had overheard stage hands whispering that he was still proficient in bed. The rationale was there—something that wouldn't be disloyal to Carl, not really. If Jason gave Seeley what he obviously wanted, maybe Seeley would give Carl the job. Wasn't that what Seeley had hinted in extending the invitation? Even Jason knew the job wouldn't last that long. Carl was deteriorating fast. But it would be some form of victory—that he could still win a position. And over Halem the Magnificent.

In the trailer, Seeley sat on the side of a narrow bed and Jason knelt between his spread thighs and sucked the man's cock to a throbbing erection. He really was nicely equipped, Jason had to admit. And Jason had done this maybe a hundred times before he met Carl. It was no big deal considering the favoritism it could get for Carl.

Both men were naked and Seeley was strong, so it involved little effort when he felt that he was ready that Seeley reached down and grabbed Jason's waist and lifted the small blond above him as he lay on his back on the bed and brought Jason down into his lap and onto the throbbing cock. The older man groaned and grunted as Jason leaned his torso over Seeley's chest, dug the heels of his hands into the older man's beefy pecs, and rode the cock.

Afterward, with Jason still saddled, Seeley shocked him.

"You know that I can't give the position to Carl, don't you?"

"But . . ." Jason said.

"You know as well as everyone else does that he's on his last leg. I'm a businessman. I can't make a decision like that just to have you here to ride my cock when I want you."

"I don't . . . why then . . . ?"

"I do want you here riding my cock. So I'll give you a job with the circus. A good one. A better one than you have now."

"I'm sorry, I can't leave Carl," Jason said with a choked voice. He climbed off the cock and padded over to where his shorts and T had been discarded on the floor of the trailer.

"Come back here. I'm not finished with you."

"I think I'm finished, though. If you won't sign Carl's act, there isn't anything more to say."

"There's the check I haven't cut to cover you coming down here for the trials, yet. You want me to give that to Carl, don't you. And with a consolation bonus and some comforting words on how hard it was to make the decision, and maybe even an offer of an administrative job for him too. You'll come back over here for that, won't you? I'm not done with you."

Jason stood there, considering. And then he meekly walked back to the bed.

Seeley fucked him brutally this time, Jason on his back, with his head bouncing off the wall of the trailer and the trailer rocking, as Seeley grabbed his ankles, split his legs wide apart, and took him with long, deep thrusts. Jason loved every minute of it.

When he was walking gingerly back to the dormitory, though, the first thing that caught his eyes were the swirling red lights. Lights on top of a police cruiser and also on top of an ambulance.

"Oh, no," he muttered, as he broke into a run.

They were bringing a stretcher down the front steps of the dormitory before he got there. There was a body, under a sheet, on the stretcher. The face was covered by the sheet.

"Carl," he said in a weak voice, knowing instinctively that it was Carl.

He felt hands gripping his arms from behind and he leaned back, knowing from the musky smell of him that it was Bud, the lighting technician. Jason looked around. An old Sebring convertible was pulled up next to the curb, the driver's door open.

"That's—"

"Yes, I know, It's your Carl," Bud said in a low voice. "They called us over at the auditorium. Looking for Seeley . . . and for you." He made no accusation, probably not needing confirmation for what he knew Jason had been doing, trying to save Carl's job—but also because the small blond was so randy.

Well, so was Bud. He was hard again. He was hard for Jason despite the circumstances.

"Come with me. Come back to my place," he murmured. "You need a bit of time to get your head around this."

Jason sobbed quietly. "He needs me."

"He doesn't need you anymore, Jason. I need you. And you need me. Come home with me. We'll take care of last things for Carl later. Both of us."

"He said he'd never retire from the circus. That he'd die in the circus."

"And that he did. He went the way he wanted to go. He would want you taken care of too. Come with me."

Jason didn't resist, as Bud turned him and guided him around to the passenger side of the Sebring. Jason had no illusions about what he and Bud would be doing within the hour. But Bud was right. It's what Carl would have wanted for him. He had told him so just the previous night.

* * * *

170

It was dark in Bud's bedroom and they had been going at it for hours. Jason was on his back, near exhaustion, all cried out. It was what Bud had said he needed, and he knew Bud was right. Bud was crouched between his thighs, his knees under Jason's raised buttocks, his cock moving slowly in and out, in and out, of Jason's channel. Bud had an arm under the small of Jason's back, raising him, with the young blond's torso arching back, Jason's weight borne on his shoulder blades. Bud was smoothing Jason's brow with his free hand. Their faces were close together, Bud closely scrutinizing Jason's eyes to watch the effect of the slow, deep thrusts of the cock.

"I'll take care of you, baby. You'll always have me."

Jason smiled up at him. That was good to hear. But he knew that Bud wouldn't be enough. He knew he was unlikely to ever have a full relationship again like the one he'd had with Carl. But there would always be the sex. That would compensate to a great degree until he too grew old. And if all of this had taught him nothing else, it had taught him that the sex was important to him.

Bud was nice. But there was Clyde Seeley too—with the offer of the job and a sexual relationship, and—and now Jason grinned—there was Halem of the magnificent cock, who would be getting the magic act position with the circus.

His thoughts went back to Carl. Yes, he thought Carl would approve.

The German

I was met in the baggage area of the Munich international airport by a florid, slightly oversized man, obviously Germanic, who apparently knew who I was, although I didn't have a clue who he was beyond him having introduced himself as Hans when he approached me. They obviously wanted it that way and I was at their command. I didn't actually have any luggage beyond my carryon, but I had been told I would be met in the baggage claim area.

Looking in all directions at once as he took a firm grip on my elbow, he guided me out of a side door and into the arms of a black Mercedes. I was taken to a nondescript row house in the center of the city and thence to a second-floor bedroom.

The obligatory interview was tolerable, after which I was told to take a bath and to nap until 7:00 p.m. The formal clothes I was to wear that night were laid out on one side of the bed. Alone, I blissfully sank into sleep on the other side of the bed.

Hans helped me dress. He stressed that I was to wear gloves throughout and produced several different pairs for me to take with me. I understood the necessity of those, which largely were for my own protection.

Night had fallen already when he guided me into the Munich National Theatre, some twenty minutes after Mozart's *The Magic Flute* had already started. We silently entered the darkened box, and Hans gently pushed me down in a chair set somewhat behind that of the only occupied chair. He leaned over the shoulder of the man sitting there, who turned and gave me a piercing look.

"This is the American," Hans whispered in the man's ear, and then he withdrew. I was never to see Hans again. Not something I particularly regretted, however. The interview hadn't been all that comfortable.

My first impression of the man in the theater box was elegantly coifed hair, dark on top but gray over a large expanse at the temples, and piercing dark eyes—black in this lack of light. A ruggedly handsome face indicating a man in his fifties who had led a life in which hard work had fought with privilege and wealth and resulted in a well-dressed man who also was well formed.

He said, in a low, bass tone, "I am Horst and you are . . .?"

When I answered that I was Logan, having been instructed to give no more identification than that, he merely responded with an, "Ahh," and turned back to the opera, in which he quickly appeared to be fully engrossed.

A car, yet another black Mercedes, was waiting for us in the alley beyond the side door we exited after the conclusion of the opera. When the man had stood in the theater box, he proved to be tall and on the thin side—and the epitome of rich elegance. A muscular, rather menacing looking chauffeur, bald and bull necked and more than somewhat thuggish in appearance, was standing at the open door to the backseat. He handed me in, then he handed in the patrician older man, Horst, making me slide over to the far window. The chauffeur then moved around to the driver's door and glided the sedan out into the street at the front of the theater, cutting through the departing theater crowd like a warm knife through butter and giving the impression that the man sitting beside me was a Moses in the response that his car received from the well-heeled theater goers on the street.

That impression never left me throughout the weekend. I had expected the man to sit closer to me in the backseat, but he did not do so. He was taking it slow; I would

174

be here the entire weekend. He was never identified as anything other than Horst, but I read the newspapers—in my line of work, it paid to know what was what and who was who. He was Horst Tielman, a major German industrialist. His reputation was one of ruthlessness and perhaps in having his fingers in more financial pies than were publically acknowledged. It was interesting that he didn't bother to use a false name with me; I certainly hadn't given him my real name.

He had said nothing to me during the performance or afterward other than to tell me which direction we were to walk in, which almost hidden door we were to use to leave the theater, and that there was a car waiting for us. He had, though, given me a scrutinizing lookover when the lights went up in the theater, and I could tell that he was pleased. It was my business to please, and I knew I cleaned up very well in evening wear— almost as well as I did in a Speedo.

He loosened up—to the extent that a reticent, almost military stance patrician German could do—while we rode in the car to a somewhat more stately looking row house in an older section of Munich than the house I'd been taken to from the plane. He chatted, initially in general terms, and then more specifically when he found that I was knowledgeable concerning the art of the opera we'd seen, an example of the uniquely Germanic Singspiel. And he spoke of his favorite composers of operas and other musical works—Weber, Wagner, Strauss, and, of course, Mozart for operas; Handel, Gluck, Beethoven, and, again Mozart, for music in general. As with all Germans I'd met, his revealed sense of what was German extended well beyond the borders of today's Germany.

He seemed quite taken with all things German. I don't remember him having gone out of this context the entire weekend.

In the house, the chauffeur deftly turned into the butler and all other forms of manservant, coming back from the garage in a black suit, as Horst and I shed our outwear in the first-floor foyer and Horst continued his discourse on what was uniquely German, and therefore superior, in opera.

175

His arrogance about Germany's place in the arts brought to my mind how I thought the elite in German in the 1930s viewed the world. It wasn't my place to question or argue, though—just to please.

We were guided up a floor to where the public rooms were, and a fire had magically been laid in the fireplace of the thoroughly masculine, but immaculate and tidy, study we were led into. There surely were other servants about, but I encountered none of them.

We sat across from each other, with the fireplace to one side and sipped brandy from snifters as, slowly, what Horst had to say about German music wound down. He seemed to have prolonged the discussion from the delight of finding that I could answer almost at the same level of understanding as he did—and that I demurred from what he was saying only infrequently. As that discussion wound down, though, his close scrutiny of me and the look of interest and arousal in his eyes increased. The music in the background was muted, but I recognized the mysterious strains of Wagner's *Der Ring des Nibelungen*—the Ring of the Nibelung—which I knew would grow wilder and more intense as it spun through its four cycles.

He merely had to gesture for me to understand, to place my nearly empty snifter on the table beside my leather club chair, and to kneel in front of him and unzip his trousers. I extracted a cock so long that I gasped, even though I had enough experience not to be surprised by much of anything along these lines anymore. He cupped my chin with the hand not holding his snifter and raised me up to engage in several kisses as I stroked the cock with both hands, bringing it to an almost-cruel up-curve hardness.

He disengaged my lips, gave me a stark little smile, and muttered, "Now." I went down on my haunches, took the cap of the cock in my mouth, and was rewarded with a slight shudder and low moan when I squeezed it with my lips. He placed the snifter on the table beside him, cupped the back of my head with both hands, and dug his fingers into my scalp. For the next fifteen minutes I sucked the cock, with Horst making every effort—accompanied by gagging on my part—to

176

force me to swallow the cock to its root. There was no physically possible way I could do that, though, no matter how well trained I was, and he seemed to realize and accept that I couldn't without backing away from trying to make it happen. He only seemed to want me to make the effort and to have some limited success at it. He released my head eventually and told me to stand up and disrobe.

I undressed, standing in front of him. Knowing it was what he would want, from his Germanic sensitivities, I neatly folded my clothes as I took them off and arranged them in a pile on the chair I had vacated.

As I disrobed, he sat there, eyes slitted, and sipped from his snifter. His cock, which almost curved back to meet his chest somewhat north of where his navel would be, remained rock hard. When I was down to my bikini briefs and my socks, and had hesitated, he said, in a low growl, "All of it."

I fucked myself—with the help of the pull and release of his strong hands on my waist—on his cock, sitting in his lap, facing him, with my legs draped over the arms of his club chair. He didn't wear a condom. I knew he wouldn't. I was certified clean and my handlers had made sure he was as well, specifying the doctor who would do the test in Munich if Horst wanted this type of service. His stroke was strong and his cum prodigious. It spouted in three heavy spurts that bathed my insides at a depth I'd never experienced before. He was at least three inches longer than the norm I sheathed.

He had not permitted me to stroke myself and he had not done so either, so I had not ejaculated. At the point of his ejaculation, the music in the background had swelled to its loudest. It had progressed through Wagner's bombastic Ring series to the point where Horst released his strong stream of seed at the height of the screaming of the Furies in *Die Walküre*. Immediately afterward, the volume had fallen. Either Horst had a dramatic sense of timing and admirable control or someone had been watching us and had been controlling the musical accompaniment of the fuck.

The whole process seemed detached and clinical— except for the feel to me of his cock working inside me at an impossible depth—mechanical, and unemotional, as if

177

believing that the act of ejaculation with another man rather than self masturbation was just a periodic health necessity, like brushing one's teeth. If I had expected or sought an emotional attachment in any way in exchange for letting a man fuck me, I would have been sorely disappointed. However, I didn't and was actually relieved that I could perform my role without complications.

After a few moments of holding there in postcoital embrace, each of us savoring the fuck and the load he had given me, he rang a bell on the table next to him, and the bullet-headed manservant appeared. There was not a twitch of surprise in the man at finding me naked and plastered to the pelvis of his employer.

"Draw a bath and then come back and take Logan there, if you will," Horst said.

The bath was for both of us, in a large tub inside a gigantic bathroom on the next floor up appended to what must have been Horst's bedroom. Horst reclined at one end of the tub, and I at the other, my legs overlaying his thighs, that were muscular, if not thick—like the rest of him—and it was in this position that Horst, his eyes glued to mine to catch the effect, stroked my cock with both of his hands to an ejaculation.

As he stroked me, which he did expertly, edging me, bringing me to the point of explosion and then backing off, holding me rigid until the need to shoot had subsided, and then building the arousal and need again, he spoke of German writers he admired: Goethe, Günter Grass, Bertholt Brecht, Thomas Mann, Herman Hesse—and that he wanted me to admire too. I told him I did, very much so, except that I hadn't read Hesse. It was good I had been truthful in my responses, as he quizzed me enough to be comfortable that I had, indeed, read the others.

Once again he showed his surprise and pleasure that I could hold my own in the conversation—not to mention that I could do so while he was jacking me off. I was trained to do so; I was chosen and kept at the height of my profession for being able to do so. I had been classically trained in the arts— but only the arts. I could only produce dumb looks on the topics of science and math.

178

I'd been a child actor—on stage and television—my career prolonged because I was so slight of stature and, as one critic expressed it, not complementarily, as I was playing child roles until just the previous year, that I suffered from having a "perpetual cuteness." Indeed, legally I would have been termed a boy not much more than a year ago.

I was where I was today because I was so young looking and trained to the role play. What stage critics liked to giggle about behind their fanned hands played to the interest of some men—rich and powerful men—who enjoyed pursuing the appearances of a certain fetish without facing the legal ramification of indulging in the pure form of the fetish. So, whereas I could not be termed a boy, I could be described as being boyish in aspect.

Let's just say I had no trouble remaining gainfully employed and eagerly sought out by men of a certain preference—some would say perversion.

I didn't intend on doing this work forever. I had never gone to an organized school, having been schooled on the set, in topics focused on the arts with only a minimal bow to what would enable me to pass the standardized tests, but I did plan to parlay this into university studies. Like a fashion model, I couldn't do this highly specialized work for long, not at the peak of the art. If I realized my schedule, I wouldn't be too far behind my peers when I entered the university.

Horst fucked me next in the second bedroom, the only other room on the level that the master bedroom and bath nearly fully encompassed. Still naked, I was guided to the room by the manservant. When Horst entered, a light, silky robe was draped over his shoulders. It wasn't closed in front, though, and for the first time I saw him, standing tall, and somewhat gaunt, if well enough muscled. There wasn't an ounce of fat on his body, nor were there wrinkles, which was impressive for a man his age. And, speaking of impressive, his cock dangled almost to his knees when he entered the room, although it began to harden almost immediately when he saw me lying on the bed.

I might have risen to greet him, but I was bound to the surface of the queen-sized bed, my buttocks at the edge of the foot of the bed. It was a four poster, and the manservant had secured my limbs to all four corners with restraints, my arms stretched out above my head, and my legs raised and spread. Leaning over my chest and staring intently down in my face, Horst gripped my waist in his hands, worked his cock inside me, and fucked me in long, deep strokes, replacing the pool of cum deep inside me that had been washed away in the bath.

Once again, he mined me impossibly deep and expertly, taking me to the edge and then making me wait for a climax, bringing moans and groans and begging for a finish out of me that went well beyond any role playing on my part. Allowing me to strain at my bonds and buck against his thrusts to bring on my climax and then holding me still until the wave of completion had passed. Kneeling between my legs and giving me head until I was ready to blow again, and then holding me still, before thrusting inside me to start me up the stairs to heaven again. When he let me cum, it was with an explosion that lifted my pelvis off the bed, seeking to be skewered even deeper yet on the cock. He came only after he had let me do so.

He left me there, still bound, for more than a half hour, but returned and fucked me again, as expertly and on the edge as before, murmuring that he found me almost irresistible and that I would "do" nicely, that I would "do nicely indeed."

When the manservant helped me up yet another flight of steps to a floor of smaller, less well-appointed bedrooms, I thought that he would remain with me and fuck me as well— his eyes and the sneer on his mouth told me that he certainly wanted to. And I had been told that there would be more than one, multiple ones. But other than copping a feel of my bare buttocks as he guided me into a small bedroom, with an adjacent shower bath, he left me alone.

I made the rounds of the environment of my small prison—the door to the corridor had been locked—and found, to my confusion, that the closet was nearly full of men's clothes. The clothes were of different sizes but not radically larger or smaller than the sizes I wore. I could have selected a wardrobe from here. Some of what was in there was provocative clothing, as was some of what I found in the

180

bureau drawers. I wondered who this clothing belonged to—or whether it had been supplied for a succession of small men like me, playing similar roles to what I now was doing. I rather thought this was the case.

I slept the sleep of the dead, knowing that tomorrow would be the important—and taxing—day.

* * * *

"When the Arab rides away from us, I wish you to follow him and give him what he wants." Horst whispered this to me as we rode a horse path at the base of the Bavarian alps, where the manservant had driven Horst and me on Saturday morning. Horst had a large chalet on the side of the mountain, where three male guests already had gathered.

He told me little about what would happen this day and why I was here, but my handlers had told me to do what Horst wanted this weekend and that it would entail being fucked by multiple men.

There was an Arab, wearing one of the white robes many Arabs wear that are called dishdashas. The robe didn't seem to hinder his ability to sit in the saddle, maneuver the horse, and look good doing so. The other two men were middle-aged East Europeans of somewhat swarthy and unsavory appearance. They were muscular but going toward pudgy. The Arab, although older, was of larger and more commanding stature than they were, and, although having a cruel look about him, was in much better shape than the other two and much more adept at riding a horse.

He also proved adept at riding me.

I had known when I'd come out of my bathroom that morning that the day's activities would either involve horseback riding or a costume party. The manservant had laid out a riding outfit complete with frilly white blouse and skin-tight riding pants, as well as shiny black boots rising almost to my knees. The fit of the pants was snug—I'd almost say provocative—but they did fit.

At Horst's bidding I had ridden a bit behind the others, but if he thought that meant I couldn't hear the business they

181

were transacting, he was sadly mistaken. I suppose I was taken just as a bimbo woman would be who was brought on outings like this to hand out to clients one was trying to sell to. I guess I was considered too young looking and cute to have a brain and to understand deals being discussed of exchanging East European contraband weapons for drugs controlled by Middle East terrorists. But I wasn't dumb, and I wasn't here because I was dumb.

The Arab and I hadn't ridden too far away from the others, only into a copse of trees with a babbling brook running through it, before he pulled up and said, "Let us rest the horses here for a bit."

He was already dismounting when he was saying it and left no doubt who was in command, so I came down off my horse too. I thought it was a bit too much accommodation to the resting of the horses when he unsaddled his—expertly— until I realized why he had. He fucked me doggy style on the grass beside the brook, with my belly bent over the seat of the saddle he'd placed on the ground there and him riding my ass hard and pulling my arms back painfully on either side of his torso.

Neither one of us was disrobed, although it turned out that, other than an easily discarded loincloth, he was wearing nothing under the dishdasha other than a condom and only needed to bunch the robe up around his waist to be in fighting form. I would gladly have peeled my tight riding pants off, but he preferred slitting the seam running down the center of the buttocks with a curved knife he'd had strapped to his calf and inserting, first, his fingers, and then his cock in the rift thus created. I hadn't worn briefs of any sort under the riding pants; it had seemed futile to have done so and none had been laid out by the man servant.

He rode me hard and cruelly with a noticeably thick cock. When he released my arms after having worked himself deep inside me, he also used his riding whip on me while he fucked me, although still having my clothes on took away much of the sting of that.

He claimed to have been pleased with my servicing, but that didn't stop him from just jerking the saddle out from underneath me while I was still lying there, moaning and trying to catch my breath, quickly resaddling his horse, and riding back to the chalet without me.

I had no trouble understanding that use of me was part of what Horst was providing his clients, to gain a favorable deal as a broker of the arms-for-drugs trade, and I wondered if the arms dealers would be included in this sweetening.

I found out Saturday evening.

At Horst's command I danced a pole in his dining room for dinner entertainment while the four man sat around me in a semicircle on pillows and ate their dinner off tray tables. Obviously the Arab was the one Horst was trying to impress the most, as signaled by the Middle Eastern manner in which they were eating.

I had been supplied with a gold lamé G string and had been told that the Arab was the one I was to play up to. The music was Middle Eastern, and I played the dance up in what I considered would be Middle Eastern moves, taking my cue from visions of belly dancers. I had danced a pole before, briefly and recently, after I found when I came of legal age that my manager had walked off with all of my stage and movie money that I hadn't already frittered away myself. I knew how to dance a pole and make the most of it.

The business negotiations between the men continued in a low burble under the music I was dancing to, and it seemed that we weren't far from the after-deal celebrations. I knew exactly what I was there for.

Horst beckoned me to dance closer to the Arab, so I did. Horst signaled to me to crouch over the Arab's thighs and give him a private lap dance, so I did. The Arab himself decided to bunch his dishdasha up around his waist, rip off my G strip, and put me on his cock. I let my torso arch back toward the dining room carpet, my arms dangling across the carpet, while the Arab pulled me on and off the cock. As he fucked me, the two East Europeans gathered closer, smacked their lips, pulled out their own cocks, and masturbated to the dance the Arab now was doing inside me.

He no sooner was finished inside me when, at a signal from Horst, the manservant appeared, tossed me over his

183

shoulder, and I discovered, with the rest of the men following us, that there was a dungeon in the basement of the chalet.

The two East Europeans were beside themselves with lustful need, so I was given to them first, each in succession, as I lay in a sling suspended from the ceiling. Neither of them was anything special, but fulfilling my role and purpose, I made noises and met their thrusts with counterthrusts to convince them that they were.

The Arab, who had already fucked me twice, wanted something a bit more special—and more taxing. I had to admit that I had been told by my handlers that it might get a little rough. I was suspended from the ceiling on a chain with a restraint holding both wrists together, and the Arab got his jollies by flogging my back and thighs—raising red welts but not as far as bloody cuts—before he saddle up to me from behind, lifted and spread my thighs, and fucked up into my channel until he had filled the head of a condom inside me for the third time that day.

I wound up bent over on my belly on a pommel horse-type contraption, with my wrists and ankles bound to the legs of the apparatus, none of my appendages quite reaching the floor, and any of the four men taking as many pokes at me as they wanted. I knew Horst participated in this part, because he was the only one not crowned with a condom and giving me his cum.

They trooped upstairs when they were satiated, leaving me there, my service to Horst's business needs finished, but not before I had figured out why I had been here and what these men were up to.

After about half an hour, the manservant appeared, unbound me, threw me over his shoulder, and took me up to one of the bedrooms of the chalet. He put me under the shower head in the adjacent bathroom and turned the water on—not too hot and not too strong. It stung like hell on my back and thighs, but I was glad to be getting clean.

He dried me off with a big, fluffy towel; told me to bend over the foot of the bed, stiff arming my weight on the heels of my hand; and applied some sort of soothing salve to my back and thighs. I was wondering how often he had to do

184

this—whether Horst provided incentive candy such as me with all of the business deals that were beyond the normal scope of his overt industrial operations.

When I was getting all soothed and comfortable, the big bruiser took hold of the back of my neck, shoved my face into the surface of the bed, mounted my ass from behind, and fucked the stuffing out of me in hard, rapid, brutal strokes. All fight had been fucked out of me earlier, so I just lay there, moaned, and took it from him—nearly every hour for the rest of the night.

I figured that Horst truly didn't need me for his business scheming anymore if he was handing me out to the servants. I just took it. My contract hadn't specified by name who had privileges. The services were just listed "as desired."

* * * *

My meeting with Horst the next morning, on Sunday, was almost incidental. I was standing in the foyer of the chalet, waiting for the manservant to bring the car around to take me away, and Horst wafted through on his way from one room to the other. He did a double take, as if he was surprised to see me still there. It couldn't have been the clothes I was wearing. I'd taken them out of the closet of the room I'd been locked in after the manservant finally was finished chain fucking me. There were almost as many clothes about my size in the closet here as in Horst's Munich townhouse.

He gave me a look as if to say he thought I was willingly hanging around for more—but I'd had enough that weekend of the "more" he had to give.

"I paid up front," he said.

"I understand that," I answered. "I'm just waiting for the car to come around."

"Oh," he said and started to walk off. But then me turned and said, "You were great. A great and enduring lay. I'll commend you to your service."

"Thank you," I answered, and then added, because it was the truth, "You have possibly the longest and most

185

talented cock I've ever had inside me. If you do this again, feel free to ask for me specifically."

"Oh . . . thanks," he said, clearly pleased. To show that he really was pleased, he dug into his back pocket, came up with a wallet, extracted a hundred-euros note from it, and handed it to me.

"You don't have to tip me," I said, but both of us knew I was just being polite. I'd already taken the banknote.

The manservant/chauffeur drove the Mercedes, which had smoked windows, half way down the slope until he was out of sight of the chalet, pulled off the road, climbed into the backseat, and set the car rocking fucking me again, crouched between my spread thighs, with my feet leveraging off the interior roof. I didn't begrudge him the fuck. The contracted day wasn't over yet. It reminded me who and what I was, and he wasn't half bad at it.

He delivered me to a specified café in downtown Munich and left me there. A whole new contact from my handlers in the States showed up. I was half expecting to see Hans, but it was an Italian. I knew he was Italian, because he told me he was Italian and that his name was Paulo.

"Let's leave. The coffee in here sucks," he said, standing up from the table.

"Where are we going?" I asked.

"I'm Italian. Where would you think we're going? You're doing the quick rounds of Europe. In and out before the authorities get a whiff of you. Didn't you understand that? We're going to Italy. To Portofino for now and then over to Sicily. Your next client is known as The Sicilian . . . then The Turk after that, I think. But you get a week off in Portofino so your back can heal."

"My back? You knew I'd be flogged?"

"That probably did come up when the order was made, yes. It was in the contract I saw."

"And no one told me?"

"Who the fuck cares what you think about it?"

"That's a point, I guess," I answered.

186

We took the train from Germany to Italy and had a carriage room to ourselves. Somewhere in the Alps, Paulo pulled the shades down to the corridor, and turned to me.

"Why did you pull the corridor shades down?" I asked.

"Didn't I mention that I was Italian?" he answered with a smile.

I sighed as he pulled me up on his lap after I'd knelt between his thighs and given him hardening head, and lap fucked me. Yet another 'interview' not much different from the one Hans had given me when I arrived in Munich.

I made no protest. Even in the world of high-class international male escorts, the pimps take their pound of flesh.

Carnival at Viareggio

"I've never looked out on the Tyrrhenian Sea before. All in all the beaches of Viareggio surpass those we have visited in Venice. Perhaps we should just stay here longer."

"I couldn't help but overhear you, sir," a well-dressed young gentleman, complete with white suit, vest, and white bowler hat and shoes called over from under a nearby beach umbrella. "You said Tyrrhenian Sea. That, I am afraid is a common misconception of the tourist to Italy. That's actually the Ligurian Sea out there. But it's just a natural mistake. I would agree that the beaches here are better than those in Venice, though."

Hugo Von Stoben had been talking to a different, younger man sitting with him under a beach umbrella, who stood as Von Stoben's attention went to the nattily dressed— and quite incongruently attired for the beach, he thought— young man who had just corrected him on the body of water they were facing. The younger man stretched and sauntered down to the sea.

He was dressed for the seaside as any well-formed young man of the 1920s would be—in a one-piece, form-fitting, short-legged woolen costume topped by an athletic shirt adhering to the young man's muscular chest and with deep arm slits and neckline. Such bathing suits apparently had been meant for modesty but had neglected to provide anything that hid the obvious line of the young man's left-dressed cock and the curve of his balls. To most young women and a certain kind of man, the young man was breathtaking in his innocent beauty.

Both Von Stoben and the formally attired young man watched him walk down to the surf—the view from behind of the pert, but bulbous buttocks being as interesting as the frontal view—and start stretching his body. Within minutes he walked into the surf up to his knees, executed a beautifully arced surface dive, and started swimming out to sea in strong, sure strokes.

"You have a handsome son, sir. You should be proud of him."

"I am quite proud of Eric, yes."

"He's a strong, elegant swimmer."

The young man had swum out some distance from the beach and was swimming laps parallel to the beach between the wave-breaking rock walls at either end of the beach. He kept his curly mop of platinum blond hair above the water, as he did the pert bulbs of his buttocks, and his arm strokes were regular and pulled him a long distance with each stroke. In the water, he looked much taller than he did on land.

On the beach, Von Stoben and the young man he was talking with weren't the only ones watching Eric swim. On the other side of Von Stoben, a canvas chair under an umbrella was just now being occupied by a German doctor, Gerhard Mueller, from Hamburg, who was large-boned, a bit on the heavy side, and had a florid, redheaded complexion. He was perhaps in his forties. He, and the man sitting on the other side of him, an older French Catholic priest, fully clothed in black clerical garb and a high, white collar, Father Jacques, had met the Von Stobens here on the beach the previous day.

"Not the Von Stobens of Munich?" Mueller had asked when they were introduced, and when they allowed as how they were, indeed, those Von Stobens, Mueller had attached himself to them like glue.

To that point he had been staying close to the fifth man in the little bunch in canvas chairs under five beach umbrellas. The Englishman, Sir Reginald Chamberlain, a man appearing to be in his fifties, was tall and rugged looking,

190

almost cadaverous in appearance, but with piercing black eyes. There had been a hint at the introductions that he was in Tuscany convalescing from some wasting disease, but the discussion had not yet delved deeper into that topic. Nor had it explored the depths of what the French priest, a professor at the Faculté Notre-Dame Catholic seminary, in Paris, was doing on the western coast of Italy in March of 1924 beyond that his order had determined he needed to take a sabbatical.

All four men sitting with Von Stoben, even Dr. Mueller, as he arrived on the beach, being the only one of the group who said he came to the beaches on Tuscany's Riviera della Versilia every spring, were scrutinizing the young man swimming in the sea. Only Von Stoben was looking at the men he was talking to during their disjointed chatting.

The only one of the group who wasn't watching the swimmer, and the only woman present, was Ingrid, who sat immediately to Hugo Von Stoben's left, but set back behind him under a separate umbrella. Like the young gentleman in the white suit, she was fully dressed in a somber, long-sleeved dress that ran up to a choke collar, pinned with a large cameo broach, and down to the ground, with the points of black leather boots peeking out from under her multiple petticoats. She paid little attention to the men, keeping her nose in a series of Victorian Romance novels. The impression given was that vacationing at a Mediterranean beach hadn't been her idea, and that she didn't wish for Hugo to forget that.

"We've been in Viareggio for three days now, and the architecture hasn't ceased to amaze me," Hugo said to the young man sitting to his right. "I was led to believe it was an ancient town, but I don't think I've ever seen a larger collection of Art Noveau-style buildings."

"Ah, that would be explained by the fire we had seven years ago that leveled much of this area of the city. Only the Grand Hotel Principé di Piemonte survived. Perhaps you've seen the hotel?"

"We are staying there."

"A good choice." The young man raised his eyebrows. Only the very rich stayed there. "I have one of the Art Noveau buildings myself."

191

"You? You live here? I took you for a fellow tourist," Hugo said. "Your accent. I thought—"

"That I was an American, right?"

"Yes, I confess I did think that."

"I am, as a matter of fact. But a displaced one. I am Martin Biddle, and I have an antique store here on the Piazza Puccini, not far from the Grand Hotel." He briefly looked away from Eric swimming in the sea to shake Hugo's hand and then looked back. "My family thought it safer for their reputation for me to live abroad," he added.

Hugo didn't pursue this point, but he did register it in his mind. He turned his head and took another look at the young man. He was quite handsome. Trim, but with good musculature. And obviously sophisticated and refined—and well to do, as he was expensively dressed, if overdressed for the seaside. And perhaps knowing now that he lived in Viareggio explained why he was fully dressed. It was unusually warm for the beginning of March in Tuscany, but that was all relative. It was warm enough for bathing wear for the likes of Hugo and Dr. Mueller and the English nobleman at this time of year— and even for the sixty-year-old, gaunt French priest, who was, to use a pun, sticking to his habit—but it likely would still be too cold for the beach for a local inhabitant.

Eric came out of the water but remained on the hard sand at the water's edge. He was, indeed, a beautiful young man. Short, but trim with a boyish body that, nonetheless, had good torso definition and strong looking arms and legs, as he would have to have to have been swimming as strongly and expertly as he had been. He was Germanic, light blond, with striking blue eyes, and a dazzling smile when he wasn't looking shy and withdrawn into himself—or aloof to the scrutiny he obviously knew he was being given from the line of umbrellas.

A sigh went up from the cluster of men sitting around the Von Stobens as Eric unbuttoned the straps on the shoulder of his form-fitting one-piece swim suit and let the top of the suit drop to reveal his smooth, both boyish and well-muscled torso. Seemingly entirely blind to the multiple sets of eyes capturing and mentally caressing his form from the line of umbrellas, he started doing stretch exercises again to step down

192

from the vigorous swim in the sea—and then a few mild calisthenics.

"Did I overhear right, that this is your first visit to the Riviera della Versilia?" Biddle asked Hugo—although his eyes were glued to Eric.

"Yes, we are doing the rounds of beach resorts this year. January was the Turkish beaches, the island of Cyprus in February. Italy was reserved for March and April. We will go to Venice, where we have gone before, after our visit here. And later in the spring we'll take in the French Riviera. Eric wants to swim in the sea, and I love to spoil Eric."

"I can well see why," Biddle murmured. In fact he could only wonder at the effort Von Stoben must have to make to keep men's hands off the young man. His own hands were twitching at the prospect, which he hoped to be able to pursue. The young man must know the effect he was having here on the beach. In a louder voice, though, he said, "But how can your young son be out of school for such a long time?"

"He's not as young as he looks," Hugo said, with a small laugh. "He finished his basic schooling last year. He wanted to take this year off to perfect his swimming skills. He enters the Universitat at Heidelberg in the fall—a year older than most entering students—but the difference certainly won't be seen in his visage; he still look years younger than the others. He wants to swim competitively for the Universitat, but he believes, because of his size, that he will have to convince the coaches with his skill. They invariably will say he is too small just from looking at him."

"Ah, I see," Biddle said, giving a little smile and slitting his eyes as he peered at the young man. His interest was diminished in one respect, but the lessening of the risk involved compensated—almost. And the young man *did* look quite young. "He does swim like a fish, and so elegantly."

Eric returned to the chairs, with the eyes of at least four men following him, but only long enough to gather a towel, which he took out to the sand between the watchers and the sea, and then reclined, his torso raised a bit by the set of his elbows in the sand—his beautiful small body pointed at the line of umbrellas—and flopped his curly haired blond head back so that his face and torso and legs were exposed to the best advantage to the rays of the sun.

"Do you and your family plan to join with the Carnival of Viareggio festivities tomorrow, Herr Von Stoben?" Biddle asked in a low, gravelly voice.

"The carnival? They have a carnival here?"

"Yes, of course. Tomorrow is Shrove Tuesday—we also have a Mardi Gras parade. It's been celebrated for nearly fifty years here every year and rivals the one in Venice in enthusiasm if not in expense. It's a time for our people to let loose and show their true selves. There's a parade and dancing in the streets and partying in the wine shops. Partying in the streets too, for that matter, before the celebration is finished."

"Show their true selves?" Hugo asked. "That's an interesting way to put it."

"Yes, it's a time that they can wear real masks but act as themselves, rather than showing their faces and masking their needs, desires, and deepest sins."

Hugo looked at Biddle with interest, but Biddle was looking at Eric.

"I hadn't known about the carnival. And we have no costumes or masks."

"I could quickly fix that," Biddle said, turning a dazzling smile on Hugo. "There are many Mardi Gras costumes in my antique store. And masks aplenty. I would be happy to let you and your wife and son borrow what you need. Your family really must not lose out on our carnival."

Hugo laughed. "I'm afraid that Ingrid would rather walk on burning coals than go out into the street in a mask and a gaudy costume."

"Then you and your son. You must visit my shop this afternoon and pick something out. Here, here's my card. I won't take no for an answer."

* * * *

Hugo explored Biddle's antique store with fascination after Biddle had picked out costumes and masks for them. Hugo would go as a Roman senator.

194

"I think perhaps a young sailor—or cabin boy—for young Eric here," Biddle had said, carefully helping the young man try out several costumes. He certainly did look arresting in the sailor suit, with a white tunic that came down only to his midriff and tight, white trousers with a square buttoned codpiece. A blue and white scarf tied around his neck and a sailor's hat set at a jaunty angle on his blond curls completed a look that, yes, was arresting, although sensual might have been a better term for it.

The choices completed and Eric changed back into his clothes, the young man joined Hugo at a case that had drawn Von Stoben's admiring attention. The showcase gleamed with gold and contained an array of expensive-looking gold chains and watch fobs. Von Stoben pointed to a fob with three deep-red rubies inlaid in it that he particularly admired.

"Let me show you something over here," Martin Biddle said, as he put an arm around Eric's shoulders and guided him to another part of the shop. They had their heads together in conversation as they leaned over another case. Hugo was aware of them but devoted most of his attention to admiring the gold chains and watch fobs in the case in front of him.

All three men were smiling when Eric and Hugo left the shop.

* * * *

The parade and the Carnival of Viareggio raucous celebration in the streets lived up to its billing. The Torre di Via Regia seaside promenade and Viareggio Avenue and the blocks off this parade-route were teeming with boisterous, mostly drunken revelers in every conceivable costume and, as the festivities chugged on, lack of costume that one could imagine.

Hugo and Eric were parted by a stream of revelers meeting a counterstream of revelers, all shoulder to shoulder and hip to hip, moving in no discernible direction in the streets as the last of the parade floated by. The serious partying was starting now and wine was flowing on the promenade.

195

Eric could hear the noise of the celebration from only a short distance away from where he was suspended off the ground and pressed up against the wall of a shop in an alley off Viareggio Avenue behind a stack of wine casks. The sounds closer to hand were the grunts and heavy breathing of the devil pressing him to the wall and his own moans and groans as the buried cock of the man in the devil suit slid Eric's back up and down on the rough shop wall with the strength of the cruel upward thrusts in Eric's channel. The front flap of Eric's sailor trousers was open and slapping back against the wall between his raised and parted legs. His knees were hooked on the devil's hips, and his hands tightly grasped and then released their grip on the devil's biceps through the red velvet of the devil's suit, matching the rhythm of thrusts of the devil's cock up into his channel.

His head was thrown back against the rough bricks of the wall, and his mouth was open as he gulped for breath and moaned deeply.

The devil's hands were under the half tunic of the white sailor shirt and gripping the sides of Eric's torso as he lifted the small body and slammed it down on the up-thrusting cock. Lifted and slammed. Lifted and slammed.

The devil was muttering what a nice little piece Eric was, how tight his passage was, while Eric whimpered, "Yes, deeper, harder. Fuck me hard."

The noise of the crowd beyond the alley ebbed and flowed, but the pace of the cock thrusts steadily increased as did the intensity of the two coupling bodies in a mutual effort to explode, which Eric did first, with a little scream in unintelligible German, whereupon he collapsed in sighs and groans as the devil fucked on for several more minutes before realizing his own shuddered release.

When he was finished, the devil swirled away, leaving Eric in a sighing heap at the base of the wall, where two nearly drunk Italian fishermen revelers found him and each took their turn with him before staggering off, surprised as the fine little piece of tail had held his own with them rather than struggling.

When Hugo and Eric somehow managed to reunite in the milling crowd, slowly wearing down from the height of its partying, nothing was said about the short interval they had been parted.

Late in the night, when Martin Biddle had finished his inventory and redisplaying in the antique store downstairs, locked the front door to the shop, and mounted the stairs to his flat above the shop, he found Eric standing at the open wardrobe in his bedroom, fingering the velvet material of the devil's costume hanging therein.

"Where? How?" a shocked and confused Biddle asked.

"You were in the back of the shop and I just walked in and came up here without you seeing me," Eric said. "But do you really want to have a discussion at this moment?" He opened his other hand to reveal that he had found Biddle's stash of Sheik lambskins.

Biddle didn't see the need to discuss anything. He enveloped Eric in his arms, and while they were kissing deeply, he unbuckled Eric's belt, unbuttoned his fly, and pushed the young man's trousers down to his ankles. He went down on his knees and buried his face in Eric's belly, kissing and tonguing the young man's navel.

Eric placed his hands on the back of Biddle's head to hold the man, not much older than he was, to his belly. He gave a little laugh and murmured, "Eat me out, suck me. Fuck me."

With a low moan, Biddle palmed Eric's buttocks and closed his mouth over the small blond's cock. After a while, he turned Eric and stroked Eric's cock with both of his hands, encircling the young man's hips with his arms, and snaked his tongue into Eric's asshole.

The first fucking was on the bed, with Biddle sitting on the foot of the bed and holding Eric's wrists, as Eric's legs streamed out around and behind Biddle's hips, and his torso cantilevered out over the floor beyond the foot of the bed, giving him the aspect of a thrusting figurehead on the prow of a boat. Eric used the leverage of his feet to fuck himself on Biddle's cock, remarking that it was just like barebacking.

Biddle used lambskins precisely for that effect, but he wondered—with wonder—how the young man knew what barebacking felt like.

197

After a rest, their bodies entwined on the bed, Biddle pushed Eric over on his belly, wrapped an arm around his waist to bring him up onto his knees, mounted his hips from above, and fucked him deep and rapidly like a dog.

Eric demonstrated in no uncertain terms that he was getting exactly the attention he wanted.

As they cooled down afterward, Eric said, "I'd better go before I'm missed."

"How can you not have been missed?" Biddle asked.

"I have a separate room at the Grand," he said.

"Ah, then, it's still early," Biddle murmured, as he pulled Eric's rump into his groin, raised Eric's leg to give himself a better angle, and entered him strongly and deeply again.

* * * *

The little group fell into a set pattern over the next several days. They would all be out on the beach in the late morning, with Eric doing his swimming exercise ritual, and four sets of eyes—those of Biddle, of course; Sir Reginald; Dr. Mueller; and Father Jacques—watching Eric closely and somewhat greedily, if guardedly. Both Hugo and Ingrid were buried in books most of the time.

All would go back to their respective abodes in the mid afternoon for siestas but would be back on the beach for a second round of swimming exercises and sighing gawking in the late afternoon.

Then during the night, Eric would slip out of the hotel and lie under the young, sexy American antique dealer in the flat above his shop, expending lambskins at an alarming rate.

On the fourth afternoon, though, Eric came out of the surf holding his arm and nearly close to tears. Hugo rose from his canvas chair and came down to the surf to meet him.

"He's scraped his arm on rocks," Hugo explained to the others when the two came back to the line of umbrellas. "He swam too close to the rock breaker wall out there to the north of the beach."

198

Dr. Mueller, full of concern, rose from his chair and went to Eric and examined the arm. "It doesn't look too bad, but it's easy to get infection from such cuts in this circumstance," he said.

Hugo turned to Biddle. "Is there a clinic nearby?"

"No need," Dr. Mueller interjected. "I had disinfectant in my room at the Grand. The boy can come back with me. What do you say to that, Eric? I will take you for an ice cream afterward, before we come back to the beach, if you promise not to cry at the sting of the disinfectant."

It was obvious that the doctor wanted to see Eric as a small boy.

An hour later, after listening briefly at the door of the doctor's room at the hotel, Hugo used a skeleton key to quietly open the door and slip into the room.

Dr. Mueller didn't see or hear him at the beginning. He was otherwise energetically occupied.

Eric was lying on his back at the foot of the bed, his legs raised and spread—his ankles in the grip of Dr. Mueller, as the doctor, naked, as was Eric, huffed and puffed at the effort of pumping Eric's channel with his hard cock. A box of the newly marketed rubber Trojans lay at his feet, packets of them strewn out on the floor.

Hugo cleared his throat, and the doctor whipped his head around in shock and fright, although he couldn't stop himself from continuing to pump. He was about to come and wouldn't be denied. He gave Hugo a panicked but greedy look and fucked on. Eric was gripping his hips on both sides with his hands and crying out for the doctor to finish him.

When he had, the doctor pulled out of Eric's ass and turned to the side, hunching in on himself and covering his genitals with his hands.

"I don't mean . . . I wouldn't . . . the boy was egging me on . . . I was just . . ." Mueller muttered incomprehensibly. His face was as red as a beet and the flush had spread over the rest of his pudgy torso.

He really looked pathetic. Eric raised his torso on his elbows and turned his gaze on Hugo.

199

"You were just introducing the lad to a new brand of French Letters? To disinfect a cut on his arm? But I think we can fix this. I think we can make an accommodation," Hugo said.

* * * *

"I guess that gets them all except the young American, and we can move on to Venice soon," Hugo said later that evening. "It was a good haul here—nearly enough to cover the expenses of the entire season. The priest paid as much as the other two put together. I guess this is what his seminary sent him here to avoid and he doesn't want them to know he can't kick the habit."

Both of them gave a little laugh at that.

"The priest should have paid double. He was the cruelest of all," Eric said. But then Eric, who was really named Kurt, added, "We can move on now, if you wish, Horst. I've taken care of the American."

"He's already fucked you?"

"Repeatedly." Kurt was smiling.

"So, that's where you went at night?"

"Yes."

"I'm not surprised. He is the youngest and sexiest of the group. I rather thought he would be fucking you by now. I don't begrudge you having it off with a muscular man nearer your age. But you gave it to him for free? Is that what you're saying?"

"No, go look in the pocket of my trousers."

Horst rose off the bed and padded over to the chair where Kurt's clothes were neatly folded. He fished around in the pockets, and a big smile was planted on his face when he came up with a gold chain and watch fob with three deep-red rubies embedded on the fob. "You noticed that I liked this."

"Yes. I lifted that the first night I let him fuck me." Kurt saw no reason to mention the elaborate assignation between Biddle and him for the fuck in the alley during the carnival—nor to mention the two muscular, hung fisherman afterward. He did wonder, with some amusement, though,

200

when those men realized that they were missing their money clips. "He's either never noticed or has written it off as being owed to me for the cocking. I have a few other trinkets that should be worth a bit too."

"Tomorrow morning, then," Horst said, as he returned to the bed, gently pushed the stretched-out naked body of the son who wasn't his son onto his belly, mounted the young blond's buttocks, and began a slow, deep, bareback fuck. Kurt moaned deeply—but not deeply enough to disturb the reading of the woman in the adjoining room, who was Katie, not Ingrid, and wasn't related to—or particularly interested in—either of the men as long as they paid her regularly for her easy pretense.

David Vance Poses

I was making an effort, but if there was a rise to be had from Dominic Castilano, it wasn't happening for me. The well-known and hunky Italian had bought the Thai garment factories my company's line of men's fashion designs used as a major supplier. And the scuttlebutt was going around in San Francisco that Castilano was gay—and an aggressive top. But, though I had confirmed he was a hunk, having met him on this "touching base" and buying mission to Bangkok, I hadn't confirmed that he was gay—not to mention someone who would meld with me. And that was from no lack of trying.

I came to Bangkok frequently. Ostensibly I came here to coordinate with the local factories on the production of our male fashion line, but behind that was Bangkok itself. I could let myself go in Bangkok. I not only did much of the garment buying for our company, but I also was a model for the clothes—Devon said that if the clothes didn't look good on me, he didn't want to offer them in the line. So I was the one sent to Bangkok to close the deal on the acceptability of the cutting and sewing of the new line.

But even beyond that, I came here for a break from Devon. Devon didn't only own the fashion house; in many respects he owned me too. He was my sugar daddy. I lived with him, often felt smothered by him, and occasionally needed to get away from him and his possessiveness and to kick up my heels.

That was what Bangkok represented for me—the opportunity for some no-entanglement one-night stands with an aggressive muscular hunk in a city of "whatever gives you pleasure."

When Castilano bought the Thai factories, I looked him up wherever I could find him and found that, in media photos, at least, he was a hunk and a half. I decided then that he would be my "thrill" goal for my next company shopping spree to Thailand.

"Yes, I can see that it's a good material for that lounging robe for your company's next year's collection."

Castilano was standing close beside me at the meeting in his Bangkok factory when we were pairing off materials with the sketches for the new line, and I was aching for him to put his arm around me and palm my hip—to show me some sign that bore out the rumors. But he didn't do it.

That disconcerted me. Any other man who was interested in doing me—which was just about any man who did men—would have moved an arm behind my waist and laid his hand there. If I liked the man, I needed no more gesture than that to follow him to a nearby bed. My appetites were such that this even was so in San Francisco, which no doubt explained the tight leash Devon put on me there. I have no idea what he thought I did when I went to Bangkok, but what I did here was open my legs to any good-looking muscular man who showed me he wanted me.

Castilano left both hands on the cutting table surface. He didn't even feel the silky yet gauzy fabric to allow the sensuousness of the material, and the evocativeness of the sketch of the skimpy lounging robe, rev his engines up.

Devon himself had made that sketch and designed that robe in his mind as he was fucking me—to be rendered in material just like this was. He had caught me, standing in the sunlight at the bedroom window, in a robe cut like this, but from entirely different, less-sensuous material. I had been wearing loose sleeping trunks in the same gauzy material, and upon entering the room, Devon had remarked that the material was sexily transparent with the morning sunbeams behind it.

204

He had walked over, taken the coffee cup from my hands, walked me back to the bed, and laid me on my back. He brushed the robe back from my torso and pelvis while telling me that it was the wrong material and describing what he would make such a robe out of. He kissed my nipples and worked his way down my body with his mouth, while he pulled my sleeping shorts off.

And then he fucked me.

It was, I'm sure, more enjoyable for him than for me. I'd already experienced what this scenario could produce, and although Devon provided very well for me in most aspects of our relationship, his performance on the bed that morning didn't prevent me from craving my little fantasy vacations in Thailand. Rather, it brought the image of the earlier cocking, by the big brute in Bangkok, under similar circumstances to mind.

I couldn't help thinking of that, as we—Castilano, his material designers, and I—were selecting the material for the new robe design there in the center of the noisy, dusty factory floor in Bangkok. I was trembling at the remembrance and was sure that Castilano could feel that and hear my ragged breathing—that, if he were gay and a top, as rumored, he surely could catch and appreciate the encouragement of that. I'd never had a gay top not show interest in me. The image of the connections of the lounging robe design with what now was the ideal material for it had my heart racing. And Castilano was twice the hunk that Devon was—even hunkier than that earlier man in Bangkok had been.

How could he not know, not feel it too? If he was an aggressive gay top? He must have been able to tell that he could have lifted me, laid me on the cutting board table, and fucked me there in the noisy, dusty factory with the corrugated walls and lofty ceiling, in front of all of his workers, and I would have opened to him and loved every thrust of his cock.

But after two hours of handling sensuous material together to realize evocative men's fashions with, and doing so hip to hip, the most of a rise I got out of him was a statement that he certainly hoped I would attend a dinner with his factory managers and him at his home that evening.

205

* * * *

I was seated at one end of the table and Castilano at the other end in his Thai-style house, elevated on teak columns and located on one of the main canals, known as klongs, in a city called the Venice of the East. The setting was surprisingly traditional for an Italian not long in residence in the city. The house consisted of a series of roofed pavilions with snake skin-like tiled roofs, many of them open sided. The dining room was in one such open-sided pavilion. The lush jungle foliage came right up to three sides of the pavilion, giving the impression of steamy privacy.

I was in unrequited heat for Dominic Castilano, and thus found the atmosphere intimately sensuous—and frustrating.

The frustration was accentuated by Castilano playing the attentive host to nearly everyone at the long teak table but me. I was more than a bit irritated by that because I was the buyer here, the one who a new factory owner, who relied heavily on the orders of my company, logically should be trying to impress.

I was achingly impressed with him, because he was clothed only in a Thai silk sarong skirt knotted at his waist, and his torso was magnificent. I had been warned it would be a traditional Thai dinner—served at a long, low table that we knelt, cross-legged at—bare-chested and wearing sarongs. This had been quite all right with me. I looked great in a sarong and eagerly permitted myself to be redressed in a guest room when I arrived.

Several of the Thai factory managers looked good in their sarongs too, and a few of these eyed me during dinner like they'd like to throw me down on the table right there and fuck me. If I thought it would have kindled Castilano's interest in me, I would have encouraged them to do so.

The rice wine was going around the table freely, and toward the end of the dinner, I had the insistent urge to piss. I asked, interrupting Castilano's boisterous conversation with the man seated at his right, and was directed, with only a cursory glance and a wave of his hand, to a pavilion at the back of the complex, where he said there was a Western-style bathroom.

The bathroom was attached to what must have been the master bedroom. It was a richly appointed room—the bedroom was—with shimmering maroon and dark orange-stripped draperies, a sisal rug underneath, and a huge four-poster teak tester bed in the center, also draped with Thai silk in the same colors and design. This possibly was the most enclosed room in the house, with polished teak walls and conventional windows, albeit the windows were shuttered, the louvers loosely spaced so that the lush green of the jungle could be seen beyond, behind the open draperies rather than covered with glass panes. The draperies rustled softly and the air moved languidly, heavy with the musky scent of the exotic flowers pressing at the walls of the pavilion, from the melodic "wok, wok" whisper of two paddle fans moving overhead.

What accosted me and made me stop and my jaw to drop when I entered the room were the lighted art photographic prints—large and framed—arranged strikingly around the walls.

They were evocative male nudes, high-art prints, the young, well-built men all in provocative poses. I was fascinated by the effect of the overhead paddle fans, moving the highlighting and the shadowing of the beams of light directed on the photographs, giving the effect that the men were moving, if ever so slightly. At any movement I expected one of the young men to turn a thigh or hand slightly and show me his genitals. What struck me the most, though, was that I knew who the photographer was. There was every reason why I would know who the photographer was.

I had hooked up with Liam Ryan, an Australian fashion photographer, in Bangkok two years earlier. Devon had decided to backdrop his men's fashion line with lush Bangkok foliage that year, and I had been sent out to be one of the models. I had been the signature model of Devon's collections for three years at that point.

Liam was a big-bodied hunk, a rough and demanding, cocky, hung bastard, who had been covering me and fucking me hard within an hour of our having met and whose cock I

207

couldn't get enough of. He had been exactly what I took these Bangkok trips to find.

He was striving to emulate the renowned photographer David Vance in his own work. Vance photographed celebrities and magazine layouts—in addition to having a line of male nudes in an extension of the Robert Mapplethorpe evocative style. Because he was a mean son of a bitch, Ryan couldn't help putting an extra twist of demanding sex in his photographs.

Ryan performed the fashion design shoot very well—and afterward he did me royally in a private, male nude shoot, which included a rough, complete fuck before or after each pose. I had never been fucked so many times in one afternoon—at least not by just one man.

A good third of the framed and lit photographs on Dominic Castilano's walls were of me—from Ryan's photo shoot. My eyes immediately went to the one of me standing at a window in an open, gauzy robe, backlit by the morning sun, which I myself had suggested and had emulated for Devon earlier this year to rev him up. I had posed the scene myself to try to relive the fuck with Ryan, to push Devon to new heights of satisfying me.

The fucking Ryan had given me after shooting that, though, made Devon's cocking pale by comparison. Ryan hadn't taken me to the bed. He had fucked me right there, my back pressed to the frame of the window, my knees hooked on his hips, and his palms cupping and spreading my butt cheeks to help me accommodate his hard, thick, thrusting cock.

Another photograph was of me face down on the bed, chest pressed into the surface, and pelvis raised, my face showing the awe and fear in my eyes at the sight of a naked and magnificently erect Ryan, coming at me with a camera firing off, before he dropped the camera, mounted my hips, and fired off himself. A third was taken after sex, with me lying on my back, legs open, arms akimbo, a silly grin on my face, and eyeballs swimming in cum.

I was barely able to make it into Castilano's bathroom before I had to ejaculate into his toilet. I then stood at the sink, looking into the mirror, checking out whether I had changed at all in facial features since that photo shoot. How could

Castilano be so aloof from me? Was he blind to the comparison of the photos he had on his wall and me in the flesh? Had he just not looked directly enough at me to make the connection?

I splashed water on my face, set my facial expression as much into nonchalance as I could, and returned to the dinner table.

Castilano did look up at me as I approached the table, and he gave me a little sardonic smile that could have meant almost anything.

But soon thereafter, the dinner party was breaking up—and the guests were departing rather than prolonging the evening. I stood, ready to go back to the guest room where I had changed and to change back into my Western clothes.

But, to the sound of men preparing to leave and saying their good-byes to each other, Castilano's voice floated out over the hubbub.

"Evan, would you be good enough to stay on a little longer? We have more to discuss, I think."

At the edge of the entrance pavilion, as the head of the last guest disappeared down the stairway to the ground, Castilano came up behind me and put his arms around me. He already had unknotted his sarong and let it fall to the teak boards underneath. I leaned back into his chest, my head buried in the hollow of his shoulder, and sighed, as he unknotted my sarong and let it too fall, with a whisper of silk, to the floor.

I moaned, knowing he was going to fuck me, feeling the strength and size of his hard cock at the small of my back. And, indeed, as I felt him pull my feet off the floor with the strength of his hands fanned out under my thighs and his effort to roll my pelvis forward and my butt cheeks up, that he was going to put me on the cock and fuck me right here, right now.

I barely heard the whisper at my ear, "I bought the factories because of those photos—because of you. May I—?"

"Oh, yes, yes, please," I murmured in return.

My thighs climbed his, and he cantilevered my torso out, moving the hands that now were on my waist and then up to my pecs, palming them, as I arched further out, raising my buttocks even more, gasping and panting as the hugeness of him fought to enter me. And then when he had, I moaned as he moved up inside me, and then groaned as he began to pump.

Atonement or Exorcism?

By the time another business trip came up to cross the Atlantic, I was ready and grabbed at it. It was back to my old stomping grounds when I'd worked in that European branch—and when I'd been with Cal. And when I'd been such a wandering ass that I now couldn't forget about my sins against Cal. The trip would give me a chance to atone for my sins—to confess and take my punishment—or, I don't know, exorcise my demon. Who knows? I'm not Catholic, but this seemed to be a very Catholic thing I needed to do to square myself with Cal. Not in person, of course. That wasn't going to happen. But at least to myself. I had just been waiting for this chance to go back to the scene of my crimes and erase what I could.

I didn't seek out the Jazz Club immediately upon landing, but pretty close to that. I checked into a hotel and was almost immediately out on the street, walking the familiar pavement. I'd picked a hotel closer to the club than to my company's offices. It was clear to me what my priorities were in coming here. I had two days to get this done before I had to appear at the office. And I'd had two years to plan what I had to do.

The Jazz Club—the signage in English, I guess to appear more cosmopolitan—was a basement venue reached by a door at the head of an alley in the old town, where the buildings were three and four stories, flats above and

211

businesses below, that were an architect's delight and an engineer's nightmare.

I could hear the strains of the saxophonist from nearly a block away—a rendition of Billy Joel's "Just the Way You Were," pretty much the way Cal used to play it. I slipped into nostalgia almost immediately, even before descending the steps into the cave-like room where those who loved jazz—and particularly jazz played on the saxophone—gathered nightly. I stopped on the stairs, closed my eyes, and imagined that Cal would be on the small stage under the haze of smoke when I got down there. And that I could just enter the club and reenter his life with an entirely new attitude—not be the shitty little snip I was when we parted, or, rather, when I'd flitted off in a snit and taken the first transfer available back to New York.

The musician had moved into the Stan Getz arrangement of the "Girl from Ipanema" before I reached the bottom of the stairs. It was another one of Cal's standards. This wasn't going to be easy on me. But maybe that was part of what I needed for this act or atonement, or exorcism, or whatever.

The saxophonist the club now had certainly was no Cal. He was short and pudgy, black and wrinkled, and wore a beret on a wild-haired wooly black-shot-with-gray head. He may have sounded like Cal, but he certainly didn't look like my tall and thin handsome Aussie.

I sat at a table near the back of the room, which was three-quarters full of patrons here for the music, rapt in the sweet tones of the sax. When I was seated, I braved a look toward the bar that ran nearly the full width of the room along the back wall. I wasn't sure if I wanted him still to be here or not. He had become the most important element of this ritual I had decided I needed to go through, so, for that reason, he still needed to be here—and still needed to have the wants he had expressed to me while I was with Cal, and most pointedly when Cal and I were having difficulties. But if he wasn't here, maybe I could take that as a sign that I didn't need the ritual confession of my sins and punishing atonement for them at all.

But he was there, behind the bar, where he worked as one of the bartenders and also as the club bouncer, not that this club needed a bouncer. The patrons were sophisticated, well heeled, and here for the music. The saxophonist had moved into "Take Five" in the Dave Brubeck version from his *Time Out* album. The patrons would be floating on that for some time. They wouldn't be paying any attention to what was happening at my table.

The big Slav, Horst, saw me from behind the bar, did a double take, and then smiled. He raised a bottle of Scotch, and I nodded in assent. He fiddled under the bar for a few seconds, but quickly had added two glasses to the bottle and was moving toward my table. He was as monstrously big as always—a head or more taller than I was, broad shouldered, and muscular. Completely unlike Cal. It was weird that I was planning to use him to make atonement—in my mind, at least—for how I had treated Cal, but somehow it had seemed fitting. The last thing Cal had said before I flounced out on him was, "If I don't satisfy you, go fuck Horst."

But Cal did satisfy me. He always did. I just didn't know it at the time. I was always after more—mostly more attention to me. I had grown since then, but I couldn't square that directly with Cal now. He was departed. Not in the sense of the final last breath, but back to Australia, which was as close as he could get to being dead to me and still breathing.

"You came back," Horst said, as he sat down, precariously, on a chair meant for a much more normal-sized person than he was.

"Yes, I came back," I said as he poured out two stiff glasses of Scotch. He'd brought good Scotch. He was still interested, on the make, which fit into my plans, even if it sent a chill up my back. Besides the magnificently muscled oversized body, Horst was pug ugly with a bald head resembling a bullet and a face that only his pug could love.

"He's not here anymore," he said. "Went back to Australia not long after you left."

"I know. I didn't come here to see him. I came here to see you."

That obviously pleased the big Slav. He smiled and took his wallet out of his pocket and placed it on the surface of the table. He immediately pulled a photograph out of it, but I knew he'd placed it on the table so that I could see the indentation the condom disk made in the leather of the wallet—a very wide condom disk, a Magnum size. He had done this signaling before when he'd been trying to make me. He wanted me to know he required a Magnum—and that he went everywhere prepared to use it.

That's what he'd done when he saw that Cal and I were having difficulty and he wanted some of what Cal got—some of what some others were getting, which was at the root of the problems between Cal and me. He'd slapped the wallet, showing the indentation, down on a tabletop, drawn my attention to it, and said, "You want a real man? I'm a real man."

He flipped the photograph over and showed it to me. "Nice blond little piece, isn't he?" Horst said. "Curly hair just like you. Cal had him in here almost before your seat at the table had gotten cold. That didn't last long, though. None of his progression of cute little pieces like this twink and you lasted long with Cal. He pulled up stakes and returned to Adelaide soon thereafter."

"Soon after what?" I asked.

"Soon after I'd fucked the stuffing out of this one," Horst said with a grin. "Squealed like a little pig, he did. He loved it but couldn't walk straight for days afterward. Cal was pissed."

I know, I know, I screamed in my mind. You have a big cock.

He was rubbing a finger over the indentation of the condom disk. He was trying too hard. I'd come in with the intention of using him as punishment. He wouldn't know it, but he didn't have to sell himself to me. He poured us both another shot of the Scotch and asked me what I'd come here for.

I was honest—to a point. I told him I'd come for him, that I hadn't stopped thinking about him since I'd gone back to the States. This was half true. I couldn't stop thinking about

214

Cal and what I'd done to him, but Horst did fit into those thoughts—and then, increasingly, into my plans for atonement.

Horst was pleased and put a big paw on my thigh, high up on my thigh. I didn't push him away. I confessed my sins to him, although he probably thought I was just nervously babbling, working up to taking that big cock he was advertising. If he was listening to me, it probably didn't turn him off to hear that I had fucked indiscriminately and like a rabbit when I'd lived here before. If he was Catholic, which I doubted, he might have seen the ritual in what I was doing. I wasn't Catholic, but I thought of this in those terms: confess my sins; seek penance, which Horst's challenging cock would provide; take my punishment; and walk away cleansed—and, I hoped, able to forget and move on with my life.

It all sounded great to Horst, and I tried not to make it sound too churchy when I went through the litany, leaving the walking away happy bit out of it, naturally. I'd carefully rehearsed it all, and he was so anxious to get into my pants that he spent more time filling my Scotch glass and thinking he was seducing me than paying attention to how much I was controlling this.

He probably had no idea that a young-looking blond half his size could be controlling anything when he was the one with the huge cock.

He fucked me in the dark stair hall just behind the bar through a door covered with a beaded curtain. The saxophonist moved into Ray Charles' rendition of "Unchain My Heart" about the exact time Horst stuck it in me—although that took some doing.

He was crouched down against the wall to bring his face down to the level of mine and possessed my mouth with his, sticking his tongue in my mouth and forcing me to suck on it, while his hands unzipped us both and he unbuckled my trousers and pushed them and my briefs to the floor. I lifted my legs off the floor and hooked them on his crouched thighs. He fisted our cocks together, and I moaned at how much larger his was than mine. I was grateful for the dark and not being able to see his face clearly and being able to concentrate on the cock play.

215

I heard more than felt or saw him fiddling with his wallet to extract the condom and the wallet falling to the floor next to us.

"You," he whispered in a low, hoarse voice. "You want it, you crown it." He pressed the condom disk into one of my hands. Taking his big cock in punishment for my sins against Cal having been the whole reason for coming here, I rolled the condom on the cock.

Part of what he brought from the bar must have been a tube of lube, because I felt the heel of his hand under my ball sac and then slick fingers at my hole. I grunted and jerked when a finger entered me and began working on opening me to him. This was going to take some time, I knew, so I unbuttoned his shirt and lay my cheek in the cleavage between his bulging pecs. I worried his taut nipple near my mouth with my fingers for a moment or two before moving my mouth to the nipple and suckling it while he worked my channel opening with, now two, slicked fingers.

He must have found this arousing, because he came up from his crouch, with my knees clinging above his hips for dear life, rolled my buttocks up to him, and pressed his huge mushroom cap at my opening. I grunted and tensed up.

"I don't think I'm ready for it yet," I whimpered.

He muttered, "Ya gotta relax or it's gonna hurt like hell."

I relaxed as much as I could, but it still hurt like hell, as he got the cap lodged inside the opening and pressed in. I wanted to scream, but he was holding me tight and had a big paw clapped over my mouth. I panted and he was breathing heavily and grunting at the effort to spike me.

It hurt like bloody hell and I was sure he was going to split my walls. But he didn't. Slowly they gave way to him, at least enough for him to fill me up—or so I thought. I reached down and felt maybe five more inches that weren't inside me.

This would not do. The punishment was to take all of him. I felt filled, but this wasn't enough.

He maybe pressed in another inch, but that was all, before he started to slow pump me. I was wearing a vest with a metal buckle at the back, and I gauged the increasing rhythm of his pumping by the clicking noise the metal made when it hit the wall behind me.

It still hurt, but there was pleasure in it now too. The pleasure of being filled, and taking what I had inside me, as impressive in girth as it was in length. I concentrated on the fuck and the cleansing intent of it and began to bang him back, trying to pull all of him inside. Nothing less would do in this atonement or exorcism, or whatever my mind had decided it had to be. But a good part of my life was spent being fucked, and once I was into the rhythm, the fuck was all that mattered. We were fucking to the rousing strains of "Second Balcony Jump" on the sax beyond the beaded curtain.

But, with a jerk and a grunt, he came, filling out the bulb of his condom.

He held there for a full minute, both of us breathing hard, me feeling down there to be sure he was only half inside me, which he was. "Shit," he muttered. "Been thinkin' of this too much, I guess. Came too fast. You didn't come. Wanted to make you come."

"You still have the flat a couple of flights up from here?" I asked. "Can you get away from the club?"

His breathing was ragged, his heart racing, I knew, at me asking for another fuck rather than he having to figure out a way to get it. I felt the little lurch in his cock inside me, the promise that it could recharge quickly when sufficiently aroused. I took his head between my hands, gave him a deep kiss on the mouth, and then whispered, "Take me upstairs and fuck me all night. Make me come—again and again."

It was a chore. There was bad news and good news. The bad news was that his early ejaculation wasn't an anomaly. He was a fast shooter, each and every time. The good news was that he had balls the size of lemons and could reload fast.

The chore was that, as idiotic as my needs were, I had to have him all inside me for a fire off or the atonement or exorcism wouldn't be complete. It didn't matter if it made sense or not; my mind had to be satisfied. I had to open enough to him to take him all in a fucking before he ejaculated.

We sixty-nined, stretched out on his bed. I gave him a Cal special—or tried to—sucking on his bulb and flicking his

217

piss slit with my tongue until his hips involuntarily went into motion. Then I tried to deep-throat him. I could with Cal. There was no way with Horst. And he shot off without warning to either of us, filling my mouth with his cum. It took him several more minutes to bring me off, but he was determined to, and did so. While I built up to blow, I played with his huge balls with my hands and teased a few after spurts out of the cock. I measured the cock with my hands, fisting it like a baseball bat and getting the sensation that it was that big.

He'd brought the Scotch bottle upstairs and we finished it off as we waited for him to reload, which didn't take long.

He couldn't sit, but nervously pranced around the room, seemingly filling every available space with his magnificent muscular body, no muscle of his less magnificent than the one between his legs, which might have reached to his knees if it weren't perpetually erect, reaching out and curving up from his body, giving the impression he was trying to press it into the walls across the room.

"Of all Cal's pieces, you were the nicest," He said, standing over me and looking down. He was already rolling a new condom on his cock—a second one he took from his wallet. "Great little body, always so young and innocent looking. But we knew you weren't innocent, didn't we?"

Yes, we did, I thought. Cal was never enough. "I should have stuck with Cal," I said.

"Of all the guys you let fuck you, why was it never me?"

"You should know why, Horst? Look at me, how small I am. I was scared stiff of it."

"What? This cock?"

"Yes, of course."

He clearly was pleased that his cock cowed me. "But now you want it?"

"Yes. Now I want all of it. I want you to keep fucking me until I have taken all of it." He didn't need to know why— that it wasn't because I loved his cock but because taking all of it was the penance I had to pay for being at peace with how I had treated Cal.

218

"You want it, you got it," he growled as he grabbed me out of the chair I was sitting on with hands on my waist and pulled me right onto his cock. I arched my back toward the floor and he tucked my knees under his armpits. He seemed aroused at the unusual fuck position; I had the experience to know a million of them. He pulled me on and off his cock with the strength of his arm muscles, but he didn't last any longer this time than he had down in the hallway. He wasn't fucking me at much more than a six-inch depth before he ejaculated.

He muttered another, "Sorry," but added, "But there's more." And indeed he was still as hard as ever.

He lay me on the side of his bed, opened his nightstand drawer, took out another one of those Magnums, and rolled the used one off his cock. His eyes went wide as, standing between my legs, which were bent, with my heels digging into the edge of the mattress, he was rolling on the condom and I was reaching into the drawer and pulling out two more condoms and laying them on the top of the nightstand.

"All night long," I murmured. "I don't care how many times you have to come, I want to take it all."

He groaned, crouched over me, pressing his forehead into mine, grabbed and raised and spread my legs wide, and started working his cock inside me. I moaned and reached down and spread my buttocks as open as I could, wanting him all inside me. He'd given me maybe seven inches before he was moved to start pumping—and then, shortly, firing off.

We were both exhausted and slept for a couple of hours, stretched against each other, me cuddled into his groin, inside his embrace. Late in the night, I woke and slipped a hand between us. He was snoring quietly, lost to the world. In this world, though, his cock was hardening at my touch.

He wasn't fully erect, but he was erect enough to handle a condom when I gently rolled him on his back and continued to stroke him. He remained asleep. He was erect enough for me to straddle him and press the cock head to my hole while he was still in deep sleep. He was moaning, though, having a wet dream that he hadn't connected yet to reality. It helped make him rock hard.

219

I had most of him inside me before he even started to wake up. He was fully awake, though, when I had taken all of him and was able to feel the scratchiness of his wiry pubic hair on my buttocks. And he was immediately game for the fuck, grabbing my waist and pulling me up and slamming me down as I went into a wild rodeo ride of his dick—of all of it. Taking it all, pain deep inside me, but pain that was subsiding into the sheer pleasure of taking a cock that big and long. I both felt and listened to the slapping of his balls on my buttocks in time to his thrusts, savoring it as victory music.

I felt the guilt flowing out of me. The plan, as idiotic as it was, was working. Cal was great, but I wasn't his one and only. He probably had already recovered. According to Horst, he had recovered and gotten back onto the small blond twink circuit within days after I had walked out on him.

It was only my guilt I had to deal with. And the punishment I had chosen had turned into a glorious cleansing. I had never taken it so deep.

Horst jerked and cried out and came deep inside me. But he wasn't the only one doing so. I came with him, giving me assurance that I was free and had picked an appropriate ritual to free myself.

I lay, crouched over him, panting. He was looking up at me in wonder, holding my arms in his hands.

"All of it," he muttered.

"Yes, I took all of it. Has that never happened before?"

"No, never," he said, his voice still in awe.

I knew the secret now. I wouldn't tell Horst—that he had to be three-quarters buried before he was even aware he was being fucked. This wasn't about Horst, and I didn't really like Horst all that much.

But I think I could come to like Horst's cock. Very much. I had never felt so possessed.

He started to struggle up from underneath me, but I whispered, "No, don't. We're already there. Let's take advantage of that."

He groaned and lowered his torso back on the bed. "I don't know if I can. We've done it so much."

"I think we can," I said. I lowered my mouth on his, sucked his tongue into my mouth, moved my hands to his nipples, and started tweaking them. At the same time I put my hips in motion. Not rising or falling too much, as I wanted to keep the depth of him, but moving back and forth in a wave motion.

Champ that he was, he was ready to go again right away. He grabbed my waist and began slamming me up and down on the cock again and thrusting up with his hips. When I reached back and grabbed and squeezed his balls, he fired off three salvos, gave me a deep groan, and sank back onto the mattress, exhausted.

I lowered my cheek to the cleavage between his pecs and smiled a little smile, still moving my hips in a gentle wave motion.

That was for you, Cal, I thought, even letting my lips form the words. Fulfilling the last thing you told me to do. And now we're good. Good-bye and good luck to you.

"Are we finished?" Horst asked, with a moan.

"Not by a long shot," I answered. "I said all night." That was for Cal, I thought. The rest of the night is for me.

He groaned—but he was still hard inside me.

~

221

About the Author

Habu is one of the pen names of a former supersonic spy jet pilot, intelligence agent, male model, movie actor, and diplomat. A wild youth in South East Asia was spent enjoying whatever sexual opportunities came his way, and much of his gay male writing is about recalling incidents from those days and inventing ones he'd perhaps have liked to experience. He now leads a very quiet and ordinary happily married family life.

An American, he is a published mainstream novelist and short story writer under another name and in another dimension of his life. He has written or cowritten (with Sabb) approaching 1,000 published short stories and over 100 published erotica e books, primarily of gay fiction but also memoir, straight fiction and ménage fiction. His hand and creative writing can be seen in stories and books by habu, sr71plt, Dirk Hessian, Shabbu, and Stephen Kessel—among unrevealed others that might surprise readers. The fictionalized GM memoir *Flying High, Diving Deep* is loosely based on his life experiences. He can be found at the adults only gay male site www.BarbarianSpy.com, which he shares with Sabb and Dirk Hessian.

Our authors always like to receive feedback, and appreciate it when readers post reviews at distributors and other sites.

BarbarianSpy

FOR LITERARY HEAT

Not all books listed below may currently be on release.
* indicates the book is available in paperback and e-book.

BOOKS BY DIRK HESSIAN

Xtreme Erotica
The King's Men
Shores of Tripoli
Prophecy of Noto
Pretender's Fate

General Erotica/Romance
Fire Down the Valley*
Constantinople*
The Beautiful Way*
Blue and Gray
Colonel's Treasure
Beginning of Time
Labyrinth

BOOKS BY HABU

Gay Erotica

Memoir Faction
Flying High, Diving Deep*

Xtreme Erotica
Apyko: The Greek Pimp
Visits of the Schlange
Second Coming: Emile La Cour Unleashed
Vortex: Sacrificed by Curiosity*
Dark Angel Sounding *(in e-book & included in Sounding:Ultimate Control Paperback)**
Sounding: Ultimate Control (*Print Only*)*
Sounding Five *(in e-book & included in Sounding:Ultimate Control paperback)**

General Erotica

Romance
War is Hell and Heaven

225

Ravens Roost
Caribbean Cruise Top to Bottom
Arena Stage
Trading Partners (Valentine's Day)
Friday Nights with Lenny (Christmas Romance)
Snowy, Snowy Nights (Christmas Romance)
Four Coins
Lower Than the Heart (Valentine's Day)
Brambleton
Gotta Keep Trying
Finding Amnad
Platres Conclave
Other Novels/Novellas
Stallion Station
Racing With the Devil (espionage suspense)
Cruising Gigolo (bisexual)
Prepared in Cape Verdi
Gilded Cage
House on Park
Anything for Ambition
Dance of the Ravishers
Hard Knocks U*
My Neighbor's Spa*
Man's Man: Tales of a High Priced Gay Hooker*
Trip Money
Clint Folsom Mysteries Compendium Volume 1*
Death to Blonds - Stolen Judgment (Clint Folsom
Mystery)*
Clint Folsom Mysteries Compendium Volume 2*
The Indian Doctor
Sailorboy
Home to Fire Island
Choke Hold
Gay Erotica Anthologies
Eleven to the Dogs
Fifty Seventy*
Spy Tails 001*
Spy Tails 002*

Doubled*
Doubled Again*
Tails in the Tropics*
Tails in the Med*
Tails in the West*
Rough Riders*
Grab Bag 1*
Grab Bag 2*
Grab Bag 3*
Grab Bag 4*
Grab Bag 5*
Beyond the Beaded Curtain*
Habu's Christmas Balls
The Sporting Life*
Fetish Galore!*
Literary Gay Erotica
Cairo Surrender*
The Handyman*
Homeward Bound
Journey to Mirage*
Menage Erotica
Cruising Gigolo
13 Ways for Halloween
Luther*
The Indian Prince
Literary GLBT Fiction
Summer of Denial
BOOKS BY SHABBU
Velvet Interrogation
Finding Jason
Dirty Pool
Operation Black Jade
Cigars!*
Angel in the Barn
Gayly Complicated*
Despoiling David
The Tree of Idleness*
I Met a Man

Rough Road to Happiness

BOOKS BY SABB

Hiring in Hollywood

The Legend of Holleystone Grange

Surprise Encounters

She is He

Wrong Man

Loyal to his King

Barbarian Tales - Book One - Traveler's Tales*

Barbarian Tales - Book Two - Journeys Begin*

Barbarian Tales - Book Three - The Inheritance*

Barbarian Tales - Book Four - Road to Persepolis*